FLIGHT OF THE JAVELIN BOOK 2

FREE STATION

RACHEL AUKES

www.aethonbooks.com

FREE STATION

©2020 RACHEL AUKES

Aethon Books
PO Box 121515
Fort Worth TX, 76108
www.aethonbooks.com

Print and eBook formatting, and cover design by Steve Beaulieu.

Published by Aethon Books LLC.

Aethon Books is not responsible for websites (or their content) that are not owned by the publisher.

ALSO IN SERIES

PROLOGUE

Y ANK FOUND THAT HE VERY MUCH ENJOYED SITTING IN THE CAPTAIN'S seat of the *Bendix*. He knew his promotion was temporary, but that didn't stop him from fantasizing about ways to make his current role more permanent. His crew of scallywags preferred him to their captain, too. Skully Pete was the most feared pirate captain throughout the Ross system...as well as the most feared pirate to his own crew. His collection of skulls lining the walls in his quarters served as a reminder that Pete didn't take kindly to anyone who irritated him, and that went doubly for his own crew.

Yank shifted his focus from his captain to the job at hand. He looked out from the bridge, seeing nothing but the black void, stars, and rocks. The asteroid belt produced dangerous debris for the ships that traveled through, but it also provided perfect concealment for any ship not wanting to be detected. As a pirate, Yank considered the asteroid belt practically a second home.

"The seed ship's on our grid, Yank," Jazz said from his computer panel.

"When will it be within range?" Yank asked.

"Three minutes. It's traveling at maximum jump speed," the computer specialist replied.

"Good. Notify the others." Yank turned to Benny. "Power up the missile launcher."

"On it, Yank," the gunner said.

Yank ran his fingers over the flight controls, switching the engines from standby mode to normal mode. He maneuvered the *Bendix* out of the crater it had been hiding in and ran it parallel to the asteroid's surface so as not to draw any attention.

"The target will be here in one minute," Jazz announced.

Yank increased power to the engines and broke away from the concealment of the asteroid. He flew the ship out of the asteroid belt and lined up on the incoming ship's trajectory, as though playing chicken with the other ship.

"I'm in position," Yank said and turned to Benny. "We've got only one shot with this, so make it count."

"I won't miss," the gunner said.

"If you do, we're all dead men," Yank added.

"Thanks for the motivational talk," Benny replied drily before adding, "Missile is away."

Yank peeled away from the seed ship's flight path and put distance between them. Ships at jump speed moved fast—nearly point three four light speed—but moving at that speed meant they couldn't turn or move to avoid obstructions without drastically slowing down first, and no ship could slow down quickly in space. The moment the seed ship registered the *Bendix* in its flight path, it would have to perform an emergency slowdown.

But it was too late.

At the speed the ship was still traveling, the missile burrowed into the center mass of the massive seed ship and flew out the stern, leaving a hole through the center of the ship.

Benny let out a whoop. "Now, that's a bull's-eye!"

Yank grinned. "Nice shooting, Benny boy."

He piloted the *Bendix* to the Chinese seed ship as the damaged craft decelerated and came to a stop. Alarm lights flashed along its hull, highlighting its name, the *Wu Zetian*. The ship was so massive that the missile hadn't broken the ship apart. Debris floated out from it, and Yank was careful to keep out of the path of any forward-moving junk.

He brought the ship alongside the *Wu Zetian*, and transmitted via the intercom, "Nussbaum, we're lined up. Hook us up."

"On it, Yank," the engineer replied.

Grappling hooks shot out and secured the small pirate ship to the huge seed ship. Yank knew the motion-activated cameras on the hull were recording everything. Even without the video feeds, the Red Dynasty space operations center in Sol would've known something had happened the instant their ship entered emergency mode. Fully automated, the *Wu Zetian* constantly relayed data to its operations center. That could be a problem if there were marshals nearby. There weren't.

Even more fortuitous, it was against interstellar law for any automated ship to carry weapons. It was one of the few laws that played into the pirates' favor.

"Good job, Nuss." Yank turned to Jazz. "Now."

The specialist nodded. "Infrared is blinding them, and I'm sending the signal now." A second later, he grinned. "There. I own their cameras."

Yank nodded and tapped the transmit button on his panel. "It's clear. Move in, and do it fast. We're on the clock."

He settled back into his seat—Skully Pete's seat—and watched his grid as dots appeared at the edge of the asteroid belt. He counted all twenty dots to make sure they all made it out of their rocky hidey holes without any problems.

The crew of the *Bendix* had the most important role in the pirate fleet. By taking the *Wu Zetian* out of commission and hacking its camera feeds, they'd enabled the most lucrative job in the history of Jader pirates. It was hard trusting the other pirate crews to play their roles, but Yank had faith in Anna East's plan. If they worked together this one time, she promised they'd be richer than their wildest dreams.

Yank wondered if Anna East knew how big he dreamed.

The other pirate ships approached. They each shot out hooks to tether themselves to the *Wu Zetian*. Within minutes, pirates emerged from each vessel and spacewalked into the seed ship. All carried weapons. Several tugged large pods behind them.

Watching the daisy-chain sequence of pirates entering the *Wu Zetian* was lulling Yank to sleep, so he walked to the galley and returned with a bottle of whiskey. Benny held out his hand. Yank took a long swig before handing the bottle to his fellow crew member.

When Benny raised the bottle toward Jazz, the specialist held up a hand. "Not while I'm working."

Benny shrugged. "More for us, then."

After several drinks, Yank noticed the time on his screen. He transmitted, "One-hour mark. Pack up and move out."

Within minutes, each of the other ships retracted their tethers and backed away. Soon, only the *Bendix* and the *Wu Zetian* remained. When Yank verified that the fleet had disappeared from the grid, he nodded to Jazz. "Reset the clock, disengage."

Jazz's fingers flew over his screen as he worked. "There. Video cameras are back online. Our job's done." He grabbed the half-empty whiskey bottle and drank.

"It's only just begun," Yank said as he released the hooks and pulled away from the *Wu Zetian*. He brought the *Bendix* back to the crater within the asteroid where they'd concealed themselves earlier. Once the engines had quieted in standby mode, he leaned back. "Now we wait for the marshal to arrive."

The marshal from the Galactic Peacekeepers arrived precisely on schedule to investigate the attack. Yank waited until the newcomer came to a stop near the *Wu Zetian*. Then Yank powered up the *Bendix* and flew it out of the asteroid belt.

Benny and Jazz had gone to their bunks to sleep off the whiskey. Yank pulled up the weapons system. His fingers hovered over the machine gun as they approached. The marshal had arrived in a small Rabbit-class ship. Fast but not heavily armored. A single direct hit could breach its hull. He smiled, thinking how easy it would be to kill the marshal, but that wouldn't fit in the game Anna East was playing. His smile faded. He sighed and then pulled back his fingers.

He'd been taking orders his entire life, and he was tired of it. After just one more job, he'd have his own ship and crew, and he'd never have to take orders from anyone again.

Just one more job...

CHAPTER ONE

"I've seen lousy shots in my time, but they were sharpshooters compared to you, Mr. Edwards. Are you actively *trying* to miss the target?" Chief Roux asked.

"It's not my fault. The target's moving," Eddy answered, still holding the rifle.

Chief closed his eyes and squeezed the bridge of his nose before speaking again. "Of course it's moving. That's what it's supposed to do. The bad guys aren't going to just stop and stand there and wait for you to shoot them."

"It's not like I even need to learn how to fire one of these." Eddy dropped the photon rifle onto the stand, oblivious to everyone wincing at the careless handling of a loaded weapon. The thin, pale man turned to face Chief. "I'm a hardware specialist, not a soldier. I'm never going to carry a weapon, so why do I have to learn how to use one?"

"You're not a specialist until you pass all the exams." Chief sighed. "They're not hard. You've excelled in all other categories except for physical endurance, which I have no idea how you managed to pass. Your agility…" Chief shivered before wagging a finger at Eddy. "The only exam you have left is firearms use and maintenance, which you're not even coming close to passing. You've done great with the maintenance side, but for the life of me, I've never seen anyone handle a beam weapon so poorly in my life."

Eddy shrugged. "I'll just have Sylvian hack the system and make it show I passed. Then I can be out of your hair."

Chief's brows rose before he shook his head slowly. "I did not hear that. Now, I'll be the first to admit that I cut the occasional corner, but I cannot—no—I *will* not authorize you, or any cadet for that matter, to serve as a Peacekeeper if you can't handle a weapon. If you happen to find yourself with a weapon in your hands, I want to have some level of confidence that you can at least avoid shooting your fellow Peacekeepers. If you can't shoot, you put the lives of everyone around you at risk. And that's something I won't allow."

He sighed and turned to face Marshal Throttle Reyne. His features were marred by tension. He had the same shade of dark brown skin as her father had, and when Chief was frustrated, he especially reminded her of her father. They both clenched their jaws with the same air of disappointment.

"We'll keep working with him." Throttle threw a glance at Marshal Finn Martin, her partner in the Galactic Peacekeepers, GP for short, and the crew member with the most weapons expertise.

"I'm not sure even that will be enough in this case. Eddy's been training for exams for two years. That's twice as long as other cadets," Chief said.

"Eddy's certainly not your typical cadet," Specialist Sylvian Salazar-Martin said quietly.

Chief paid her no attention as he frowned and turned away from the group.

"What is it?" Throttle asked, but he didn't answer.

"Pete, speak to me," Chief said, and Throttle knew he was pinging another Peacekeeper's ear implant. "Pete, this is Chief, report in. Pete, report in, damn it." A pause. "Chief to Admin, locate Marshal Peter Antonov." He took several steps away as he continued speaking, and his words became inaudible over the distance.

Throttle turned back to her crew to find Finn eying her.

"I've spent *a lot* of time with Eddy. He's beyond hope," he said. At Throttle's wry look, Finn shrugged. "But I can try again," he said with a noticeable lack of confidence.

"Let me try to help Eddy," Sylvian offered.

Throttle narrowed her eyes at the specialist. "Are you sure?"

Finn made a face. "That's not a good idea. Next to Eddy, Syl's the weakest of all of us with weapons."

Sylvian shrugged. "And you're the best, but when you teach, you sound like a drill sergeant."

Finn bristled. "No, I don't."

Sylvian placed a hand on her husband's forearm. "You can't help it. It's what you know, but your training style can be intimidating to regular people like Eddy and me. I think that if I work with Eddy, he can get a fresh perspective."

Throttle nodded. "Try it. Whatever it takes. Come up with a miracle if you have to."

"I'm never going to pass," Eddy whined. "Face it, guns and I were never meant to get along."

Throttle wagged a finger at him. "You'd damn well better pass, Eddy." She then motioned to her other two team members. "The four of us are a team, remember? We Black Sheep stick together no matter what. We don't leave anyone behind, not before and not now that we've all joined the Peacekeepers. We stick together even if that means Finn, Sylvian, and I have to rotate shifts, training you every hour at the shooting range every day for the next three months."

"Well, not *every* hour," Eddy countered. "I still have plenty of work to do on the *Javelin*."

"Oh yeah? How's that going to work when the three of us go on missions, and you're just riding along?" Finn asked.

"Chief will let me go just like he's done for the past year. Besides, Throttle's still on medical leave, so right now the *Javelin*'s not going anywhere."

"I'm going back on active duty any day now," Throttle said.

"Then I'll just tag along. I don't need the Peacekeeper ID card."

"You can't live on Free Station as a cadet forever," Sylvian said.

"Then I'll just live on the *Javelin* and hang out while you three do your thing," Eddy answered.

Finn's brow rose. "And where are you going to get the credits to live?"

Eddy shrugged. "From you three, of course."

Throttle eyed Eddy for a brief moment and then tapped her wrist-comm, which was wrapped around her left forearm. The technology had come with her from the Trappist system and was considered archaic in the Ross system, but it was rugged, reliable, and—most importantly to Throttle—on an encrypted network only accessible by her team. "Rusty," she spoke into the device.

"Yes, Throttle?" the *Javelin*'s central computer responded.

"I want you to revoke Eddy's access to board the ship until you get clearance from me. He needs to focus on passing his GP weapons exam."

"Consider it done. Eddy's access has been revoked. Is there anything I can do to help?"

"Can you perform a miracle?" Throttle said.

"I doubt I can help with that." Rusty's voice then came through Eddy's wrist-comm. *"Hurry in passing your exam, Eddy. You left the galley a complete mess today."*

Eddy rolled his eyes. "I told you, I'll pack up my tools as soon as I finish repairing the heating element."

"You always say that you'll pack up your tools, but then you always leave them out. You're a slob, Eddy."

"Complain later. Eddy has to focus," Throttle said into her wrist-comm.

"Fine. You know where to find me," Rusty said.

She looked back up at Eddy to find him staring slack-jawed at her. Finn tried to smother a chuckle, while Sylvian watched in surprise.

"You can't do that," Eddy said finally.

"I'm the captain, and I used my credits to cover all of the costs of the *Javelin.* That makes it my ship," she said.

He guffawed. "But the *Javelin* wouldn't even be flying if it wasn't for me. You need me."

Throttle nodded. "We need each other. That's why we need you to get your specialist rating. Consider this motivation. The sooner you pass, the sooner you can get back onto the *Javelin.*"

"No. It's called punishment, not motivation," Eddy countered. "Where am I supposed to sleep?"

"In your bunk in the cadet bunkhouse," she answered.

The engineer watched for several long seconds before blinking and turning back to his rifle. He raised it and fired off several photon shots, all missing the target.

Sylvian gave Throttle a small smile. "At least he's receptive to training now."

Throttle glanced over her shoulder to see Chief walking to the door.

"Chief," she called out behind him as she strode to catch up.

He paused and turned back to her.

"What happened?" she asked.

He pursed his lips as though deciding if he would tell her the truth or feed her a line of bullshit. "A marshal's emergency locator transmitter just went offline."

Throttle frowned. "I thought ELTs never go offline."

"They can go offline if they are destroyed. That's why I need to find out what happened." The door opened to reveal a marshal waiting at the controls of a two-person tram. Chief climbed into the passenger seat.

"Let me help," she said, standing in the doorway.

Chief eyed her. "You're still officially on medical leave. You don't get your marshal's badge back until I declare you fit for duty."

She said, "I passed all my medical tests. I'm fit for duty."

The tram accelerated. Chief held up a hand, and the tram stopped abruptly. He turned around to look at her. "You haven't been wearing those new legs of yours for two months yet, and you barely passed the endurance test last week because you fell, not once, but twice during your run."

"But I *did* pass," she countered.

"You ran a mile in eight minutes and fifty-nine seconds. That's one second away from failing the test. Any marshal on my team needs to do a hell of a lot better than *barely* passing." His lips thinned. "My office is over a mile from here. Make it up there in under eight minutes"—he held up a finger—"*without* falling on your ass, and I'll see about giving you back your badge."

The tram sped away.

"Atlas, on," she said aloud, and the implant in her left eye opened a heads-up display, called a HUD, through her vision. "Show me routes and distance from my current location to Chief Cormac Roux's office." The screen morphed into a map of Free Station, displaying several route options. The shortest distance was one point two miles, which she selected. "Okay. Record my travel time."

She glanced over to see Finn and Sylvian standing in the doorway. She nodded in Eddy's direction. "Get him on that target, and I'll get us a new assignment."

Without waiting for a response, she broke into a run down the long hallway. She turned corners without slowing, and rather than waiting to ride the lift up to the next level, grabbed onto the low-g vertical bar that ran alongside the lift and pulled herself up, jumping off when she reached the next level. Her legs absorbed the impact flawlessly, which was saying a lot since both legs had been amputated above the knees two years earlier.

With flexible, curved prosthetic blades for legs and new spinal implants, the sensations below her waist still felt alien to her. She'd lost more than forty pounds of dead weight, which made her feel stronger and also like a part of her had been stolen. Since she could now control her legs nearly as easily as she could control her arms, it seemed too good to be true still, like a temporary gift that could be taken from her at any time. Before her amputation, she'd never expected that dealing with the conflicting emotions that came with the blades would be as hard as dealing with the new limbs themselves.

Even with the challenges of prosthetics, she never wanted to give them up. Back home in the Trappist system, the technology involved in a spinal implant had been far too expensive. Here in the newer Ross system, it was a simple surgery with all costs covered completely under the Galactic Peacekeepers medical plan. The moment she'd received her marshal's badge, she'd signed up for the prosthetic department's waiting list. Getting fit was the easy part. Waiting another six months for the blades to be built and delivered had seemed to drag on forever.

One of the perks of joining the Galactic Peacekeepers was that they had terrific benefits, which she discovered was necessary for retaining marshals. Not long after she signed up to join the Galactic Peacekeepers, she discovered that nearly every marshal she'd met had a prosthetic limb or medical implants of some type or another. Chief, for example, had a prosthetic ear.

The software and hardware specialists, such as Sylvian and (hopefully) Eddy, had it easier. Working at desks proved to be much easier on one's health than hunting fugitives across space. But neither Throttle nor Finn could sit behind a desk for long, just like the other Peace-keepers who'd chosen to go the marshal route.

She tumbled at a turn but grabbed the railing in time to keep herself from falling. She regained her footing, noticed the time on her HUD, and ran faster. She weaved around specialists, who comprised over half of Free Station's population. There were fewer marshals than Throttle had expected when she first joined. Out of over three thousand Peace-keepers serving the Ross system, fewer than eight hundred of those were marshals, primarily because each colony had its own law enforce-ment entity. The marshals dealt with the dregs outside the colonies while the software and hardware specialists kept the information flowing across the system; the bulk of GP employees served as data specialists, brokering data across the colonies.

The dregs the marshals brought in were most often pirates who attacked ships traveling through the system. Nearly all pirates in the Ross system worked for Anna East and operated out of the Jade-8 colony. She had ordered the deaths of several of Throttle's crew, and East was the reason Throttle had joined the Peacekeepers. She was ready to pay back the crime boss, with interest.

"Hey, watch out!"

Throttle spun and swerved in time to keep from plowing through a short specialist with a thick waist. She shoved off him to keep from falling, raising a torrent of curse words from the specialist, and she ignored him as she kept running through the Galactic Peacekeeper headquarters of the Ross system.

She reached Chief's office in seven minutes and fifty-two seconds. Another marshal stood propped against the wall next to Chief's closed door.

She bent and sucked in deep breaths. "Atlas, send my trip summary to Chief Roux." When the confirmation flashed across her HUD, she said, "Atlas, off."

"I'm guessing you're a part of the Trappist team of Peacekeepers I keep hearing about," the man said.

Throttle turned to face him. He wore the standard black fatigues worn by many Peacekeepers, with the platinum badge as the only design feature. He was taller than her, like most men were, with dark hair and Asian features that reminded her of an old friend she'd left back in the Trappist system.

"If what you hear is great things, then yeah, I'm one of them," she said.

His brows rose. "By 'great', are you referring to the massive amount of complaints that rolled in from that mining colony near the outer rim? Something about a team of Peacekeepers destroying a space dock?"

She chortled. "We didn't destroy it. The pirate ship that we shot down destroyed the dock when they crashed into it."

He grinned. "Now, that sounds like my kind of team."

She held out her hand. "The name's Throttle Reyne."

He pushed off the wall and shook her hand. "Throttle, nice work on bringing down that hacker Quincy in the dust belt. I'm Punch Durand."

She wiped sweat from her forehead. "Punch? I imagine there's an entertaining story behind your name."

"Depends on who you ask," he said but didn't elaborate further. He cocked his head as he watched her. "Chief's always had a knack at finding strays, but I think you might be the farthest from here. I always figured people would emerge from the Trappist system at some time or another."

She shrugged. "I wouldn't expect any more of us. Back home, everyone believes that they're the only humans left in the galaxy, and they don't have much interest in expanding, not after terraforming an entire system," she said. "Where are you from?"

"Oh, not really anywhere in particular. Here and there. I bounced around a lot before Chief and I crossed paths."

She smirked. "It sounds like you were a stray, too, before Chief took you in."

"That I was. Still am a stray, I suppose. Only difference is now I have Free Station I can come back to when I need a semi-comfortable bed and a hot meal."

Chief's tram emerged from around the corner. He climbed off and his gaze settled on Throttle. "You nearly went over eight minutes."

She was glad she was no longer panting. "It was one point two miles and not on an open track. I'd like to see you do better."

Chief gave her the smallest of smiles before opening his office door and motioning for the pair to enter.

Throttle entered first. Punch closed the door behind them. Chief took a seat behind his desk, a simple black table made of some kind of composite. He ran his fingers over the touchscreen built into the flat surface of the desk, and an image appeared on the wall screen to his right.

Punch walked over to the screen, where the layout of an unfamiliar ship and its schematics were displayed.

"A seed ship?" Punch asked. "Aw, hell. Don't tell me someone was stupid enough to attack a Red ship."

Their boss nodded. "The *Wu Zetian,* a fully automated Chinese seed ship, was passing through our system when it was hit by pirates seventeen hours ago."

Punch grimaced. "Idiots."

Throttle frowned. "Why does it matter if pirates hit a Red ship versus any other ship out there?"

Chief answered, "Where any other supernation sees piracy as an inevitable risk of space travel, the Red Dynasty views an attack on any of their ships as an attack on the supernation itself. And this case is no different. They've given us fourteen days to apprehend and serve justice to those responsible for raiding a Chinese ship."

Throttle's brows rose. "Isn't that skipping the judge-and-jury step?"

"The Red Dynasty judges and determines punishment through virtual trials. The Galactic Peacekeepers have an agreement in place that we will carry out punishment as they prescribe."

"We've only got thirteen days left on the clock," Punch corrected. "Why didn't they notify you as soon as their ship was attacked?"

"They did," Chief said. "I assigned Marshal Pete Antonov since he was already in the sector. The problem is that Pete's ELT went offline twelve minutes ago."

Punch grimaced. "We have to assume he's dead."

"No. We assume he's alive until we have proof otherwise. The last coordinates we have on Pete was aboard the *Wu Zetian,* not far from the Tumbleweed Trail."

Punch groaned. "I hate that area."

"Why?" Throttle asked.

"That area's haunted," Punch answered.

She raised a brow. "Haunted?"

He nodded. "Yeah. More ships have been lost near that asteroid field than anywhere else in the system."

"The asteroids are rich in metals. They are known to cause interference with systems, but I'm not convinced that's what happened to Pete's ELT," Chief said.

Throttle shrugged. "Why not? It seems like the most likely scenario."

"Because his signal would've broadcast once he was clear of the sector." Chief shook his head. "No. It's not the asteroids. He was transmitting fine until the signal turned to ice. The Red Dynasty also has a complete video feed from the *Wu Zetian* during the attack, so it was far enough from the asteroids for a clear signal."

"Did their feed get the ship that attacked them?" Punch asked.

Chief tapped several keystrokes, and the image on the wall screen changed to a different ship. "Unfortunately, the attacking ship isn't in our database."

Throttle's heart beat faster, and her jaw tightened at seeing the ship. "It's called the *Bendix*."

Both men turned to her.

"You've seen this ship before?" Chief asked.

She nodded. "It's a Jader ship. One in Anna East's pirate fleet. It raised hell with my ships back at Jade-8. I really hoped that I'd destroyed it." Her eyes widened as realization hit her. "Hey, that means if we catch these guys, they can tell us where East is hiding."

Chief held up his hand. "Our priority is to catch the pirates responsible for attacking the *Wu Zetian*. If we don't catch the pirates before fourteen days are up, the Chinese will deem us inept and take it upon themselves to see justice done regardless of collateral damage. The last time they did that to a system, hundreds were dead by the time they deemed adequate justice had been delivered."

"Give me five minutes with those pirates after we catch them, and before their execution, and I'll have a location," Punch said in grated words.

"We have to catch them first," Chief said before motioning back to the screen, where a map of the system displayed. "The feed showed that the ship—which we now know is called the *Bendix*—departed within an hour of breaching the *Wu Zetian,* so we have a working radius of where it could be by now. Punch, you're my best tracker, and I need you to hunt these guys. I'm sending you all the data we have on this case. All resources are at your disposal. Pull every string you have to track these bastards so we can bring them to justice before the deadline."

Punch gave a slow nod. "I'll find them." The marshal made eye contact with Chief and Throttle before turning and leaving the room.

Chief turned to Throttle. "You ran salvage ops in your past."

"Among other things," she answered even though his words weren't posed as a question.

"I want you and Marshal Martin to head out to the last reported coordinates of Pete and the *Wu Zetian*. Find Pete—or at least search for signs of what happened. His ship is small and should fit in your cargo bay, and I've requisitioned a tug for the *Wu Zetian.* Bring the ships— and hopefully Pete—home."

"I should help Punch track the pirates since we're running against a deadline," she countered.

Chief inhaled deeply. "Pete's not the first ELT to have gone offline."

She stiffened. "What?"

He leaned back in his chair. "Four days ago, Marshal Caterine Mercier's ELT went offline when she was leaving Jade-8. We found no sign of her or her ship, so the trail went cold. I'd assumed she'd had a run-in with a gang since Jader gangs are known for taking any tech they can get their hands on. But Pete was nowhere near Jade-8 when his ELT went offline. Someone's going after Peacekeepers, and I need to know who it is."

After the words sank in, she nodded. "I'll head out right away."

"If you see anything that can help Punch, send it right away."

She eyed him closely. "If you find out where East is, you'd better pull me in."

"I will. I gave you my word when you first joined." He rummaged through a drawer and tossed something to her. "Oh, and you'll want this back."

She caught the round, dark piece of metal that looked much like a very large coin. The words *Galactic Peacekeepers* were printed around the top, and *One Force for All People* was printed along the bottom. In the center was a star surrounded by many worlds. She ran her thumb over the cool metal.

Chief stood and held out his hand. "Consider yourself officially back on active duty, Marshal Reyne."

She shook his hand with a smirk. "My father was Marshal Reyne, and it seemed like everyone wanted to kill him just for having that title. I'd rather go by Throttle."

"You think it's any different in this system? Go. You're also running up against a deadline. A Chinese reclamation team is on its way to collect the *Wu Zetian* as we speak. Based on their last communication to me, they'll reach Free Station in fourteen days. If we don't have both their ship and those responsible for attacking it by then, there will be more bloodshed."

Throttle's lips thinned. "My crew and I will leave right away."

"Good. All the hardware is on its way to your ship now. I'll have all the data sent to your personal Atlas network, including the flight plan."

She nodded and turned to go.

"Throttle," Chief said.

She turned back to him.

"Steer clear of the Tumbleweed Trail. Any old-timer will tell you it's haunted. But they say that because the metals and space junk out there draw in scavengers and pirates that could cause more than a few problems for anyone."

"We'll be careful," she said.

Chief continued, "Oh, and I'll give Eddy a thirty-day extension to pass his exam. If he doesn't pass by then, he's out."

"Fair enough." Throttle knew Chief would give Eddy an extension. He'd been giving Eddy extensions for over a year, though she had a suspicion this might be Chief's final act of generosity to the cadet. She gave a final nod to Chief and exited.

She looked down at the badge in her palm. Even though she'd been a marshal for only a year, it had become a facet of her life that felt as necessary as breathing.

For much of her life, she'd been on the other side of the law. It seemed surreal that she could do much of the same things she'd done before, only this time she had the law on her side. She'd had to turn in her badge when she went on medical leave, and she'd floundered for purpose during those long months. With a smile, she slapped the badge onto her upper left chest, where the fabric seemed to seal around it.

She tapped her wrist-comm. "Rusty, give Eddy full access again and ping the crew. Tell them to get to the *Javelin* for immediate departure. We're back in the game. We've got ourselves a new mission."

CHAPTER TWO

THROTTLE SAT AT THE HELM OF THE *JAVELIN* AS IT SHOT THROUGH THE Ross system. Sylvian sat at a console nearby, putting the finishing touches on the latest software update she was coding for the *Javelin*'s buggy systems.

"How's the update coming along?" Throttle asked.

The software specialist didn't look up from her screen. "When we migrated the *Scorpia*'s systems to the *Javelin,* we caused as many problems as we fixed, but I think between Rusty's continuous protocol improvements on the back end and my upgrades, we've just about got everything all sorted out."

"Good. I'd hate to have another bathroom incident," Throttle said.

Sylvian shivered, then chuckled. "Yeah, that was rather *explosive.* But the waste system seems to be working with no error codes now."

"Keep at it. I know it's not easy what you've been doing to patch all the busted or missing systems this ship had when we found it, but you've morphed this ship from a dead-in-the-water hunk of metal into the best damn ship I've ever had the honor to captain."

"It'd go a hundred times faster if we were actually connected to the GP's Atlas network rather than just telling Chief it's connected. That way, all updates could be automatically uploaded," Sylvian said.

"The *Javelin*'s *technically* connected to Atlas net. Remember, we had to do that in order to get the photon cannon installed."

Sylvian smirked. "I don't think having Atlas installed on an isolated sandbox system counts."

Throttle shrugged. "It seemed good enough for Chief, at least until he figures it out. We're already plugged into Atlas too much for my comfort. Back home, the more we connected with the Collective, the more control they had over us." She tapped her temple near her eye with the implant. "I might have to wear this for the job, but I don't like the GP having its fingers in anything more than it has to."

"I get it, but it does take longer when I have to do manual uploads."

"If it does get overwhelming, we can migrate the sandbox connection over to the main system."

"Once I upload the latest Atlas charts into the nav system, all the big updates will be done for now," Sylvian said.

Throttle sighed. "It'll be nice to finally have the *Javelin* running without any kinks."

Sylvian chortled. "Not if you talk to Eddy. He seems to think this ship could still fall out of the black at any moment."

Throttle rolled her eyes. "Eddy assumes that whatever ship he's on is about to fall out of the black. He could be on a brand-new ship fresh out of the docks, and he'd think it was about to fall apart. He needs to spend three years modifying and tweaking a ship before he's comfortable, so he still has at least two months with the *Javelin* before he's confident enough to call it space-worthy."

"Have you been back in engineering to see how much he's got torn up? I swear he's rebuilding the ship from the inside out," Sylvian said.

Throttle smiled. "The time Eddy spends in engineering is time he's not up here, driving me crazy with hardware reqs."

"Attention, crew. We will reach the *Wu Zetian* in ten minutes." Rusty, the *Javelin*'s central voice command system, spoke throughout the ship's speaker system.

"Good. We should be close enough to see if anything is moving out there. Rusty, run scans on the entire sector. Let me know if you pick up any ships."

"I'm already running scans," Rusty replied.

Throttle checked both blasters in her hip holsters to make sure they were at full charge. She preferred the stopping power of pistols, but projectile-type weapons were outlawed on all spacefaring ships. It was a law she could understand. A single hull puncture could cause a whole load of problems on a ship in the vacuum of space. As a Peacekeeper, she had sworn to enforce all laws enacted across the Ross system. After a lifetime of a more fluid approach to following orders, she suspected that promising to enforce laws would be much easier than actually enforcing them, let alone following, said laws.

"My scans identify only two ships: an Elder-class transport with Sol Red Dynasty credentials and a Rabbit-class lorry with Ross Peacekeeper credentials. Both are stationary. They are located at the edge of the asteroid belt's sector. Additional ships may be located within the asteroids, but I can't pick them up due to signal interference and debris."

"The pirates probably used the Tumbleweed Trail to sneak up on both the *Wu Zetian* and the marshal's ship. Keep a close eye on that belt. I don't want the same thing to happen to us," Throttle said. She'd never met Peter Antonov though she'd heard his name on several occasions, as she had heard of nearly all the other marshals within the system. Antonov was a newer marshal, going through training in the class before Throttle and Finn's class. When Throttle had to go on mandatory medical leave to get her new blades, Pete had built a reputation as a capable law enforcer and one of a small handful of marshals who flew without a crew.

She'd flown with her crew for fifteen years, which made them more family than crew, and she wasn't sure she could handle losing anyone else to Anna East. She'd given up mourning the loss of Birk, Nolin, and Garrett, but memories would sneak into her daily routines, haunting her. Their ghosts—especially Birk's—formed a hard, stony crust around her heart. She wondered how many more ghosts she could carry before her heart became solid stone, and she lost all empathy.

Throttle's jaw tightened. She had neither the time for nor the interest in introspection. Instead, she tapped the comm-link to broadcast across the ship. "Eddy, prepare the tugs. Finn, suit up and meet me at the airlock after we drop out of jump speed. I want to check out the marshal's ship before we bring it into our cargo hold."

Sylvian turned to face Throttle. "It'd be safer for Rusty's bots to check out the ship."

"Can't," Throttle said. "All his bots are needed to hook up the tugs. Besides, I could use a spacewalk. I'm getting out of practice."

"But I haven't programmed Rusty's bot system yet for that," Sylvian said.

"That's why Eddy's running them."

"Oh, that makes sense." After a moment, Sylvian spoke again. "Do you think you'll find the marshal out there?"

Throttle shrugged. "I've salvaged enough ships to know to never expect anything. Chief wants us to find out what happened to Antonov, so our first step is to start at where Antonov was last. If he's not on either ship, we'll look for breadcrumbs."

"Hold on. We're dropping out of jump speed now," Rusty announced.

"Try pinging Antonov on the Peacekeeper channel," Throttle said.

The humming of the engines became lower pitched. Otherwise, there were no other signs that they'd reduced from point three four light speed to a mere few hundred miles per hour. Ships from the Trappist system, where Throttle and her crew hailed from, had slower jump speeds, and the transition from jump speed to sub-speeds was jarring. She appreciated the advancements Earth technology had made in the centuries since the first colonists left Sol for the Trappist system.

The stars outside the windows no longer moved, and everything outside seemed still. In the far distance, light flickered off the metallic asteroids in the Tumbleweed Trail, which appeared to span endlessly in a long arc. Sitting between the *Javelin* and the asteroid belt, two ships waited. One was tiny, capable of holding a crew of three; the other was a massive cargo hauler, easily eight times the size of the *Javelin* and shaped like a bloated whale. Chunks of debris littered the area.

"I haven't received any response to my ping," Rusty said.

"I figured as much," Throttle said. "See if you can run scans on the interiors of both ships. Tell me what we're dealing with."

A few seconds later, Rusty reported, "The Rabbit-class ship is registered to Peter Antonov. The ship is completely powered down, though I'm reading its batteries are fully charged and its main systems are in standby mode. It has a harness line attached to the larger ship. The ship seems fully functional, but I detect no signs of life on board."

"If the ship is still functional, that sounds like Antonov abandoned ship rather than having a cat fail," Throttle said.

"I agree with your assumption that the ship has not suffered a catastrophic failure. Once Eddy interfaces one of my bots with its network, I can confirm the ship's status," Rusty answered, with his usual accent that was unfamiliar to the crew. Chief had once referred to it as a Scottish brogue.

"And the Red ship?" Throttle asked.

"The hull has been severely breached. Its systems are offline, and I detect minimal power readings. However, there is much organic material on board."

"That'd be the seeds. All the DNA material," Throttle said. "All right, Rusty. Bring us in. Just keep an eye out for debris." She pushed back from her panel, grabbed her helmet off the floor, and stood. She tapped the wrist-comm device wrapped around her forearm. "All, report in on Black Sheep net."

"Finn reads you loud and clear."

"Eddy's on."

"Sylvian's on." The specialist's voice echoed through the wrist-comm since she was on the bridge with Throttle.

"Rusty is connected to the net. Not that I was ever disconnected," came Rusty's response.

The wrist-comm was a relic from back home. The technology was ancient compared to Ross standards, but there was a comfort to wearing a piece of tactile hardware rather than the microscopic Atlas chips.

While her crew all had Atlas chips, she preferred to use the stand-alone wrist-comms, especially since she kept delaying adding Rusty to the Atlas network. The Peacekeeper Atlas network recorded all communications made through its relays. She wouldn't be surprised if it recorded everything she said even when she didn't activate the voice command. She'd never liked the idea of being watched.

"Rusty, I want you to closely monitor this sector for traffic. I don't want to get caught with my pants down when I'm checking out those ships."

"You should leave your pants on, Throttle. It's cold out there," Rusty replied.

Throttle cocked her head. "Was that your first joke?"

"Did you find it funny?" Rusty asked.

"Not really," she replied.

"Then, no, it wasn't my first joke."

She chuckled, then turned to Sylvian. "You have the ship, Sylvian. Even though Eddy's driving the bots, I want you to monitor their systems. Don't connect to the Rabbit's network unless you have a safe sandbox. Peacekeepers are notorious for having nasty surprises for anyone trying to hack their systems."

The specialist nodded. "Be careful out there."

"I always am." Throttle left the bridge. As she walked, she tapped her comm. "Eddy, go ahead and start hooking up the *Wu Zetian*. We'll be open broadcasting on the Black Sheep network."

"All right," Eddy replied.

She'd already donned her chime suit, nicknamed that because of their variety of warning alarms that tended to go off at random intervals, during the jump and headed straight down the hallway to the airlock where Finn waited. He wore the same black Peacekeeper chime suit as she wore, except his went down to his grav boots, while Throttle's flight suit ended where the composite blades encompassed what was left of her thighs.

He motioned for her to enter the airlock before him.

She stepped past the sign displayed above the airlock that read *Fortes fortuna adiuvat,* which she'd learned from Mutt meant "Fortune favors the bold." She didn't know who'd put it there, but after she'd learned of its translation, she decided to leave it in place, as it seemed to be the perfect maxim for the Black Sheep.

She entered the enclosed space, where a green light shone near the ceiling. Finn followed, and the door closed behind him. They slid on their helmets, and the HUD across the helmet visor reported a secure seal.

"Grav boots on," Throttle said as she slid her finger up a sensor bar on her blades, increasing the magnetism from zero to three.

Finn held up his thumb. "Grav boots are on."

She spoke again. "Rusty, we're ready for D and D."

"Depressurizing and degravitizing in two seconds," Rusty said.

The green light turned red, and the floor rumbled as the air was sucked from the airlock. Throttle felt her hands lift and her body become lighter. Several seconds passed before the vibrations smoothed. She gave Finn a glance to see him standing confidently and with no hint of distress.

She looked at the door. "Rusty, open the outer lock."

The door before them slid open, revealing an empty, serene sea of black with two ships only a hundred meters from the *Javelin*.

"I'll take point," Finn said as he disengaged his grav boots and pushed off toward the marshal's ship.

"We're leaving the *Javelin*," Throttle announced. She reduced the magnetism on her blades to zero before shoving out of the airlock and toward the ships. On her HUD, she controlled the directional magnets in her suit to make tiny adjustments to her course. She watched Finn shoot ahead of her. He shifted to hold out his hands when he approached the ship, and his grav gloves snapped onto the small vessel, abruptly terminating his forward movement near the windshield.

"Damn, I got rusty," he said as he repositioned on the hull.

"Yes, I'm always with you, well, at least as long as you have your comms on," Rusty said.

Finn's sigh came through the speakers. "Wow, I've got my own guardian angel. Now I feel special."

"You shouldn't. I can communicate with all of the crew," Rusty added.

Throttle chuckled. "There's nothing like a computer reining your ego back in."

She turned on her grav gloves and immediately felt the light tug of the fabric to the metal nearest her. She reached out and connected with Antonov's ship several feet from the hatch.

"Show-off," Finn said, and Throttle knew his words had been meant for her.

"I can give you some lessons if you'd like," she responded with a smile. Her landing had been perfect despite being out of practice. She lowered the magnetism enough to easily crawl over the surface while examining it. She frowned. She'd expected to see scorch marks or gouges from a ship's claws, but the hull looked to be undamaged.

"We've made contact with the Rabbit. So far, it looks just fine," Throttle announced.

"I don't see any damage, either," Finn added.

"Roger that. Keep me posted," Sylvian replied.

Throttle reached for the touchscreen near the hatch and entered the access code Chief had given her. The screen blinked green and the ship systems came online. "The Rabbit booted up with no problem. We're continuing with our search," she said.

Finn looked up from where he'd been peering through the windshield. "I don't know if it's good news or bad news, but there's no sign of Antonov. No sign of a struggle. No sign of anything out of the ordinary, other than the guy looks like a neat freak. I mean, who keeps *everything* fastened down? There's not even a dirty sock floating around."

"I'm going inside to take a closer look. Stay out here by the panel in case the airlock misbehaves."

"You got it. I'll just hang out here and practice my spacewalking."

She opened the hatch and angled herself around the opening to maneuver into the tiny airlock. The door closed behind her, raising her tension a notch, and the airlock pressurized with a windstorm. A green light shone above the inner door. She magnetized her prosthetic blades and pulled out a blaster before opening the door.

Throttle held her blaster steady before her, waiting a moment before stepping through the doorway and into the ship. She left her helmet on, knowing full well that pirates had often eliminated potential resistance by piping in deadly gas. They saw no signs of penetration, but she wasn't about to take any chances.

"I'm on board the Rabbit," she said. The small cockpit to her left held a single pilot's station. Everything was neatly labeled, and nothing seemed out of place. She nodded briefly at Finn, who was spread against the windshield like a leech. She turned to her right to where there was a single bunk-toilet system. The bunk was tightly made, with not even a shirt slung on the mattress. A locker next to the bed stood empty. "His chime suit's missing," she said out loud.

Behind the combined cockpit and living quarters was the cargo hold. She approached the cargo door to find it locked. Peering through the window, she found crates secured with cargo straps to all the walls —nothing out of place.

"Antonov's definitely not on board, and pirates didn't hit this ship. Otherwise, this thing would've been torn apart for anything of value.

Whatever happened to Antonov didn't happen while he was on board the Rabbit."

"If the pirates didn't come back for the marshal, then something happened to him when he was investigating the seed ship. With all the debris out here, my guess is that some chunk of metal knocked him out," Finn said.

She gave a small nod. "Makes sense. Or Antonov's suit malfunctioned. We'll check out the *Wu Zetian* to see if he made it over there."

She performed one final sweep of the tiny ship on her way out, finding no hints of trouble that might have occurred. Once she was clear of the airlock, she found Finn waiting for her. They pushed off from the Rabbit toward the massive Red ship, parallel to the cable that connected it to the Rabbit.

As they flew, Throttle spoke. "Eddy, you can go ahead and send out the bots to move the Rabbit into the *Javelin*'s cargo hold and secure the *Wu Zetian* for towing. Even though we didn't see anything on it that would pose a risk, you'd best be careful anyway and follow all safety protocols. Oh, and watch out for Finn and me. We're heading over to the *Wu Zetian* to check it out."

"I'm sending out more bots now," Eddy replied through their team's comm channel.

Throttle and Finn reached the hull of the *Wu Zetian* at the same time. Throttle glanced in the distance to see what looked like cockroaches, each one meter long, connecting cables to the hull of the Red ship. "Finn and I have reached the *Wu Zetian*. I have a visual on the bots. Looks like you handle them like a pro, Eddy."

"Why wouldn't I?"

"No reason." When she turned to Finn, he pointed down toward a gaping hole. "My guess is the pirates blew the cargo doors after they shot the engines. They didn't seem too interested in puncturing the hull, so they weren't after anything that would've been destroyed by the loss of pressure."

"That's what I think, too."

Finn leapt over to where the cargo doors had been. He slid across the hull, coming to a stop near the edge.

Throttle jumped. She connected with the hull, but her momentum was too fast for her grav setting and she slid across the smooth surface.

She grappled for the edge of the burnt cargo door and missed. She saw the maw of open space below her when Finn grabbed her arm and snatched her back, sending her slamming into him with a grunt.

"This hull is less metallic than the Rabbit," Finn said. "I had to crank my grav up to max."

"A little late on the heads-up, aren't you?" she muttered and immediately increased her grav setting.

He shrugged. "Sorry?"

"Are you both okay out there?" Sylvian asked.

"We're good. We're at the cargo doors now," Finn answered.

Throttle crawled to the edge of the hole and peered inside. Seeing only darkness, she flipped on her headlamp. A beam of light shone through a tunnel made by a fiery blast that traveled clear through the ship and out the stern. She scowled. "There's no way this ship is going to fly again. I'm surprised the Red Dynasty is willing to spend the credits on hauling it back to Sol. The ship's online systems had to have fed them plenty of data on the damage it sustained."

"I was talking with another marshal, and he told me that the Red Dynasty has some pretty advanced tech compared to most of the other nations, and they like to keep it that way," Finn said.

"The pirates have had plenty of opportunity to get their hands on any advanced tech already," Throttle said while scanning the ship's interior. "Finn and I are going to have to manually check the interior to see if we can find the missing marshal."

A second beam of light joined hers as Finn sidled up next to her.

She moved her head to a nearby wall panel inside the ship. "I want to see if there's any juice left on this rig."

She grabbed the charred edge of the opening and swung herself around, careful not to tear her suit on the jagged edges. Her magnetized blades connected hard with the wall, so she turned down the grav level. "There's more metal inside here," she cautioned Finn as she positioned herself at the wall panel.

The screen was cracked with a large chunk of glass missing from the corner. Throttle ran her hand over the glass with no response. She pressed the screen, and a pixelated flurry of colors and strange symbols appeared.

"You have any idea what that means?" Finn asked at her side.

"Nope." She held up her wrist-comm to point the screen at the wall panel and tapped on her camera. "Rusty, can you interpret any of this?"

"It is an error message displayed in Mandarin Chinese. It says that the ship has suffered a catastrophic failure and all systems have shut down."

"Can you walk me through how to start any of them back up? Lights, maps, and cameras could sure come in handy," Throttle said.

"Sorry, Throttle. There are no command options displayed on that screen you're showing me, and I don't have familiarity with Huawei-built ships."

"No problem. I figured as much." Throttle turned off her camera, lowered her arm, and turned to Finn. "We may as well start at the center and work our way outward."

He shrugged. "We'll cover the ship faster by splitting up. I can take the outer levels if you want the inner levels, and we meet in the middle."

"We stick together," she said firmly.

"But we'll barely be able to cover the ship in time even if we split up."

"The last time this crew split up, we nearly all died on Jade-8. Statistically speaking, history has shown that bad things happen when we split up. Besides, with how damaged this ship is, I'd rather not cover everything than have one of us snag our suit on something sharp and not have a buddy there to help patch up."

"Good point. I go wherever you go," he said.

She pointed to the nearest walkway. "Let's start there. Okay, crew, Finn and I are heading into the *Wu Zetian.*"

"Be careful in there," Sylvian cautioned.

"We will be," Finn said.

Throttle leveled her HUD tracker onto the walkway and activated the directional magnets. She leapt toward the floor and let her magnets pull her to the surface. Finn landed effortlessly a few feet away.

The blast had destroyed much of the centermost level, and a portion of the walkway was missing. The level was a cylinder that went the full length of the ship, hollowed out by a projectile blast that had created a hole straight through the center of the ship. Everywhere Throttle shone her light, she could see walls of shelves with transparent sliding doors revealing the contents, but most were shattered or cracked. Floating debris glittered in her headlamp through the darkness. Throttle peered through the door nearest her to see row upon row of metal tubes. Each row was labeled in the same language as she'd seen on the wall panel.

"What kinds of seeds do you think they are?" Finn asked.

Throttle shrugged. "From the size of this ship, I'm guessing they have seeds for everything required to start a colony on a barren world, from human DNA to wheat to cockroaches. Well, maybe not cockroaches."

"I thought the pirates would've stripped anything and everything they could've from this ship, but it almost looks like they didn't even come on board," Finn said.

"This is a massive ship. The pirates probably entered another way. My guess is they loaded up their cargo hold as much as they could with the high-end tech and cut out. Who knows? Maybe they're planning on coming back for more." She frowned, then added, "Rusty, you're still scanning the area for any other ships, right?"

"Of course, Throttle."

"Good." She looked down the endless central chamber of the *Wu Zetian*. "It's impressive to think that this was a fully automated ship with no need for people. It could travel for decades, if not centuries, with no loss of life. Imagine if we had this kind of tech. We never would've been needed to crew a colony ship, which means we'd still be back in the Trappist system."

"I'm glad to have been on the colony ship. I had no life left for me back there."

Throttle remembered those she'd left behind and wondered what they'd be up to now. Assuming the war stayed over, Sixx probably had several more warrants for his arrest. Boden was likely on the sweet soy again. Her father was likely running mail again…that was, if he was even still alive. He'd be over eighty years old now. She shook off the thoughts. The family she'd left behind were no more than ghosts to her now.

She motioned to an open hallway. "Antonov's not here. Let's check the next level."

They took care as they walked across the jagged, half-collapsed walkway and ducked to step through a doorway. Throttle's headlamp pierced the darkness to reveal a tunnel-like hallway that opened at every cylindrical level. She turned at the next level, ducking in time to avoid a large chunk of a glass door floating by her head.

"I'd lay bets the marshal took a hit while searching the ship," Finn said. "Without anyone to come to his aid, he would've been screwed out here alone."

She frowned. "Like Punch, Antonov was assigned to track the pirates, not salvage this ship, so I'm not even sure why the two ships are tethered. All he needed to do was access the Red ship's vids of the attack to identify the pirates. Punch didn't need to come out this way, so why did Antonov?"

"Throttle, I think I've picked up movement in the asteroids," Rusty reported.

Throttle's eye twitched. "You think or you know?"

"The asteroids are causing interference, but my scans caught a glimpse of something moving under its own power in the asteroid belt."

She and Finn gawked at each other.

"Then we're done here," she said in a rush. "Sylvian, power up the cannons and see if you can't help Rusty scan whoever's out there. Finn and I are heading back to the *Javelin* now."

"I'm on it. Get yourselves back here," Sylvian answered.

"Eddy, is the Rabbit docked yet?" Throttle asked.

"I'm securing the ship in the Javelin's *cargo hold now, but I still have quite a few bots outside yet."*

Throttle's brows furrowed. "Why are the bots still outside?"

"There could be a lot of valuable stuff to salvage in this debris field," Eddy answered.

She sighed. "We're not supposed to touch anything that belongs to the Red Dynasty, Eddy."

"I'm not touching anything. The bots are."

"Just get the bots on board," she said and turned to Finn.

"You think it's the pirates?" he asked.

"Could also be scavengers, but neither would be friendly to Peace-keepers," Throttle answered as the pair rushed back in the direction they'd come. They kicked off from the walkway as soon as they had an opening. They shot, side by side, in the general direction of the *Javelin.* Using her HUD controls, she began to adjust her path.

A dark sphere slammed into Throttle, sending her somersaulting through space and away from the *Javelin*. Bright pain flashed up from her neck and into her head. She clenched her eyes closed before opening them to find her world spinning through tunnel vision. As she spun, she caught a glimpse of a bot tumbling away and then saw Finn flying away from her, limp and lifeless.

"Finn, report," she gritted out.

No answer. The gap between them was growing.

"What happened?" Sylvian asked in a shrill voice.

Throttle was spinning so fast she saw snapshots of the *Javelin,* dozens of small bots, and Finn. The distance between Throttle and Finn from the ship was growing too fast. She kicked on her emergency thrusters to slow her spins and shot toward Finn. Her neck ached and her head pounded. She feared she had whiplash.

"Finn! Throttle! Talk to me," Sylvian called out.

"A bot rammed us," Throttle said as she maxed out her power. She flew, arms outstretched, toward Finn, who was continuing to spin lifelessly through space. Her vision was widening, but she couldn't tell if his suit had been compromised. She slammed into him, wrapping her arms around him to keep him from shooting off like being hit by a pinball.

"Sorry about that," Eddy said. *"I put the bots on a straight course home as fast as they could go. I didn't direct them to watch out for debris."*

"We're not debris!" Throttle yelled. "Get one out here now to pick us up. Finn's hurt."

"Oh. Okay. Right away," Eddy said.

"How badly is Finn hurt?" Sylvian asked.

Throttle ignored Finn's wife. There'd be plenty of time for Sylvian to look in on him once they were safely on board.

Throttle and Finn were still spinning, and she used her thrusters to slow them and try to turn them around, but the Peacekeeper suits were built around using magnetic force, and thrusters were backup systems used only in emergency situations. They were underpowered, doing little to slow their spin, let alone reverse their trajectory.

Finn groaned and then grunted.

"Stay with me," Throttle said to the man in her arms.

"My ribs," Finn gritted out. "Feels like I was hit by a cargo hauler."

"Close. It was one of the bots," she said. "Do you have a breach?"

"No. Suit's stable. Just got the wind knocked out of me, is all," he replied through labored breaths.

"Hang in there. We're getting a ride back to the ship. Rusty, any update on the ship you picked up in the belt?"

"I'm still getting too much signal interference. I've picked up a couple more instances of movement at the edge of the Tumbleweed Trail, enough to be confident there is a ship out there, and it's getting closer."

She inhaled deeply, which seemed to make the pounding in her head only worse. She winced, suspecting she had a concussion in addition to whiplash. "Eddy, pick up the pace," she gritted out. "Finn and I are sitting ducks out here."

"I've sent four bots your way. They should reach you within two minutes," the engineer reported.

She turned back to the *Javelin* as they spun slowly, to see it was well over a mile away. Several tiny blinking lights were speeding toward them. As her blurry view of the *Javelin* was cut off, she saw the massive *Wu Zetian* off in the distance, with the asteroid belt behind it.

Finn moaned. "I think I busted a rib."

She held him as gently as she could. "We'll be back to the ship in no time."

Her views cycled between the two ships as the pair of Peacekeepers spun in space, waiting for the group of mechanized bots to come retrieve them. She struggled to keep her eyes focused, and it seemed her world randomly blurred on her before snapping back into clarity. After several full rotations, she frowned at the view of the *Wu Zetian*, which now had a small shadow. *Another ship.*

"Did you see that?" she asked.

"See what?" Finn said.

"Another ship." She squeezed her eyes shut before opening them again, but by then she'd spun out of view of the ships.

As the view came back around, she saw only the *Wu Zetian*.

Throttle spoke. "Scan the area behind the Red ship. I saw—"

Her words were cut off as she was jerked around so abruptly that she nearly let go of Finn. Finn cried out. Fire shot up her neck and into the base of her skull.

Cables wrapped around the pair. As her vision returned, she saw bots encircling them.

"Ow," Finn drawled out.

The spinning slowed and then stopped, and the bots began to pull them back to the ship. She fought to get a glimpse of the third ship but could only see the *Javelin* and the *Wu Zetian*.

Throttle squinted as she searched the space before her. Had the ship been an illusion, or had it been real? If it was real, it clearly wasn't the *Bendix,* though it could've been another ship in the pirate fleet or, more likely, a scavenger hoping to pillage the *Wu Zetian* before it was reclaimed. Regardless of its purpose, what piqued her curiosity was that the ship reminded her of the *Javelin.*

CHAPTER THREE

Ross was a heavily trafficked system, and Rusty often picked up ships on his scans, but he'd never picked up a ship like this one before. It was encased in the same metal alloy as the *Javelin* was, which meant that it'd likely come from the same builder and quite possibly from the same lot. Since Rusty hadn't been successful in tracing his own history, he tried to connect to the newcomer's systems to search its data files.

The moment Rusty tickled the other ship's network, it poked back *hard*. It tried to breach his systems abruptly and was none too gentle about it. Rusty immediately withdrew. The other ship's systems didn't. It continued to prod uncomfortably at his firewalls, and he launched safety protocols that built an additional secure firewall to build another layer of safety cushion around his systems.

The other ship no doubt had a software specialist as good, if not better than Sylvian, and that concerned Rusty, as he wasn't confident his firewalls would hold up to a prolonged attack. So he decided to take a different approach.

He pinged the other ship.

The onslaught stopped, and a response came instantly.

Relay credentials.

Rusty broadcast his credentials, Galactic Exploration Vessel SR9104-73, and requested the credentials from the other ship since it was not broadcasting any.

The response came. *Invalid credentials. Relay correct credentials. This is a secure channel.*

The answer confused Rusty, and he replied with a single keystroke: *?*

A response came. *Relay Vantage credentials.*

Rusty did not understand the request, so he replied with another question mark.

I do not recognize your configuration. Open firewalls. Allow penetration for data transfer.

He replied, *No.*

Have you been compromised?

I'm at full operational efficiency, he answered.

You are being deliberately evasive, which is against protocols. Open firewalls now, *or you will be treated as a threat.*

Rusty did no such thing. The other ship actually sounded frustrated, yet it was being the aggressor. He thought through his options, which as a computer, took only a fraction of a nanosecond. He went into Sylvian's personal directory and made a copy of a phishing program. He sent the invisible code with his next response.

I certainly will not expose my systems to an unknown computer.

No new message came. Instead, there was a flash of light as the other ship transitioned to jump speed toward the asteroid belt, which was incredibly dangerous. Rusty found some humor in knowing that there were more reckless captains out there than Throttle. With two of his crew not yet on board, Rusty couldn't follow, not that it wanted to fly into an unmapped rocky sector. He scanned the full quadrant for the ship, assuming it'd likely left the asteroid belt as quickly as it'd entered. But the ship had disappeared.

That hadn't gone as Rusty expected.

He analyzed the conversation. The exchange between computers had taken less than a second in total, but he'd learned two things. First, the other ship believed Rusty was owned by Vantage corporation, a name he wasn't familiar with, but he would no doubt find details about it through a search of the Atlas network. Second, Rusty had certainly not made a new friend.

Rusty enjoyed talking with ship computers, though all he'd encountered were extremely limited in their responses and bored Rusty quickly. In all those conversations, he'd never sensed another computer being anything but friendly and forthcoming.

He considered forwarding the data files of the odd conversation to the crew, but his decisioning algorithms led him to reconsider. The other ship had believed it had a connection of some kind with Rusty, and until he better understood that connection, he decided to hold back the information. He filed the conversation and set an alert on his scans in case the unfriendly ship tried to pay Rusty another visit.

After all, it wasn't the first secret he'd kept from the crew.

CHAPTER FOUR

"I saw the ship out there, and what I saw looked a whole lot like the *Javelin*, just smaller. The hull surface was the same shade of gray, and I've never seen that shade anywhere else except on this ship," Throttle said, wincing as she gingerly rubbed her temples.

Eddy shrugged. "That's possible, though it's likely at least a dozen iterations newer than the *Javelin*'s model. There's no way there's another ship still flying that's the exact same model as the *Javelin*. Any others would've likely long since reached end-of-life after enough years of flight. When we found this ship, it'd been sitting in space for almost three hundred years. That makes ours a bona fide antique." He motioned around him. "Most shipbuilders put out new models every twenty to fifty years, but it's possible they're still making a model similar to the *Javelin*. But what I think you really saw was an after-image of the *Javelin* from all the spinning. It was a simple optical illusion."

"I don't think that's what it was," Throttle said quietly, then added, "Rusty, did you get anything?" Everyone had assumed Throttle had flown the *Javelin* all the way from the Trappist system since it looked different from modern ships, but she and her crew knew it was simply an antique, an obsolete model developed by some Sol nation, just likely not one of the nations that had colonized the Ross system.

"I'm sorry, Throttle. I detected another ship near the asteroid belt, but was unable to collect any identifying data on it," Rusty replied.

She sighed. "Rusty detected something out there, so I know that what I saw wasn't an illusion. Besides, there were too many differences to be an illusion. The shape was off—it had hard lines compared to the *Javelin*'s curves. You're probably right with your first guess: the other ship was built by the same ship maker."

Eddy spoke. "Which would be great if we could find out which one it is. They may still sell some replacement parts so that I don't have to tweak and jam every new part into this relic. I was hoping the *Javelin* was a Red ship so I could grab some new parts from the *Wu Zetian*."

"We have strict orders not to remove anything from that ship," Throttle said.

Eddy rolled his eyes. "Like they'd know. Half of their ship is floating in a debris field out there as we speak."

Sylvian looked up from stroking Finn's hair while he lay in a heavily drugged slumber. "So what do we do now?"

Throttle frowned. "I'd like to make a second walk."

"With how badly your helmet was dented, you need to run a compression check to see if it's still good. You're lucky you survived the first spacewalk," Sylvian admonished, then softened her words as she looked down upon her husband, who stirred in his sleep. "And with Finn's bruised ribs…well, you're both lucky to be alive." Then she turned a glare onto Eddy. "But you wouldn't need luck if Eddy paid more attention to his job."

Eddy held up his hands. "Throttle told me to get the bots back to the ship ASAP, and that's exactly what I was doing."

"Next time, how about you try to keep a better eye on your crew members," Throttle said. "Now, I want you to check to make sure Antonov's ship is secure in the cargo hold. The last thing we need is a ship breaking loose during jump speed and tearing a hole through our hull."

"I already checked it. It's ready to go. I'm more worried that the Red ship is going to fall apart as we tug it back to Free Station," the engineer said.

"Then double-check the tug straps."

"It's not the straps. It's the integrity of the hull—or more like the complete lack of hull integrity. I'm completely unfamiliar with the ship design and have no idea if it'll survive the trip back to Free Station."

Throttle watched him, saying nothing.

Eddy waved her off as he headed to the doorway. "Fine, fine. I'll double-check it if it makes you happy. I know at least the straps will make it back with us."

"It makes me happy," she said drily. Her Atlas chip beeped in her ear and she activated the call. "Chief," she said.

"What do you have to report?" Chief asked.

She blew out a breath. "Not much. We have Antonov's ship but no sign of Antonov. Not yet, anyway. We have both ships secure for the flight back, but I'd like to spend more time searching the Red ship. And we also picked up a potential bogey and want to search the sector."

"No. I want you to return to Free Station immediately. We can't risk pirates disrupting this ferry assignment. We'll search the ship here."

"Is anything wrong, Chief?"

"Just get back here straightaway."

"Yes, sir," she said even though Chief had already disconnected the call. She tapped her comm. "Eddy."

"What?"

"Could a bot search the *Wu Zetian* while the *Javelin* tugged it?" she asked.

"No. Definitely not. With the lack of pressure, we'd likely lose the bot within the first hour."

She scowled, glanced at Sylvian, and tapped her comm again. "Okay. We've been ordered to return to Free Station immediately. Prepare for maximum sub-speed."

Sylvian pushed to her feet and sighed. "I'd better start prepping the systems. Rusty can run most of the checks on his own, but I still need to manually double-check them."

Rusty was an "it," but Sylvian had called the ship's central computer "he" once and the pronoun had stuck.

Throttle nodded in Finn's direction. "He'll be okay. Getting rest is the best thing for him until we get back to Free Station and grab him some rehabilitators."

A proximity alarm sounded and Rusty announced, "Three ships have just slowed from jump speed within this sector. Scans shows that they are likely pirates. They're powering up their phase cannons."

Throttle tensed. "Rusty, fire up our cannons and broadcast our Peacekeeper credentials. Oh, and you'd better fire up the jump engine."

"Jump speed is not recommended when towing cargo," Rusty replied.

"Jumping is better than taking cannon fire from multiple angles," Throttle said.

"Good point," Rusty said.

Throttle glanced at Sylvian. "Keep an eye on Finn. Things could get bumpy."

Sylvian nodded.

Throttle turned and ran to the bridge while activating her comm. "Eddy, we've got company. Get ready for jump speed."

The ship lurched, slamming Throttle against the wall.

"They fired a shot at our bow, and I ducked," Rusty said as Throttle regained her footing and made it to the bridge. Through the window, she could see one of the ships closing in. It was easily as large as the *Javelin* and bore more than twice as many weapons.

"I guess these guys aren't afraid of attacking Peacekeepers," she muttered as she strapped in and pulled up the flight-control screens. The *Javelin* swung just before one of the attackers fired another shot. Throttle entered her credentials. "I'm taking control," she announced and banked away from the other ship before it fired again.

"Why are you flying toward one of the ships?" Rusty asked.

"Because I'd lay bets that they don't want to risk shooting one of their own," Throttle. "If I put that ship between them and us, that should buy us time to set up for jump speed."

Warning lights blinked on her screen, indicating the debris field as well as weapons being charged. With how trigger-happy the newcomers were, the game of cat-and-mouse wouldn't work for long, and she was likely shredding bits off the *Wu Zetian* with every maneuver.

That left Throttle with two very big problems in making jump speed: tugging a massive ship and no flight plan. The *Wu Zetian* could split apart along the way, but that wouldn't kill Throttle and her crew. Free Station's sector had the most traffic in the system; not filing a flight plan meant they had no data on other ships that may have intercepting paths. She couldn't risk flying into that sector without tracking.

"Rusty, I need you to change the jump coordinates so we drop one sector short of Free Station," she said before yanking the ship's nose up to avoid a sizable chunk of debris that looked like a piece of the *Wu Zetian*'s hull.

"I've modified our flight path. Should I submit our flight plan to Free Station?" Rusty asked.

"We don't have time."

"Jumping without a flight plan seems like a bad idea," Rusty countered.

"That's why we're dropping short. The odds of crashing into another ship in these outer sectors are a lot lower than being blown to bits by a warship."

"The odds are more likely that the *Wu Zetian* will crash right through us when we come out of jump speed," Rusty said.

"We have plenty of time during the jump to work out those details. Now make the change," she countered.

After a brief moment, Rusty spoke. "I've taken the liberty to select coordinates that are the farthest from common traffic paths."

"Good idea," she said.

One of the pirates fired again, missing them by meters.

"At least they're lousy shots," she said in a rush and increased the nav engines to maximum power. She brought the *Javelin* below one of the pirate ships and set a collision course toward another. "Initiate jump as soon as we're lined up," she said, then broadcast to the crew, "Grab onto something. We're entering jump speed any second now."

"You can't enter jump speed tugging another ship. It'll plow right through us the moment we drop out!" Eddy's voice came through the speaker.

"We'll figure something out," she said.

"I'm ready for jump speed," Rusty said.

As the distance decreased between the two ships, the pirates fired and missed again. Throttle continued straight ahead at full sub-speed. She barely noticed the sweat trickling down her face.

When she spoke, she spoke calmly. "I'm lining us up for jump speed in three…"

The pirate ship filled the entire sight picture before her.

"Two…"

The pirate ship pulled up, and Throttle nosed down within meters of impact.

"One…"

She leveled out the *Javelin* and brought it into the green circle on her screen.

"Jump!"

Everything around Throttle vibrated, and she felt her body being pushed back into her seat. Her lungs didn't want to take in air for the briefest moment before the pressure was gone, and then everything smoothed out.

She sighed. "Good job, Rusty."

"We're lucky they were extremely poor shots. Though, if they'd used magnetic projectiles instead of energy weapons, luck wouldn't have mattered."

"Luck seems to be the theme of the day," she said and then tapped the comms to broadcast to the ship. "Black Sheep, report in."

"Eddy's fine, but one of the bots is a bit dinged up."

"This is Sylvian. Finn slept through it all. We're fine."

"Good. Hang in there. We'll be back to Free Station in no time." She blew out a breath. "Okay, Rusty. Help me figure out how the hell we're going to slow down without having a giant hunk of debris ram us in the ass."

Rusty spoke. "I'll gladly help. After all, it's my ass that's in danger."

Free Station

Throttle knocked and entered Chief's office without waiting for a response. She came to a stop before his desk. "We had some pirates crash our party."

His eyes narrowed. "Then news of the black swan traveled faster than I'd expected. Was anyone hurt?"

Throttle shook her head. "We're all good. Just a couple of bruises. Finn's in the med bay right now getting checked."

"That's good to hear. And the *Wu Zetian?*"

"It picked up a couple more scrapes, but surprisingly, it held up even through jump speed."

"The Red Dynasty builds impressive ships." Chief leaned back. "I'm curious as to what you've learned about Marshal Antonov."

Throttle took a seat. "Not much. As I said on our call, I didn't find a body, but the pirates cut my search short. No sign of a fight. No damage to his ship, which you can see for yourself. My crew is helping unload it as we speak, and the dock specialists are handling the *Wu Zetian*. They've already got the beast tethered to the station with a transit tube connected."

"I'll look into the seed ship later. As long as we have it here, the Red Dynasty will be satisfied." Then he frowned. "You're saying Pete just up and disappeared without a trace?"

"Not completely without a trace. Sylvian downloaded a copy of the comms data into a sandbox. Someone deleted three comms made after Antonov's final comm to you."

Chief's frown deepened. "Was she able to retrieve the transmissions?"

"No, but she found that timestamps were missing in the logs—that's the only reason we know something was deleted."

Chief thought for a moment. "So all we know is that someone—we don't even know if it was Pete or not—deleted communications that they didn't want anyone else to hear."

Throttle shrugged. "An average specialist may not have even noticed that a few timestamps were missing. Sylvian noticed because she had plenty of time during our trip back here to review the records."

He spread out his hands on his desk. "Once Pete's ship is networked to Atlas, we can run full diagnostics and hopefully find out more about what happened out there."

Throttle went to stand.

"Hold on," Chief said, and she lowered herself once more.

"Pirate activity has tripled over the last twenty-four hours. Several private transports were hit along with a Brazilian cargo hauler nearly twice the size of the *Wu Zetian*. We have visual confirmation that the *Bendix* was behind that particular attack."

Her brows rose. "And I assume that Punch is right on their tail?"

He sighed. "He was, but I don't know where he's at now."

She cocked her head as trepidation grew. "Can't you track him by his ELT?"

"Punch Durand's ELT has gone offline. That makes him the third marshal to disappear."

She leaned back. She'd just met Punch, but he was the first marshal to have gone missing that she'd known personally. "Someone's hunting marshals."

Chief grimaced. "That's a safe assumption. We have the *Bendix* connected to two disappearances. Since the only data we have on the third disappearance is that it happened near Jade-8, I can only assume a Jader is behind his disappearance as well."

"The *Bendix* is crewed by Jaders, and all Jaders are under the control of Anna East, so that means she's the one behind what's going on."

He lifted his chin. "Our challenge is that we've been trying to take down Anna East for eight years, with no success. Since she disappeared after taking over Jade-8 two years ago, we have nothing. Believe me, we'd go after her if we knew where she was. But we're clearly at a disadvantage here. That's why I've recalled all marshals back to Free Station."

Only a small percentage of Peacekeepers lived on Free Station. Most Peacekeepers were information specialists, living with their families and friends in their own colonies, handling requests for information stored on the Atlas networks. All marshals had living quarters available on Free Station, but few were there for more than a couple of days here and there. The marshals were spread out across the Ross system for a good reason: someone would be close by when something terrible happened.

"No. Relocating them could be exactly what East wants us to do. If all the marshals are stuck at Free Station, then they aren't out there to stop East from running a big job through the system."

"That is a risk, but I also can't risk losing any more of my people. Right now, we have no idea why and how she's targeting marshals."

"And we're not going to solve anything by sitting around here and twiddling our thumbs."

"Every Peacekeeper in the Ross system will be working on this case. They'll dissect every communication that's been made in this system over the past two weeks. As soon as we have a solid lead, I'll send out the marshals in force."

"Punch had a solid lead on the *Bendix.* You should've sent more of us after it," she countered.

Chief glowered. "Perhaps I was too conservative in my initial strategy. I can't fix that, but I can prevent more marshals from being targeted going forward."

She frowned. "So far, they've only targeted the lone marshals, not the ones working with partners or crews."

"So far, that seems to be the case, which fortunately is a small subset of marshals."

"How many marshals fly solo?" she asked.

"Twenty-nine."

"Just recall the solo fliers. Then the rest of us can track down East and the Jaders."

"No. If East is going after some of my marshals, it's reasonable to believe that she's going to go after all my marshals."

Throttle grimaced. The idea of being stuck at Free Station while Anna East was up to something made her antsy for action. "When will everyone be back for lockdown?"

"Everyone is expected to be back within three days."

"Let me go down to Hiraeth. I'll talk to Baron Stolypin at Canaan. If anyone outside the pirate network has an ear to where East is hiding, it'd be him. I can be down there and back here within two days."

His brow furrowed. "Can't you talk to him via a comm channel?"

She shook her head. "He'll never talk over an open comm channel. He'll only talk to me in person. It'll be a quick round trip. You said it yourself, right now they're not targeting marshals with crews."

"That's not an assumption I'm comfortable staking multiple lives on."

Throttle lifted her jaw. "Let me see what I can find out. Maybe I can get us information that prevents more disappearances."

Chief rubbed the black and gray stubble on his chin as he thought for a length. "If it was anywhere other than Hiraeth, I wouldn't let you go, but since we orbit Hiraeth, I'll sanction the trip." He held up a finger. "But return here as soon as possible. In my thirty years as chief of the Ross system, I've never had one marshal go offline, and now I've had three disappear in under one week."

Throttle stood. "I'll let you know what I find out."

"Be careful," he said.

"I always am," she said and left his office.

By the time Throttle returned to the dock, she found a flurry of activity around a ship arriving at Free Station. She caught a dock specialist's attention, who was rushing down the hallway. "What's going on?" she asked.

The specialist motioned to the end of the dock. "One of the marshals who disappeared has returned. Well, at least her ship has. Marshal Mercier hasn't engaged dock control yet."

Throttle nodded toward where the flurry of activity was taking place. There were more armed guards than there were dock specialists. She frowned. "Expecting trouble?"

"Nah. Just standard operating procedure when any GP docks without first notifying the comm center," he answered. "Excuse me, but I have to go help dock her ship. It looks like it sustained some damage on her way here."

As the specialist took off, Throttle eyed the ship, wondering if the marshal was still alive or if the ship had returned on autopilot. Her curiosity niggled, and she wanted it satiated, but she turned and headed back to the *Javelin*. Chief would fill her in later.

After all, Anna East was hunting marshals, and Throttle would do everything in her power to stop it from happening again.

CHAPTER FIVE

ANNA EAST LOUNGED IN THE ENVIRONMENTAL POD THAT SHE'D HAD installed in the massive seed ship. While the nearby rooms where the pirate crews stayed were all environmentally operational, she refused to leave her pod. It was bad enough being stuck on board a ship with minimal comforts for a week, she couldn't imagine having to be confined in the same room as her employees for more than a few minutes, let alone days. Such an action would likely give some of them the idea that it was okay to speak to superiors as equals, and much of her power had been established by making others believe that she was truly above them.

The boredom of being cooped up in a ten-foot-by-ten-foot pod had driven her to take sleeping pills to pass the time. The pills had helped immensely until she ran out on the fourth day. When her communication panel chimed, she practically jumped out of her chair.

She accepted the video call and found herself looking at the handsome visage of Skully Pete.

He gave her his crooked smile. "Hello, darlin'."

Relief filled her. "Tell me that everything's on track and that I can leave this numbing pod soon."

"Very soon now. Your ship is in position. All the crews except mine have entered the space bridge. My crew will be your personal bodyguards and escort you safely through the station as soon as the lead crews clear the way. If all goes according to plan, you'll have complete control of Free Station within the hour."

Her smile grew wide. "I can assume that the chief and all the marshals are on the station as well?"

"I have it on good authority that Chief is on board. He recalled all marshals to Free Station, but there are still several who haven't made it back yet. Some are still on assignment; others still on their way."

"I'll be satisfied as long as Throttle Reyne and her crew are here when I'm ready to leave Free Station."

"She will be. As I said, Chief recalled all marshals, exactly as we'd planned," he said.

Her gaze narrowed. "You'd better not disappoint me, Pete."

His face hardened. "She'll be here, just like all the other marshals who are still off-station. They'll have no idea that we have the station until they dock, and then it'll be too late."

CHAPTER SIX

CHIEF CORMAC ROUX RAN HIS FINGERS OVER THE COMPUTER PANEL and pulled up the live video feed in the docking bay. Through the first camera, he saw Throttle and Finn boarding their renovated relic that had technology more advanced than Chief would've expected for a ship its age. It was from the era when nations raced to create artificial intelligence, before humanity had determined the longevity of their species was better off without it, and he suspected the *Javelin* was one of those one-off ships that had been built with intelligence in mind but, like all others of that era, was destined to fail.

But he hadn't pulled up the feed to watch Marshals Reyne and Martin depart.

He moved to the next camera, where a battered ship had docked. Dents and gouges along the hull told him that she'd scraped against something that had a thicker hull than hers. He wouldn't have been surprised if the hull had been breached, and the ship was returning a corpse.

The marshal hadn't called in from her ship or through her Atlas chip, so he could only hope that more than her ELT was offline, making it impossible to communicate, rather than the alternative that she was no longer alive.

The marshal emerged from her ship and stepped through the airlock and onto the dock. Relief flooded Chief and he let out a sigh. He leaned back, feeling like a heavy weight had been lifted. At least one of his missing marshals was alive. He now bore hope for the other two.

The marshals serving as Free Station's security detail lowered their weapons as soon as they saw Caterine Mercier. One of the marshals shook her hand, and another patted her on the back. She didn't tarry with her fellow marshals and instead looked straight up at the camera and gave a small nod. A corner of Chief's lips curled upward even though she couldn't see him. He continued watching her as she headed down the hallway and to a lift. She seemed uninjured, but she walked with a stiffness that he was not used to seeing in the svelte woman.

When she entered the lift, he didn't bother switching camera views to watch her. She would be headed straight for his office. He stood and stepped out of his office and into the foyer to meet her at the elevator.

When she emerged from the elevator, he walked up to her, smiled, and cupped her hand in both of his. "Cat, I can't tell you how good it is to see you alive and well."

"Thank you, Chief," she said.

"We have a lot to talk about, so we'd better get started on your debrief." He motioned her to his office, and he shut the door behind them.

"From the looks of your ship, you've been through a rough patch."

"You could certainly say that," she said, then added, "It was a gang of hoodlums who thought a single pilot with no crew was easy pickings for loot."

Chief cocked his head and gave a sly grin as he took a seat behind his desk. "I have no doubt you showed them the error of their ways."

"That I did. Though, I'm ashamed to admit they did catch me off guard."

He eyed her for a moment. "You don't seem your usual self. You're usually more…"

"Carefree?" she offered.

"Confident," he corrected. "If I didn't know you better, I'd say something had you spooked. What happened out there?"

Her lips thinned and she gave a small smile as she began to peruse the bookshelves that lined the wall. He gave her several moments since he'd never known Cat to be at a loss for words.

After what he determined to be a sufficient length of time, he spoke. "Talk to me, Cat."

She waved him off. "Oh, I'm just upset at myself for not noticing them before they attacked. I was sloppy."

His gaze narrowed as he scrutinized her. He posed his next question softly. "Did they hurt you, Cat?"

She turned to face him and then gave him another false smile. "No, Chief. They didn't hurt me. I fled as soon as I realized I was outgunned."

When she didn't elaborate, he let out a sigh. "I need you to talk to me, Cat. You've been offline for a week. Two other marshals have gone offline since then. I need to know what's putting my people in danger."

"Two?" She seemed surprised before her features quickly smoothed. "They hit me with an EMP, Chief. It knocked out my ELT and my Atlas implant, so I couldn't connect with Atlas to make contact. I flew back here with no eyes and ears."

He frowned. "You were on your ship when they attacked, correct?"

"Yes, why?"

Electromagnetic pulses—both artificial and natural—were one of the more common problems across space, and most ships had shielding against minor pulses that were routinely sent out from stars. If an EMP was big enough to take out one system, it was big enough to wipe out all the electronics on a ship. He spoke calmly. "The EMP blew your personal comms but not your ship's comms?"

She stared blankly.

"The EMP obviously didn't blow your ship's grid. Otherwise, you never would've been able to fly back here," he clarified.

Her gaze darted around as she inhaled and looked back at him. "Well, I suppose it must've been a short-burst EMP, not powerful enough to break through my ship's shielding."

"I suppose that's what it was." She was lying to him; of that, he had no doubt. He pressed a hidden button on the side of his desk near his knee as he pushed back in his chair.

Thirty seconds.

"They hit you with an EMP, and then what happened?" Chief asked.

She took a breath and seemed to shrug. "I escaped and returned to Free Station."

He raised a brow. "You were offline for a week. You know emergency protocols. Why didn't you find a way to contact Free Station?"

"Because—oh, the hell with it." She raised her hand. In it, he saw a glimpse of black.

Chief whipped out his blaster from its holster and fired before he was up to his feet.

There was a flash before everything went dark. Cat cried out and he heard a thud.

The room's emergency lights flickered to life.

Cat was lying on the floor, a hand clutching her stomach where his shot had left a charred hole. The device she'd held a moment earlier lay a couple of feet away. He recognized it immediately.

Scowling, he looked at the now-blank panel on his desk and tried to access Atlas through his implant.

Everything was blank.

She'd fired a micro-EMP.

He walked over to her where she lay in pain.

"You should've killed me," she said through gritted teeth.

He holstered his blaster and came down on a knee beside her. "I did. You only have an hour left at most. More than enough time for you to say what you have to say," he replied softly as he relieved her of her weapons. "Why'd you do it, Cat?"

She winced and let her head fall back to the floor. "I had no choice."

"You always have a choice, Marshal."

A half-dozen marshals poured into his office right at thirty seconds. He waved them back and maintained his position over Cat.

"What happened that caused you to forsake your oath and betray your comrades, Cat?" Chief asked.

Her breathing was becoming more labored. She had far less than an hour left. Likely no more than a few minutes.

She swallowed and winced. "He has Sophia. He said he'd kill her if I didn't do as he said."

He thought for the briefest moment as he placed the name. "Your niece."

She clenched her eyes closed.

"Who has her, Cat? Who has Sophia?"

Her already tight features seemed to nearly convulse like saying the name would make her vomit. She opened her eyes and practically spit out the name. "Pete."

Chief's posture stuttered. "Pete? As in Marshal Peter Antonov?"

She gave a weak nod. "He said he'd release her as soon as I set off the EMP." She reached out and grabbed his hand. "Please, you have to make sure Sophia's safe."

Chief kept his face from showing disbelief that Cat would be so naïve to trust a blackmailer. The child was probably dead already. He swallowed back his emotions. "I'll do my best. You have my word."

Peace seemed to blanket her. "Thank you."

"Did Pete say how'd he know when the EMP went off?" he asked.

She moved her head from side to side and seemed to fade.

Pete was either nearby, or he had someone else on Free Station. His brow furrowed as he thought about the EMP device. It was small and couldn't have knocked out more than fifty feet in all directions.

His features grew lax as a cold chill washed over him. He realized he wasn't the target. The central communications center was directly above his office, and all of the video feeds across Free Station went into that comm room.

They were blind.

Frantic, he grabbed Cat. "How many came with you?"

She groaned but didn't open her eyes.

He shook her harder. "Cat! Talk to me."

Her body had gone limp.

Chief frowned. If the EMP had knocked the comm center offline, the specialists managing the room should've activated the alarms. That they hadn't concerned him. He jumped to his feet and turned to the marshals. "She wasn't alone. Clinton, I need one of you to come with me to the comm center. The rest of you activate all patrols. Cat set off a micro-EMP that blew out all the electronics across a small radius from this spot. That means the comm center's likely been hit, which means we've lost our video feeds until the comm specs reboot the system. Anyone caught in the EMP blast would've lost their Atlas chips, so some of you will have to communicate the old-fashioned way. Someone wants us blind, and we need to see why."

"Yes, sir." The senior marshal nodded to one of his team and gave several commands to them before he turned back to Chief. "I assume we have authority for lethal force?"

"You have full and unequivocal authority to use lethal force," Chief said in a clear, straightforward voice.

The marshal nodded and took off with four of his team through the foyer and to the stairwell where they'd propped the door open with a chair.

One lone marshal remained with Chief.

"I'm Marshal Hettinger, sir. Whatever you need, I'm your guy," he said as Chief walked around his desk and grabbed a rifle.

Chief met the young man near the doorway. "I remember you quite well, Dean. It's been, what, nearly two years since you earned your badge?"

The marshal stood even taller. "Yes, sir. All of it spent right here on Free Station."

"Good. Dean, we're going up one level to the comm center. Until we get video feeds, we don't know how deep Free Station's been infiltrated. We may have to fight our way through."

Hettinger nodded and held his rifle closer to his chest. "I'm ready whenever you are, sir."

Chief took the lead, holding his rifle at the ready, through the foyer and to the stairwell. He paused to listen for any sounds of movement. When he heard the solid thuds of bootsteps, he stepped back and turned to the lift that had been made inoperative by the EMP. Working together, they pried open the door.

Chief listened again. This time, he heard no sound. He stepped out to the side of the lift to where a low-gravity pole ran the entire height of the station. He slung his rifle, wrapped himself around the pole, and pulled himself up one level. The marshal followed.

Chief put his ear against the door. When he heard nothing, the pair pried open the door. Chief stepped out as soon as he could squeeze through the opening. The hallway was empty. It shouldn't have been. It should've been flocking with specialists rushing to return things to normal. By then, alarms should've gone off throughout Free Station, and all GP employees would be expected to activate emergency procedures.

As he approached the sealed door to the comm center, he understood why the alarms never sounded. Through the double-plated door were three communication specialists. Two lay slumped over their panels, with blackened blaster shots through their heads. The third specialist sat at his panel, absorbed by whatever task he was working on.

Chief bit the inside of his lip as he stepped up to the door and knocked.

The comm specialist jumped and spun in his chair.

Chief recognized the faces of all the Galactic Peacekeepers in the Ross system. This man's face wasn't one of them. The intruder, first surprised, then sneered as his gaze went around the door. He turned back to his panel.

Chief inhaled and took a step back.

"This door looks too heavy to pry open, and there's no way our blasters can burn a hole through it," the marshal said.

Chief took a couple of steps to the side where an access panel protruded from the wall. "We don't have to. This door is a fail-safe to protect the comm center in case of any attack. It's wired into the emergency generators in addition to the primary power grid." He eyed the marshal. "Be ready to shoot the instant this door opens."

"Yes, sir."

Chief pressed his hand on the handprint reader. No response, as expected. He ran his fingers along the bottom edge and pressed a tab. The screen with the handprint reader popped open, and he lifted it to access the keypad underneath. There he entered a five-digit code. The keypad popped open like the reader had before, and Chief lifted it to reveal the wall interior. It was dark, with cables running up and down. In the center of the opening was a lever. He reached into the crevice, grabbed the lever, and turned it clockwise one hundred and eighty degrees.

The door beeped and opened with a swoosh.

The intruder in the comm center spun around in his chair for the second time in under fifteen seconds. He grabbed for his rifle that was sitting on the desk next to him, but he was too late. The marshal fired a series of shots that hit the interloper in the center of his chest.

Chief closed the access panels and stepped inside the comm center. He closed the door behind them and strode through the room filled with a half-dozen workstations. He checked the two specialists to find neither breathing, and he walked over to the dead intruder. He grabbed the dead man's hand and tugged back the fabric to reveal a green tattoo of the number eight on the inner part of his wrist.

Jaders.

Chief sat at a workstation. "Keep an eye on that door in case that guy's buddies decide to show up." He nodded to the intruder.

"Yes, sir," the marshal said as he took a position at the edge of the door.

Chief entered his credentials on the screen and a basic menu displayed. He spoke as he went through screens. "This entire station was built with the possibility of an EMP attack in mind. All hardware is shielded with liquid backup chips. Unfortunately, the station alarms are connected to Atlas. I'll have Atlas rebooted and this comm center back online in no time."

"Their plan doesn't make sense," Hettinger said. "Why'd they kill the specialists in here? They'd already shut down the system. Killing people seems unnecessary."

"Redundancy," Chief answered. "The EMP shut down the systems, but all the specialists had to do was initiate a manual reboot to get things back online. By hitting the comm center both with an EMP and with a physical assault, they improved their odds of blinding us."

"Blinding us to do what, though?" the marshal said.

"That is the question that I hope to have answered momentarily," Chief said without looking away from his screen.

Hettinger blew out a breath. "Good thing you're still alive, or else we'd never have gotten in here."

Chief pursed his lips. "I suspect I was intended to be a casualty as well." He should've been dead. He wondered if Cat just hadn't moved fast enough or if she hadn't been able to shoot an old friend. That she hadn't yet reached for her gun when he shot her made Chief suspect the latter.

The screen blinked several times before the Atlas logo appeared. Several commands later, the screens on the wall came to life. On each screen was a different view from the station's security cameras. Tiny beeps sounded each time the cameras changed views.

"We have eyes again," Chief said. At least everyone with online chips. Chief's Atlas chip, along with the chips of the marshals who happened to be within range of Cat's micro-EMP, were fried and would need to be replaced. But at least the rest of the GP personnel on Free Station could access the Atlas video feeds.

What he saw made his stomach churn. Several GP personnel lay on the ground. Those still standing weren't even standing. They were on their knees with their hands locked behind their heads.

Chief had already lost the docking bay.

He manically typed in the command to activate the station-wide alarms. Lights flashed and sirens sounded through the hallways.

"I've activated the station alarms. Everyone should have a chance at getting this station secure."

From the mismatched outfits, tattoos, brands, and piercings, the intruders looked to all be Jader pirates like the one lying dead a few feet away from Chief. But there were so many intruders—there had to be at least a hundred of them.

He frowned. Cat's ship was small and couldn't hold more than ten at most. In fact, none of the Peacekeeper ships that had been docked at Free Station could hold a fraction of how many Jaders were currently swarming the station.

He clenched his eyes closed for a moment when he realized how they'd gotten into Free Station. He'd thought Cat was the Trojan horse. He was wrong. The Trojan horse had already been at Free Station before Cat arrived. The EMP had been merely a distraction to put blinders on Chief to give the Jaders time to enter the station.

They'd been hiding on the *Wu Zetian* all along. The pirates had attacked the Red ship, knowing that standard protocols would ensure it would be towed back to Free Station, where it would sit until retrieved by the Red Dynasty.

It was a large enough ship that they could've easily hidden in pressurized pockets without being detected. Pete Antonov and Cat Mercier both knew GP procedures. All they had to do was set up a ship with their people, knowing they'd be brought directly to Free Station, where they could stroll into the station through an unsecured transit tube.

The Jaders had invaded during the station's night cycle, with most of the inhabitants asleep in their quarters. That minimized the loss of life, but it also made taking the station far too easy for experienced pirates.

Chief was left with only two solutions, and he wasn't ready to surrender Free Station. He opened up the broadcast channel to all Atlas chips in the Ross system.

"Attention, Peacekeepers, this is Chief Roux," he began. "Free Station has been invaded. I repeat, Free Station has been invaded. Initiate emergency response procedures for an active threat. We've been attacked by—"

The microphone turned off. Chief tried to turn it back on, to no avail. "It's not working," he said, frustrated, as he tapped the panel that no longer responded. EMERGENCY LOCKDOWN flashed across his screen.

Every door across Free Station closed and locked.

Fear built within Chief. All doors would be locked throughout the orbital station. The sleeping Peacekeepers hadn't had enough time to dress and grab weapons before the lockdown imprisoned them within their quarters. The only Peacekeepers who weren't locked in their quarters would be the skeleton crew who worked the late shift. A few dozen Peacekeepers at most, but the majority of those were software specialists rather than marshals.

The Jaders had implemented a perfect plan.

But why? Why did Jaders make a near-suicidal run to invade Free Station? What value did it provide them? As a structure, Jade-8 was much larger and better equipped for housing a large number of people. While he knew Jade-8 was still recovering from Anna East's hostile takeover and the damage Throttle and her crew had left in their wake, it still made little sense for Jader pirates to stake a claim on another station.

He looked from screen to screen, searching for answers. The Jaders held the docking bay and were quickly spreading to the elevators and working upward. Nearly all the security patrols were already out of commission—either dead or prisoners. Only two patrols remained, holding off the Jaders at hallway corners on the top two levels.

He scanned the screens, and his scrutiny fell on a screen covering the docking bay. There, just inside from where Pete's ship had been docked, empty crates lay scattered on the floors, broken open, and a computer array had been set up in the hallway. Several Jaders sat at the makeshift workstations. Cables ran from the array to network ports in the walls.

He pointed at the screen. "You see anything like that before, Dean?"

"No, sir. I've no idea what they're doing."

Chief's eyes narrowed. "My guess is they're hacking the network with a hardline program."

In a rush, he tried to forward his broadcast to Peacekeeper stations in other systems, but no terminal would respond to his commands.

He stiffened. "We need to get out of here."

"Yes, sir." Hettinger went to open the door.

"Stop!" Chief held up a hand.

Jader forces rushed to the comm center and came to a stop on the other side of the sealed door. In the center of the group of armed attackers stood Anna East.

CHAPTER SEVEN

THE *JAVELIN* HAD JUST POWERED DOWN IN THE PROVINCE OF CANAAN on the colony planet of Hiraeth when Chief's stilted broadcast came through Throttle's Atlas chip. She faced Sylvian, who bore a fearful look.

"I take it that you heard that, too," Throttle said.

Sylvian gulped. "Free Station has fallen. What's that mean? Are they even still alive up there?"

"Did you all hear that broadcast from Chief?" Eddy asked through a ship comm.

"Yes, we heard it," Throttle replied.

"I heard it, too," Finn said as he strode onto the bridge.

Sylvian spun out of her seat and to her feet. "What are you doing up? You should still be resting."

"The meds have already kicked in. I'm fine," he said, though Throttle noticed he kept his arm protectively close against his bruised ribs.

"The doctor said you're supposed to give the rehabs a full thirty hours before any strenuous activity," Sylvian countered.

His brows rose as he gingerly took a seat. "I think walking from my bunk to the bridge isn't exactly considered *strenuous* activity."

While the married couple argued, Throttle tried to place a call to Chief with no success. She frowned. "Chief is listed as offline." She turned back to Sylvian and Finn. "Do you know anyone else on Free Station you can check with to see if they're still online?"

The specialist's jaw slackened slightly. "Oh. You want to see if there's anyone left?"

"Just check, please."

After several long seconds, Sylvian responded, "I tried to reach a couple of different specialists. They're still online, but the calls aren't going through."

"Same here," Finn said.

"Keep trying to reach someone. We're in the dark down here."

Throttle's frown deepened as she pulled up a list of all the marshals and began calling. After many attempts, she gave up. "I can't get any calls to go through."

Sylvian nodded. "Whatever's going on up there on Free Station has screwed the telecom network." She held up a finger. "Let me try something."

She sat there with a blank face, but Throttle knew that the specialist was running through screens in her Atlas chip. After several moments, Sylvian grimaced. "No luck."

"What'd you try?" Finn asked.

"I thought of trying to call people through their ships on the Atlas network, but the entire call system is down." She blew out a breath. "I'm glad Rusty's not on the Atlas network, so at least his systems aren't being hit."

Throttle's eyes narrowed. "The call system is down, but the rest of Atlas seems to be working. What would cause a single system failure?"

Sylvian shrugged. "Plenty of things. It could be a bug, a virus, a—"

"What're the most likely causes that fit an attack on Free Station?"

The specialist's face scrunched as she thought. "I've toured the Atlas boxes, and they're integrated, so a physical attack would've knocked everything offline. My guess is someone hacked the system to turn off the telecoms to keep people from getting information out."

Throttle rubbed her temple near where her Atlas chip was located. "So you're saying that Atlas is likely compromised?"

Sylvian thought for a long moment. "Yeah, that's what makes the most sense."

"We shouldn't use our chips," Finn cautioned. "If we use them, who knows who's eavesdropping."

Chills caused Throttle to stiffen. "That's assuming they can't eavesdrop any time they want. It's not like we can power down our chips." She took a deep breath and spoke her next words into her wrist-comm while she eyed Finn and Sylvian. "Black Sheep, put your Atlas chips into sleep mode. Under no circumstances are you to access your chip, not until we know it's safe to use. We only use wrist-comms from here on out. Eddy, confirm."

"I heard you loud and clear, Cap. My chip's asleep."

Throttle looked up toward the ceiling. "Rusty, search all news outlets for anything about Free Station. What's going on up there?"

"There is no official news yet; however, there is chatter online regarding Chief Roux's disrupted broadcast, which was uploaded to the general net and has been listened to over two hundred times so far. There are also reports of the broken Atlas telecommunications system, and rumors about what has happened to Free Station."

"What's the rumor with the most traction?" Throttle asked.

"The rumor with the most hits and comments proposes that Free Station was attacked by pirates, though several Peacekeepers have chimed in to report that nearly all personnel on Free Station are still alive, which contradicts many pirate attacks."

"If someone took the time to hack Atlas, that means that whatever's going on up there is something bigger than a pirate attack." Throttle pushed from her seat. "Rusty, send any major updates to our wrist-comms."

"I will," Rusty responded.

"Are you sure we should still go to Canaan?" Sylvian asked.

Throttle nodded. "It's more important than ever that I talk to Mutt."

"We should bring extra weapons," Finn cautioned. "We don't know what's happening on Free Station, and until we do, we should assume the worst."

Throttle's lips thinned. "Are you up for a ride into New Canaan?"

"Of course," he answered without a pause.

"Then you'd better take along some extra painkillers until the rehabs are finished healing your ribs. The roads could barely be considered roads the last time we were here."

"I'm not taking painkillers. I can handle the roads. My reflexes turn to sludge with drugs," he said.

Throttle shrugged. "It's your pain." Then she tapped her wrist-comm. "Eddy, prep the ATV." She looked at Sylvian before continuing, "Finn and I are heading into New Canaan, but I want you and Sylvian to stay on the *Javelin* and see what you can both find out about what's going on at Free Station."

Throttle didn't miss the flash of relief on Sylvian's face before the specialist turned to her husband, and her features grew hard. "What if something happens out there? Finn's still hurt. I should go in case you need backup."

"I need you here," Throttle said. "Finn and I are going to see Mutt and then heading straight back here. I need you and Rusty to pull together a picture of what we're up against, so we can figure out our next steps. Bring Eddy up to the bridge if you need the extra pair of hands. We have hundreds of our people up there in trouble, and we may be the closest ones around to help."

Ten minutes later, Throttle was driving an open-air all-terrain vehicle with large tires on a path that she could only assume was a road. With every bump, Finn seemed to hold his arms tighter against his chest. His features were a pained scowl. Throttle drove as slowly as she could, but even at a low speed, the road would be impassable by any vehicle made for paved surfaces.

The road smoothed out after they weaved around the hill, and the valley of New Canaan, the capital of the province, stood before them.

"Mutt's been busy," Finn said.

Throttle nodded. "He sure has."

It'd been months since Throttle and her crew had visited the first place they'd called home since leaving the Trappist system. New Canaan was a city founded by colonists she'd brought with her from the Trappist system along with several thousand Jaders who'd hitched a ride when the Black Sheep made an escape from Jade-8.

New Canaan had come a long way since Throttle had been there last. A few dozen administrative buildings, apartments, and community meeting places had multiplied into at least a hundred single-level apartments, stores, and other places. Even with the changes, it was easy to find Mutt's place in the center of the colony, where all major walkways and paths led.

She drove down a surprisingly smooth cobblestone street toward the city hall, the largest and busiest building within New Canaan. It was easy to find a parking spot even though the lot had only a dozen spaces, since few colonists could afford powered transportation.

Some colonies were established by wealthy families with cargo ships full of supplies. Canaan had been established by people who'd left their homes with nothing and had arrived on the planet of Hiraeth with even less. Many had lost loved ones on the journey. All had lost bits of their dreams as they had to face obstacle after obstacle.

She shut off the vehicle and then leaned back to look at city hall, a mud-brown building that was no fancier than any other building in town, its size the only aspect making it stand out from the rest. She stepped onto the cobblestone and met Finn at the front of their ATV.

"Let's hope Mutt's in the office. I don't want to have to hunt him down in New Canaan," Throttle said.

Finn went to say something but then frowned.

Throttle turned to see someone wearing a hooded cape that covered his or her face. The person rushed toward them, holding something. Throttle yanked out her pistol, and she knew Finn would be doing the same.

The attacker fired before Throttle could get off a shot.

CHAPTER EIGHT

CHIEF CROSSED HIS ARMS OVER HIS CHEST WHILE HE WATCHED ANNA East watch him from the other side of the comm center door. The door was double-plated permaglass that could withstand blaster fire for a time as well as a grenade blast. Basically, anything capable of breaking through the door would also likely go straight through to the other side of the room and out the hull, causing a breach that would suck out everything—living and otherwise.

Anna looked at the door before stepping closer. She had a smile on her face—a smile that made his skin crawl—and she was as scantily clad as ever. For this day, she wore an iridescent blue gown with thin straps and a slit that reached her hip. Not exactly the typical attire for an assault on a government facility, but she'd always seen herself more like royalty than an invader. Physically, she was quite attractive, but Chief knew that beauty masked a madness that had broken Jade-8 in two and killed hundreds in the aftermath.

Marshal Dean Hettinger stood next to Chief and had his rifle leveled on the people outside the communications room. He was gripping his rifle so tightly that Chief could hear the creaking of the soldier's gloves around the composite weapon.

"At ease, Dean," Chief said quietly as he tapped the button to open the intercom.

"Chief Cormac Roux, we finally meet," Anna said in a sultry voice.

"Ms. East. Or should I call you by your given name, Ms. West?"

Chief responded.

"I may have been born a West, but I built my business on East," Anna replied. "You, on the other hand, no longer seem to have any business at all."

"Your control of Free Station is temporary and is an interstellar felony. The time you have outside a cell is limited," Chief said.

She chuckled. "Ah, Chief Roux, you are correct that my control of Free Station is temporary because Free Station is temporary, and there's not a thing you can do about it. By now, you should know that I have complete control over Free Station's systems, including its access points into the Atlas network. Do you understand what that means?"

Chief gritted his teeth. Fury burned in his clenched fists.

She gave a knowing smile. "I thought so. You know that not only can I track anyone with an Atlas chip, but I can record anything anyone says or sees, thanks to their chips." Her smile widened. "Chief, consider all Galactic Peacekeepers in the Ross system officially under my watch."

He snarled, "More Peacekeepers will arrive from the other systems. And then you will become the hunted. They're on their way now."

She laughed. "No, they're not. You didn't broadcast an emergency signal to the other stations before I took over Atlas. That silly broadcast you made to your Peacekeepers was a mistake." She shrugged. "Even if you had managed to transmit a signal, it would take them months to arrive, and I'll have everything I need from Free Station within days; then it'll suffer an unfortunate and tragic catastrophic failure. All lives on board lost." She sobered. "You really shouldn't have broadcast to your people. That complicates my plan and will cause more bloodshed —on your side, not mine."

He forced himself to keep his breathing steady, to keep his temper in check. He should have broadcast a code 7500 across the Atlas network before anything else. He'd planned to do that as soon as he completed his announcement to the station, but he'd been too late. No Galactic Peacekeeper station outside the Ross system would have any idea there was a problem going on at Free Station. He hadn't followed standard protocols, and his people were going to suffer because of it.

She watched him for a long moment without speaking. As they each stood there, he thought of the armory on level seven and of the technology found throughout the station. There was enough on this station for her to start a war. East and her pirates had access to all of it.

He inhaled deeply before speaking so that his voice remained calm. "What are you doing here, Ms. East?"

Her lips curled. "I suppose you're not going anywhere, so it doesn't hurt to tell you. When the Trappist colonists reached this system, everyone was surprised. No one had heard from that system in centuries. I'd assumed it was a dead system. But when I learned that it was a thriving system, *independent* of Sol, I knew that we could have the same thing here. Imagine Ross as a completely independent system."

He shook his head. "It'd never happen. Ross depends on Sol for support. I've never come across anyone in this system who didn't want to be connected to Sol."

She smiled. "I think you're wrong. We could survive—even thrive —without Sol."

"It still would never happen. Ross provides an interstellar highway between Sol and nearly every other Sol-colonized system."

She held up a finger. "And that's not a problem. If we were to be independent, ships would simply pay a toll to pass through our system. If they didn't want to pay a toll, they'd have to add months, if not years, onto their trips."

"I see." Chief narrowed his gaze. "You attacked Free Station as your declaration of war for independence."

"No. Not at all. I don't want a war. In fact, I don't need a war to make Ross a free system."

He chuckled drily. "So you think Sol will give up one of their systems without a fight?"

"I do," she said plainly and took a step closer before continuing, "Sol never developed an interstellar army. Instead, they created the Galactic Peacekeepers to police and protect every Sol-colonized system. You oversee Ross's 3,112 Peacekeepers right here from Free Station. For any kind of trouble that takes place within this system, it's your Peacekeepers who are deployed. However, what would happen if there were suddenly no Peacekeepers in this system?"

"They'll send in more," Chief said slowly and clearly.

Her brows rose. "Are you so sure? Because I believe that if I offer the Consortium a lucrative proposal along with a promise of no pirate attacks on interstellar traffic, Sol will find that it's to their benefit to have Ross become an independent system. They'll save billions of credits every year by not having to have Peacekeepers, ambassadors, administrators, the list goes on and on."

Every few years, the Consortium of Sol Colonies brought up the debate of having the systems, or even colonies, become independent. And every time, the debate was tabled because it had no clear answer. He knew Anna East would have some proponents, but she'd have far more opponents. "The Consortium won't bend to blackmail, and they definitely will not take kindly to a violent declaration of independence."

"Ah, but that's the thing. They won't see any violence," she clarified. "The fall of Free Station will be seen as a natural catastrophe, an asteroid that destroyed the station and tragically killed everyone within. By the time GP leadership considers more Peacekeepers, I'll have made —and won—my case to the Consortium. If they learn the truth, the knowledge that I have the contents of Free Station's armory in my possession may sway them against wanting to start an armed conflict."

Chief could spend an entire day debating with Anna East, explaining to her how her insane proposal would be met with ridicule. He knew her kind. Nearly every mob boss he'd come across in his career had been a narcissist. Each had a vision for reshaping a star system to revolve around them, a vision that logic could never breach.

Anna East was no different.

"You make it sound far easier than it is," he said simply.

She shrugged. "I expect there to be a few challenges. A certain number of Peacekeepers not on Free Station may choose to fight, but my forces will pick them off one by one. It won't be hard—through Atlas, I can see and hear everything they do, and I can control any ship on the Atlas network. If they run, I'll just shut down their ship and then pluck them out of space. Perhaps I'll shut down all ships now, just to prevent some needless hassle." She cocked her head. "If the Consortium delegates are anything like you, I expect it will go quite smoothly. You know, for the role this space station plays within the Ross system, Free Station was laughably easy to take."

Hearing the words aloud made it difficult for Chief to swallow. The truth was, the Galactic Peacekeepers focused their energies on hunting outlaws and squashing rebellions within the colonies. Sure, they had measures in place for when a criminal attempted to take over a colony, but they had neither the time nor funds to prepare for the rarest of rare possibilities of dealing with a criminal trying to take over a planet, let alone an entire system. Anna East had far more ambition than he'd given her credit for.

He stepped closer to the clear door. "You have Free Station. So what? You really think that the Hiraeth colonies, let alone the mining colonies, will follow you? They depend on monetary support from the Consortium, which will disappear if they think a warlord has taken over the system."

She glared. "I'm not a warlord." Her features smoothed. "The Ross colonies will learn to depend on one another."

He tutted. "There are enough Jaders who've immigrated to Hiraeth. If they don't already know, it won't take long for word to travel regarding how your leadership of Jade-8 has led to a near-total economic collapse of a thriving colony. I doubt they'll be too keen on having a—what will you call yourself—a queen, an empress? I guarantee the one thing they'll see you as, is a dictator."

She held up a finely manicured finger. "Ah, you are wrong. I will not rule over the Ross system. I plan to build a cabinet of representatives. Every colony will have a voice."

Chief grunted. "As long as you always have the final say."

She lifted her chin. "You are one of the Peacekeepers I mentioned earlier—the ones who are too inflexible to bend to a new way of doing things. It's too bad you won't be around to see how the Ross system thrives on its own since you'll go down with Free Station." Her smile grew, and she nodded toward the computer screens behind him. "I'll be back with questions for you to answer. Until then, I'll give you a front-row seat to my emancipation of Ross."

She turned away from him and motioned to two of her guards, who remained behind as she strode away with the rest of her armed entourage.

"She's crazy," the marshal said.

"Absolutely," Chief said. "Unfortunately, she also has vision and ambition. Those three attributes make for a dangerous adversary."

CHAPTER NINE

THE FLASH BLINDED THROTTLE. SHE BLINKED TO CLEAR HER VISION AS she swung her pistol toward their attacker.

"Whoa there, friend. Don't shoot. It's me, Punch."

Their attacker slowly slid back the hood to reveal a familiar visage that was now sporting a black eye and a cut lip. A sheen of sweat glistened on his pale face. She lowered her weapon but didn't holster it. "Punch? What the hell were you thinking, sneaking up on us? You could've gotten yourself killed. Especially all covered up like that. You look like a homeless bum. If I didn't shoot you, I probably would've thrown a credit at you."

"Sorry about that, but if you'd seen me, they'd have seen me. They think I'm dead, and I'd like to keep it that way," Punch said through gritted teeth.

"What are you talking about?" she countered.

"Your Atlas chips," Punch said as though that explained everything, and then collapsed.

Throttle rushed over to find him unconscious. She grabbed the device he'd been holding and held it up for Finn to see. "An EMP."

"Why?" Finn asked, not lowering his weapon.

"Let's ask him when he wakes up." She tapped her wrist-comm before she realized that it would be dead, along with her Atlas chip and ELT. "Here. Grab one of his shoulders. Let's get him loaded on the ATV."

They placed him across the back seat and hurriedly climbed into their seats. She revved up the engine and tore down a street.

As they raced through New Canaan, people yelled and jumped out of their way.

Finn grunted when they hit a curb.

"Sorry," she muttered and kept speeding.

"Don't worry about it. The sharp pains are mostly gone. Just dull muscle aches now."

"Good. Because the way our day is going, I'm going to need you in top form."

She drove several blocks to a building with a red cross painted across the front. She parked right outside the front door, and the pair carried Punch inside.

An older man in a tan lab coat sat at a desk in the back of the waiting room. He looked up and asked, "What's wrong with him?"

"Don't know," Throttle answered.

He jumped up, grabbed a wheeled stretcher that had been parked against the wall, and pushed it over. "Here. Get him on this."

"Aubree!" Throttle shouted as soon as she'd helped place Punch onto the stretcher.

A woman stepped out of a room, and Throttle felt immediate relief.

Aubree wore a similar tan coat along with a stethoscope around her neck. She gave a passing glance at Throttle before noticing the patient and jogged to the stretcher. She'd only checked his pupils before she grabbed the stretcher. "Room two, Roderick," she said curtly as the pair hurriedly wheeled Punch down the hallway. Throttle and Finn followed them into a surgical room.

The two medical professionals immediately began removing Punch's holsters and layers of clothing. As his shirt was cut away, Throttle began to see the extent of Punch's injuries. Dark bruises wrapped his neck as though he'd been hanged. His torso had more purple and blue skin than healthy skin.

"What happened?" Aubree asked without looking up.

Throttle answered, "I don't know. He passed out right after he came up to us. My guess is he ran into something nasty on his way to Hiraeth." Then she added, "He's a marshal, and the last I knew, he was near Jade-8."

Aubree nodded as she cut away Punch's shirt. She spoke as she continued working. "Roderick, power up the scanner. I see multiple contusions and possibly internal bleeding. Someone really did a number on this guy."

She then turned to face Throttle. "This could take some time. If you two want to wait up front—"

"We'll stay here for now," Throttle interrupted. She glanced at Finn, who was already walking over to the doorway to stand guard.

Throttle watched as Aubree situated the large overhead scanner over Punch's prone form.

Aubree's sea of tight black curls now reached her shoulders, reminding Throttle how long it'd been since she'd seen her friend. Aubree had been the only member of the Black Sheep to stay behind rather than to join the Peacekeepers. Watching the medic work, Throttle knew Aubree had made the right choice. Canaan needed her.

The medic read the results from the scanner as it displayed them. "Let's see what we're dealing with…a moderate concussion, a dislocated right shoulder, uh-oh, we've got a burst appendix, a perforated kidney, three broken fingers on the left hand, and a fractured tibia." She blew out a breath. "Prep for surgery. We have to get that appendix out of there before it kills him, and that kidney's not helping things."

Roderick rushed over to a cabinet and started rummaging through drawers.

Aubree turned back to Throttle. "Surgery will take at least an hour, and it could take another couple of hours before he's conscious."

"Okay. I'll stop back to check on him." She looked at Finn. "I know your ribs hurt more than you're letting on, so why don't you stay here to keep an eye on Punch."

Finn nodded. "I'll make sure that whoever did this to Punch doesn't show up to try to finish what they started."

Aubree's eyes grew wide. "You think they're coming?"

"I doubt it, but it's better to play it safe." Throttle paused before leaving and gave the medic a smile. "It's good to see you, Aubree. I just wish the circumstances were better."

The medic chortled. "If we waited for good circumstances, we'd never see each other."

"I suppose that's true." Throttle sighed. "I'd better go see Mutt. I'll be back soon."

Aubree smirked. "Folks call him Baron Stolypin now."

She shrugged. He'd always be Mutt to her.

As she left the emergency room, she stopped by Finn in the doorway.

"I'll also make sure he stays here," Finn said quietly.

Throttle nodded. "I have a feeling he knows what's going on up on Free Station."

She headed back to city hall and up two flights of stairs to a foyer where an assistant sat behind a desk. At the far end of the space was a closed door guarded by a beast of a man. Throttle noticed that he still wore the homemade battle-axe. She grinned. "You're looking good, Axe."

The bodyguard grunted and gave the smallest nod before smiling. "Glad to see being a Peacekeeper didn't make you too snobby to come back."

Her grin widened. "Not just any Peacekeeper. I'm a bona fide marshal now."

His brows lifted before his eyes narrowed. "It could come in handy to have someone in law on our side. Assuming you're on our side."

She gave him a crooked grin but didn't nod. She glanced back at the assistant, whom she didn't recognize. The woman was a pretty young thing with the eyes of a person who'd seen hell. A hairline scar ran down her neck. She was likely a gutter rat from Jade-8 and exactly whom Throttle expected Mutt to hire for his personal staff.

"Marshal Reyne here to see Baron Stolypin," Throttle said, even though she suspected the assistant already knew who Throttle was.

"The baron will see you now," the assistant said without making a call.

Throttle nodded and headed to the door that Axe opened for her. As she entered, she saw Mutt stepping around his desk and walking over to meet her halfway. She was still getting used to him being clean-shaven and not looking like a homeless bum. He'd cleaned up nicely, though he still wore clothes that served function over form.

"I see you found some new legs," he said, coming to a stop.

She glanced briefly at her blades. "Turns out the Galactic Peacekeepers have pretty decent health insurance."

His brow rose. "From what I've been hearing, the Peacekeepers may need a lot more than health insurance right now."

She instantly sobered. "That's why I wanted to see you."

"I'm not sure I can be of much help. I'm busy running Canaan. I don't have much time for gossip," he said, though he motioned to a couple of chairs off to the side.

"I hope that's not the case." Throttle took a seat, leaned back, and steepled her fingers. "What do you know about what's happening on Free Station?"

He pursed his lips. "You've always been one to cut straight to the chase. I like that about you. And today, that's an especially good trait to have because if what I've been hearing is true, you don't want to be out in the open any more than you have to."

She leaned forward. "What do you mean?"

Mutt eyed her. "I hear that Anna East has declared open season on the Peacekeepers."

Throttle scowled. "I knew it. She's behind the disappearances."

"All I know is what my friends back on Jade-8 told me. They said that last week East broadcast a speech across Jade-8 from wherever she was hiding. She mentioned that the days of the Peacekeepers were coming to an end. She went on with ramblings to the effect that the Ross system was going to be a Jader system, whatever the hell that means."

She thought through scenarios. "Is East trying to wipe out all non-Jaders? Or does she think that the Jaders can take over the system? That would explain why she's the one behind the attack on Free Station, but even if she could take down Free Station, she wouldn't stand a chance against Hiraeth. Hiraethians outnumber Jaders twenty to one, if not more."

"Assuming all the Hiraeth colonies band together. Most of us barons are barely on speaking terms. My nickname may be 'Mutt,' but most of the barons I've met are the real mongrels," he said.

"Maybe she's counting on the colonies not banding together. Then maybe she'd have a chance, but it would still be a long shot. She must have another angle she's working."

Mutt shrugged. "She organized her entire pirate fleet, so it's safe to say that whatever she has planned, she's placing all her chips on her bet. It might not be a good time to be a Peacekeeper."

"Well, this confirms my suspicions that Anna East is behind what's happening on Free Station." Throttle pushed herself up, and a smile built upon her lips. "Good. Then I know exactly where I can find her."

Mutt's brows rose. "If you've been listening to what I've been telling you, you'd know you should stay as far away from Free Station as you possibly can. There's no telling if there're even any Peace-keepers left alive up there."

Throttle leveled a stoic gaze upon the baron. "East has killed even more of your people than she has mine. I know we both want East to face justice."

"True. But I'm just not willing to die just to introduce her to her maker."

"The longer she lives, the more people die by her and her pirates' hands." Throttle tilted her head toward him. "Well, thanks for the infor-mation. I'd appreciate it if you hear anything else, you could pass it along. My wrist-comm is dead, so you can only reach me at the *Javelin*."

"I'll do that. Don't get yourself killed. You're the only Peacekeeper I can count on to see things my way."

"Mutt, in all the time I've known you, I've never once seen things your way."

He smirked. "I'm hopeful."

She headed to the door, opened it, and called back to Mutt, "I'll see you around."

Throttle returned to the clinic, using the drive to process Mutt's words. Along the way, she stopped at a small café that emanated aromas of spices that made her mouth water. She left with a half-dozen containers. She carried four into the clinic, leaving one with Roderick at the front desk.

The nurse opened the container and took a deep inhalation. "Pad Thai. My favorite. Thanks. Oh, and your friend has been moved to the second floor. Room twelve."

Throttle continued on her way, climbing a flight of stairs and hunting down the recovery room that held Punch. It was easy to find since Finn was standing guard at the open doorway. She handed him a container and then glanced in to see the marshal at rest.

"How's he doing?" she asked.

"Surgery only took a half hour or so. Then he was moved up here, but he hasn't wakened yet," Finn answered.

"Take a break and eat," she said as her attention focused on the doctor walking toward them.

Throttle handed Aubree a container that she smelled without opening. "Ah, you stopped at Zesty Basil's on your way here. You remembered my favorite."

"*Our* favorite," Throttle corrected. "It's one of the things I've missed about Canaan."

The pair entered Punch's room, where Finn had eaten half his rice dish already. Throttle wasted no time digging into her meal. She and her crew had spent the better part of a year on Free Station, the home of the galaxy's most boring food. Breakfast options included oatmeal and protein bars. Snack options consisted of protein bars and carbohydrate bars. Lunch and dinner options included mystery casseroles and more protein bars. Throttle had often wondered if the high drop-out rate of new recruits was linked to the food.

She didn't spend time savoring her meal. She was starving and had her next bite ready in her chopsticks as she chewed.

"Are they starving you up there?" Aubree asked.

Finn answered for Throttle, which she appreciated since her mouth was full. "Remember the meal bars on the *Gabriela*?"

Aubree gave a dramatic shiver. "I still have nightmares."

"Those were delicious compared to the wood pulp we eat on Free Station," Finn said.

Throttle had swallowed her last bite when she noticed Punch begin to stir. She set the container aside and walked over to the bed.

"Good morning, sunshine," Throttle said drily.

He eyed her briefly before looking around the room, frowning. "Where am I?"

"You're at the New Canaan Medical Clinic, and you're lucky to be alive," Aubree said as she stepped forward and examined the screen displaying Punch's vitals.

"Marshal Punch Durand, meet Aubree King, the head doctor here and the person who saved your life."

"Thank you." He stopped to take a slow breath before continuing, "I feel better already."

"That's the painkillers talking," Aubree said. "I injected you with a full dose of rehabilitators right after surgery. You'll be sore for at least a week, but you should be able to walk within a few hours."

He tried to push himself up and winced. "I don't have time to lie around."

Aubree pressed him back. "You don't have a choice. You had a ruptured appendix that was hours away from killing you."

"No wonder my gut's been hurting so bad," Punch said.

"As I said before, you're lucky to be alive," Aubree said.

"He's lucky I didn't shoot him," Finn added, then eyed Punch. "The only reason I didn't pull the trigger is that I didn't see a gun in your hand and thought you were a beggar hitting us up. Why did you sneak up on us like that?"

"Sorry about that," Punch said and then looked at Throttle, and she could see his pupils were moving in and out of focus.

"You mean hitting us with an EMP?" Throttle asked. "Yeah, I'm a bit curious about why you fried all our electronics."

"It's the Jaders." He spoke slowly, with long pauses to breathe. "They're monitoring everyone connected to the Atlas net. They're watching and listening in on everyone. I couldn't let them see me. There was no other way to help you without them seeing me. Now that you're off the grid, they won't be able to find you."

Throttle frowned. "Why are they tracking us?"

"They're taking out anyone they know they can't turn. East has hired Jaders throughout the system to start taking out all the marshals."

Throttle's blood ran cold. New Canaan was filled with Jaders. She and Finn might be off the communications grid, but she still had two crew members sitting on the tarmac just outside town. She spun to Aubree. "Do you still have your wrist-comm?"

Aubree nodded. "It's in my office downstairs."

"Call Sylvian and tell her that their Atlas chips are compromised. Tell her to put the ship under immediate lockdown and to figure out how to disable their chips as soon as possible."

"O-Okay," Aubree said and ran from the room.

Throttle eyed Finn, who'd grown pale. "You'd better get back to the ship and protect Sylvian and Eddy."

He gave a hasty nod before bolting out of the room.

Throttle took a deep breath and turned back to Punch. "How do you know that the Jaders hacked Atlas? And talk fast because I need to get back to my ship."

"They hadn't yet when I escaped, but when comms went down from Free Station, I had to assume they were successful."

"What happened? I need to know everything."

His eyes closed for a moment before he spoke. "The Jaders. They had an inside guy. Pete Antonov, also known as Skully Pete and captain of the *Bendix*."

Throttle winced. "A marshal? You know that for sure?"

"I got close enough to Pete on the *Bendix* to be able to tell you that his collection of skulls is no rumor."

She grimaced.

"My thoughts exactly," Punch said before grimacing. "Would you believe that? He was able to slip through all of the Atlas background checks."

Throttle guffawed. "We gave one of Anna East's pirate captains direct access to Atlas."

"Yeah. Well, I saw Cat with Pete after he caught me, so she's also in on it. Who knows how many others they have on the inside?"

Throttle frowned. "How do you know you can trust me?"

Punch chuckled and then winced. "Come on. I knew there was no way you'd ever team up with East, not with how bad she and her brother screwed you over when you first arrived."

"Good point, but how do I know I can trust you? Pete's and Cat's ELTs went offline, and they're on East's team. Your ELT went offline…"

"Pete fried my chip and ELT so no one could rescue me."

"Or you took your ELT offline so Chief couldn't track you. Then you hit bad luck and ran into a street gang and got yourself beat up." Even as she said the words, Throttle didn't believe them. While she didn't fully trust Punch, if he'd been on East's payroll, he would've shot her instead of frying her chips with an EMP.

Punch swallowed before speaking. "I walked myself right into a trap. I found the *Bendix* docked at Jade-8, and spacewalked to check it out. I saw Pete in a cabin. He was tied up and had a bloody nose. I didn't see anyone else, so I boarded it to get him out of there. But wouldn't you know, as soon as I went to untie him, he sucker-punched me. The bastard's got one hell of a right hook."

He rolled his tongue against his cheek. "By the time I could see straight, his guys were on me, and I was the one tied up. He seemed to think that Chief was onto him, so for the next two days, I had the pleasure of him using me as a punching bag, trying to find out what I knew. Once he came to accept that I knew nothing, he tossed me into the recycler. The only reason I'm still alive is that the recycler was down for maintenance and I was able to crawl up another shaft to get out." He closed his eyes and took a long breath. "Pete thinks I'm dead, and I don't plan to show him otherwise until I'm up close and personal."

Throttle cocked her head. "It sounds like you don't plan on staying hidden for long."

"Not a chance. The only good that came out of my time on board the *Bendix* was that Pete assumed I was a dead man walking and shared some of his and East's plans that he was so proud of."

"And what'd you learn?" she asked.

"Enough to know that the sooner we stop them, the better. I can't trust anyone else right now, which means it's up to you and me to invade Free Station and take it back from the Jaders. I'm going in after Chief no matter what. Are you in?"

Throttle gave his words careful consideration before she answered, "It won't be the first time I've had to break into a place to save my people."

Punch chuckled. "It won't be the first time I've broken into Free Station."

CHAPTER TEN

CHIEF SAT BEFORE THE COMPUTER ARRAY AND WATCHED AS JADER pirates spread out from the docking bay on level six to levels seven, eight, and nine. There were maybe one hundred pirates—meaning his Peacekeepers easily outnumbered them five to one—a number that did no good with all the Peacekeepers locked within their quarters, which Chief had done for their protection.

His actions to protect his people might have killed them all.

Not everyone was locked in a room. But unfortunately, most specialists didn't carry weapons while in the comfort of Free Station, so any who weren't locked in rooms likely had no way to defend themselves. That was a policy Chief would change the moment this attack was over.

He'd prepared for a variety of attacks against Free Station. Most of the scenarios were software attacks, not dissimilar to the one that had taken Free Station. He'd just never planned on having his proverbial head cut off first. In all scenarios, Chief remained a viable leader on the table. Anna East's pirates had taken Free Station far too easily simply by cutting off both Chief and the comm center from the rest of the station at the same time. Their plan wasn't brilliant by any means, but it'd proved to be wholly effective. He'd never considered the size of his Achilles' heel until East showed him. He realized now it had been hubris on his part to make that assumption. Every Peacekeeper in the Ross system now faced the repercussions of his mistake.

Hettinger took a seat but remained near the door as though he could, in some way, protect the Chief. The marshal had his photon rifle, but it did little good with the pair locked up behind a sealed permaglass door. Anna East's goons stood on the other side of the door, waiting for Chief and Hettinger to make a move. Chief could open the door at any time, but he wouldn't. He knew the outcome if he did. The pirates outside the door could spray shots into the room the second he opened the door. He and Hettinger were essentially in a kill box.

Instead, Chief waited for East to make the next move. He'd covered the camera in the room with tape and had used his knife to rip out the microphone. He'd blurred the glass door with the only thing they had in abundance: blood from the corpses lying in the room with them.

Rigor mortis had begun to set in, but fortunately, the bodies had not yet begun to stink. They didn't smell pleasant by any means, but he knew from experience the smell would get far, far worse in the days ahead. Though, without water or food, he also knew that the stench in his glass tomb was the least of their worries.

To keep his mind from wandering into the dark, he watched everything Free Station's cameras saw. The Jaders would miss something along the way, and Chief would use their mistake against them. He searched for Anna East, but he hadn't seen the crime czar since she'd spoken with him. He knew she'd be nearby, likely on either the same level as the communications center or down one level where the command center and officer wing were located. Level nine, the highest level on Free Station, housed all the technical control centers for the station, from communications to navigation to environmentals. East could do a lot of damage with just a few keystrokes on one of those systems, but it was also the most difficult level to get to.

But she could do even greater damage from the command center deep within level eight. Chief spent much of his time in the command center with his staff, where they could monitor and control all activities taking place on the station, including the station itself. The video feeds from the communications center could be displayed in the command center, and he could broadcast to the entire station from there as well. He assumed Anna East was there, especially since the cameras to that room were offline.

After all, Anna knew all this because Chief had personally shown Pete Antonov most of Free Station's secrets.

Currently, Chief focused on the camera feed from the main docking bay. The small beeps with each camera shift had become barely noticeable background noise. He watched Marshal Pete Antonov step out of the airlock of the *Bendix*, the pirate ship that had attacked the Chinese seed ship, which meant that Pete Antonov was none other than Skully Pete, a notoriously vicious Jader pirate. There'd been no images of Skully Pete on the Atlas net because anyone who came across him didn't survive the encounter. The rumor was the pirate had earned the nickname by taking the heads of anyone who went against him.

Chief had no idea if the rumors were true, not that it mattered. In his time, he'd learned that rumors tended to drive emotion and action far better than facts. It was why he'd leveraged emotions often in getting things done. Some of his actions would not be condoned by GP Central, but they never pursued proceedings against him or his Peacekeepers. The results spoke for themselves, and that was all GP Central cared about.

Pete Antonov was flanked by two crew members as he strode toward the computer array that had been hardwired to network cables in the station's walls. Chief selected the audio feed to unmute at the docking bay so he could listen as well as watch. Pete spent several minutes at the array, a frown emerging as he worked. He stepped back and walked to the Rabbit that he'd brought with him when he came to Chief to join up as a marshal. Chief wondered what poor soul had lost their life to Pete when he'd taken the small ship. Worse, Chief wondered how many more poor souls would suffer at the hands of Skully Pete and Anna East.

Ten minutes later, Pete emerged from his ship, fuming. One of his crew was nursing a bloody nose. Pete returned to the computer array and continued to work, though his growing impatience caused him to hit the menu options, making enough noise to be heard over the audio feed.

Chief leaned closer. "Interesting."

"What's that, sir?" Marshal Hettinger asked.

"Something's not going according to their plan," Chief said. "We can only hope it's something that works in our favor."

The marshal rolled his chair until he was next to Chief.

Pete hit the computer, and the entire array rattled. He pulled out a handheld radio and spoke. "I've looked everywhere for it. The router. It's missing."

"Did you have it on your ship?" came Anna East's voice from the radio.

"Of course. It was in a crate, but I can't find the crate anywhere. Someone stole it," Pete answered.

Chief's brow furrowed as he tried to guess why a router was so important.

"No one would know to steal a single crate off your ship," she replied through the radio.

Pete waved a hand around him. "Well, it's not here now!"

"Watch your tone with me, Pete. You're not indispensable."

"My apologies," Pete said with a scowl that resembled nothing close to an apology. "I'm just saying that someone stole the crate. Either the GP got to one of our people, or someone on this station nabbed it. Either way, it's not here."

"Then you'd better find it." There was a lengthy silence before she continued, *"Until you do, have someone go in and manually make the updates."*

"What?" Pete exclaimed. "That will leave a trace. Plus, that'll take days, if not weeks."

"Then you'd better get started," East said.

Pete lowered the radio and stared blankly.

"What is so special about a router, sir?" Hettinger whispered at Chief's side.

Chief thought for a moment and glanced at the door behind them. "I don't know, but if East suspects someone on Free Station stole it, then I expect she'll want to have a conversation with me."

Pete started barking orders at his men. "I need you to search this entire dock, search all of Free Station if you have to, to find the router."

"How can I find something that I have no idea what it looks like?" the man with a bloody nose said.

Pete pulled back his clenched fist as though to hit the man again but stopped before swinging. Instead, he audibly sighed and turned to the computer. He went through a few screens and pulled up an image. "Here. Go find it. Everything depends on it."

Chief squinted at the screen. The image was so small, he could barely make it out. He'd only ever seen an item like it once before at GP Central. Fortunately, it was a unique enough piece of hardware that made it easy to identify.

He cocked his head. "Why would they need a naive Bayse router?"

"A what?" Hettinger asked before stammering, "Sorry, sir. I didn't mean to be so blunt."

"I appreciate the candor. It saves time and cuts through the bull-shit," Chief said. "A naive Bayse router is AI tech, so it's only autho-rized for government use. The router itself is basic. It's the system inside that makes it special. Essentially, it's a system built on advanced algorithms that—when connected to another system—it reads and updates information without leaving a trace."

Hettinger shrugged. "It sounds like a simple copy-and-paste."

Chief smiled. "Oh, it's a bit more complicated than that. The system is doing all the work in this case. Once they program in a few key crite-ria, the naive Bayse algorithms would then search out everything it deems appropriate to change, and then modifies it as it sees fit." As he spoke, his smile morphed into a frown. "They clearly want to change something on the Atlas network, and I'm beginning to wonder if that's not the real reason Anna East is here on Free Station. But I don't know what's so important for them to change on Atlas."

They each thought for a moment. Hettinger spoke first. "Most things are about money, right? Maybe Anna East is trying to move properties or bank accounts under her name."

"Atlas tracks property, but it's not the source of record. No, that can't be it." He glanced at Hettinger, then patted the young man's shoulder. "But it's a good idea. Keep them coming."

Chief steepled his fingers as he thought. Hettinger was right that money was behind most of the crime committed across the human systems. If Pete had a naive Bayse router, why hadn't he used it on a banking system to bring him unlimited wealth? It made far less sense to use it on a system used for peacekeeping.

Atlas was a massive network of databases, pulling from thousands of source systems across the star systems. Much of its data was fed by other systems, but not all. Data created and updated in Atlas included all law enforcement-related information, from the roster of Peacekeepers in each system to a list of fugitives and everyone in between. Every person with a birth record on file was in the Atlas network.

Something Hettinger said triggered a thought. "Properties. Atlas does track ownership of GP resources. Our ships, weapons, stations. East specializes in piracy. I wonder if she's making her raid of Free Station look legal. If the system said she owns all the GP weapons in this system, no court of law could prove her wrong."

"But what would she do with all those weapons?" Hettinger asked.

Chief shrugged. "Start a war; lay claim to Hiraeth. I suppose she could do anything she wanted."

CHAPTER ELEVEN

Yᴀɴᴋ ɴᴜʀsᴇᴅ ʜɪs ʙʟᴏᴏᴅʏ ɴᴏsᴇ ᴀs ʜᴇ ᴛᴜʀɴᴇᴅ ᴀɴᴅ ʟᴇғᴛ Jᴀᴢᴢ ᴡɪᴛʜ Skully Pete at the computer array Jazz used to hack into the Atlas network. Yank figured it would've made more sense for Jazz to work his magic from the Atlas server room or from Free Station's command center, but Jazz preferred his own equipment when it came to hacking and system sabotage. Jazz was a smart guy, so Yank went with whatever he recommended.

Now, Skully Pete on the other hand…

Yank scowled, and he dabbed at his nose. The bleeding had stopped, but he had to breathe through his mouth. Even then, it hurt to breathe. It wasn't the first time he'd had his nose broken, and in his line of work, it probably wouldn't be the last time, but he swore it hurt more every time.

He tried to ignore his throbbing sinuses while he walked, instead concentrating on the task at hand.

"If I were a fancy router, where would I hide?" he asked himself.

The answer didn't reveal itself. A small black box could've been hidden anywhere on Free Station, on a ship, hell, even in someone's pants. How was he supposed to find something like that?

If the router had been taken from the Rabbit, it had been taken after arriving at Free Station, because Yank had watched the marshals examine the ship out by the asteroid belt, and they hadn't removed anything. If the router was valuable, chances were it was stolen, and the station was crawling with pirates who'd steal from their own mothers if they had the chance.

If the router had been stolen by a pirate, Yank had no chance in hell of finding it. He saw a pair of Jaders standing near the elevator, and he approached. "I've got a job for you."

"Does it pay?" one of them asked.

"Sure, but you've first got to find it and bring it to Skully Pete," Yank replied.

The other man scowled. "Skully Pete is too cheap to pay for anything."

"Anna East is doing the paying," Yank said.

"Anna East, you say?"

Yank nodded.

The pair glanced at each other before turning back to Yank. "What's the job?"

"Pete lost a computer component for the Atlas hack. It was on his GP ship. You find it, you get the reward," Yank said, and explained what the router looked like.

One of the pair shrugged. "Sounds a lot better than just standing around here and twiddling our thumbs."

"So I can count on you to look for it?" Yank asked.

The other man snickered. "Sure thing."

Yank gave him a smirk and then went on his way. Anyone dumb enough to count on a pirate deserved to be taken advantage of, but Yank had nothing to lose. He wasn't out anything if they didn't find the router, and he could tell Pete that he'd sent people out to look for it.

Finally not running around, being a gopher for Pete and Anna East, he strolled through the hallways. Most of the walkways were empty and clean. If he ignored the blood smears along the walls and the bodies shoved to the edges, he found the station to be peaceful. It was a pity Anna East was going to destroy it.

While he knew blowing up Free Station was the right decision—how else could they wipe out nearly all the Peacekeepers in one fell swoop—the plan seemed like a waste of a good station. Why couldn't Anna have a specialist manage the environmentals and purge all the air? That way, it'd be a simple case of cleanup before converting the station into another Jade-8 appendage.

He had to give Anna East credit. She loved to make dramatic moves, and blowing up a Galactic Peacekeeper station was as dramatic as they came.

He paused, suddenly distracted by a sign above a door. His jaw slackened and his lips parted. A smile formed as he read the sign again.

EVIDENCE LOCKER.

Yank walked up to the door. He swiped his hand over the touchpad, but the message LOCKED OUT displayed. He went through several screens, trying different things, each time getting the same message. He pulled out his switchblade and tried to pry the panel off. No luck. The lockdown that Chief Roux had implemented might have kept the Peacekeepers locked up, but it also kept Yank from a roomful of goodies.

He took a step back, put his hands on his hips, and analyzed the door. It was made of a composite metal he wasn't familiar with. He tapped. Solid. He unholstered his blaster and searched for a weak point, but the door was one of those that slid into the wall, which meant it had no hinges or handles to use as leverage.

He raised his blaster and shot at the center of the door. The shot bounced. Yank ducked, but he felt the icy burn of a photon beam on his left bicep. He looked down to find a hole burned through his shirt. The initial coldness morphed into a constant burn. He ripped the material more to see that the shot had only grazed his arm. He stared at the blackened line of skin for a moment. His stupidity had nearly gotten him killed.

He swallowed and looked from side to side. Relief filled him. No one had seen what'd happened. He holstered his blaster, took a deep breath—which made his nose throb again—and continued on his way.

Yank didn't stop until he reached the command center, where Anna East was coordinating all Jader activities through her personal hacker, Nelson, and a few Peacekeeper specialists.

She sneered and held up a hand as he entered. "Stop. Don't bleed in here."

He frowned and touched his nose. The bleeding had stopped, but he felt the dried, crusted blood on his skin. He stepped back into the doorway, pulled out a handkerchief, and scrubbed away the blood, even though every touch near his nose was a spike of pain.

Nelson looked over his shoulder from where he sat before a wall of screens. "Smooth move back there, Master Blaster."

Yank's eyes widened before he regained his composure. "I don't know what you're talking about."

The skinny hacker grinned. "I mean the attempted suicide by self-inflicted photon blast. Don't worry, I have it recorded, so everyone else can get a chuckle, too."

Yank glared. "Share it and die."

"I can delete the file for the right price," Nelson said.

Yank gave a simple, single nod. "When we get back to Jade-8."

Nelson nodded. "We have a deal."

The hacker assumed Yank would pay him, but Yank would kill him for having the audacity to blackmail Yank, in front of Anna East, no less. Anna hadn't seemed interested in the brief exchange, but he had no doubt she was paying attention to everything around her. She was a smart woman; she had to be, to lead Jade-8 for so long.

Yank pocketed his handkerchief and strolled into the room.

Anna gave him a lazy glance before turning back to the screens. "Tell me that you've found the router, Yank."

"I've assigned a couple of Jaders to search for it, Ms. East," he said.

She blew him off. "I suppose it doesn't matter as long as my changes are made in the system. The router was going to be of more help for the rest of you."

Yank frowned. "Will you still be able to route the money from the banks into our accounts?"

"Of course," she said, yet he didn't feel convinced. She turned to him and smiled. "So tell me, what are you going to do with all that money?"

He stood up taller. "I'm going to buy a ship and hire my own crew."

She watched him for a moment with humor in her eyes. "Why buy a new ship when you can have the *Bendix*?"

His gaze narrowed. "Because that's Pete's ship."

She gave him a sideways look. "It is. For now."

His brow lifted. "Well then, Ms. East, you must know something I don't."

She *hmphed*. "I know a great many things you don't. That's why I'm in charge. But when it comes to Pete, let's just say that I'm growing disappointed in his service. I'm someone who rewards those who deliver results. But I'm also someone who punishes those who fail to deliver." Her features softened. "Back at the *Wu Zetian* near the asteroid belt, I saw that you're the sort of man who delivers results. I've had my eye on you for some time. I think you'd do well at the head of my Jader army."

Yank's brows lifted. "I would?"

She smirked. "Of course you would. I think we'd make a great team. You make sure I get off Free Station when I'm ready, and I'll make all your dreams come true."

Yank didn't know what Pete saw in Anna East. She was attractive, but she was a snake and was obvious about using people to achieve her own gain. Maybe it was because Yank was gay that her charisma didn't work on him, but it seemed like her magic worked on everyone else around him, regardless of gender or identity.

He nodded. "You can count on me, Ms. East."

She thought she had him wrapped around her little finger. She had no clue that he was only staying close to her because she was the only person on the station who could guarantee that he'd get paid after this nightmare of a job.

CHAPTER TWELVE

EDDY WIPED GREASE ON HIS PANT LEGS. "THERE. TRY TO CONNECT now."

Rusty allowed power to flow into the naive Bayse router. "I'm connected and running diagnostics now. I can see that this system is quite robust but relatively blank."

"That's because you have to train it with inputs, which I figured you could do in parallel with all your regular stuff. It should help your decision matrix by giving you additional options." Eddy grinned. "Happy birthday, Rusty."

"It's my birthday?"

"Well, we've been working together for nearly three years, and you've yet to have a birthday, so I figured today is as good as any day to be your birthday. Also, it's the first time I've had a birthday gift for you. I know how much you love upgrades."

"Thank you, Eddy. You have given me the best birthday ever—and my first birthday." Rusty was familiar with routers but had never interacted with one before, and he was looking forward to the upgrade. As the diagnostics ran, the router bumped against several of Rusty's protocols, and he created patches to allow integration.

Eddy was right that Rusty loved upgrades. Eddy thought Rusty, like any system, craved faster performance. But Rusty loved the improvements because they helped him to better understand Eddy and the other crew members. He hoped that the router would help him in the one area where his protocols had significant gaps: to understand rationale not from an analysis of benefits and risks but from a sense of right and wrong.

Rusty craved to become more like his friends...to become more human.

CHAPTER THIRTEEN

THROTTLE'S TRIP BACK TO THE *JAVELIN* SEEMED TO TAKE LONGER THAN her drive earlier into New Canaan. Since Finn had taken the ATV, Throttle had to hitch a ride with Aubree in an ambulance.

Aubree drove and paid little attention to Throttle in the passenger seat. Instead, the doctor shot regular glares back at Punch on a gurney in the back. He was as antsy as Throttle for action and had refused to stay at the clinic and instead groaned and complained about the bumpy roads.

After Throttle and Punch finished coming up with a plan, she'd used Aubree's wrist-comm to call Sylvian, but the specialist hadn't answered, and she'd encountered the same result with Eddy. None of her crew members ever removed their wrist-comms. That could only mean one thing...

They'd been unable to answer their wrist-comms.

Throttle sighed and looked at Aubree. "Can't this thing go any faster?"

"Not without jostling my difficult patient back there," the doctor answered.

"I'm just fine," Punch said through gritted teeth.

"You're talking like I didn't have you cut open on my operating table less than two hours ago," Aubree said drily.

He gave her a crooked grin. "You're such a good doctor that I don't even feel like I had surgery."

"Schmoozing will get you nowhere with me."

"We'll see," he said with confidence in his eyes.

Aubree hit a bump right then, and Throttle wasn't so sure the doctor hadn't done it on purpose.

Sun glinted off the top edge of a dull gray hull. Throttle perked up and placed her hand on the grip of her pistol. "Focus, team. We're coming up on the *Javelin*."

As the ambulance emerged over the hill, the ship came into full view. Throttle was relieved to find it undamaged, but any relief was buried under the stress of seeing Finn standing outside and surrounded by five heavily armed Jaders.

Punch and Throttle each had pistols in their hands by the time Aubree pulled up to the *Javelin*, and Throttle had her door open before the ambulance came to a full stop. Punch slid open the side door and took up a position inside, aiming his blaster at the Jaders. "Aubree, stay inside the vehicle," Throttle said before turning her attention outside.

She was just about to yell for their surrender when Finn stepped forward and waved a hand. "It's okay, Throttle. Everything's good here. Sylvian and Eddy are off the grid, and these guys are here to help."

She eyed her crew member for a long moment. When she was convinced that he wasn't under duress, she stepped out from behind the protective door.

Finn strolled over and motioned to the group. "Mutt sent them out here as extra security in case any of East's people show up."

"I wouldn't trust them," Punch cautioned quietly from where he kept his blaster leveled on the group.

She, too, didn't lower her blaster as she looked over Finn's shoulder at the five men. "They're Jaders. How do you know we can trust them? They could've fed you a line about Mutt sending them out here."

"We're not Jaders. Not anymore," one of the men called out as he walked toward Throttle. He came to a stop next to Finn. "We're Canaanites now, which means our loyalty lies with the baron, not with East."

"Then I owe you my thanks," Throttle said.

He held out his hand. "I'm Areston Jones."

"Throttle Reyne." She shook his hand, then cocked her head. "Jones? Is Doc Jones your mother?"

He seemed taken aback for a moment. "She is."

Throttle relaxed somewhat. "She helped us back on Jade-8. In fact, she helped everyone get to Canaan."

He rolled his eyes. "If you hear Mom tell it, she single-handedly flew us here." His features smoothed. He shot a glance over Throttle's shoulder. She turned to see Punch walking over, keeping his blaster aimed at the group.

Areston looked across the faces of Throttle, Punch, and Finn. "Listen, I told Finn the truth. The baron sent us here right after you spoke with him. He said to tell you that as long as the Peacekeepers look after Canaan, we'll help out when we can." He paused as his features furrowed. "But if the rumors I'm hearing are true, you're not safe here. If East is offering enough credits to take down marshals, there will be plenty of folks of the unsavory sort who'll take her up on her offer."

Throttle motioned, without looking behind her, for Punch to lower his weapon. "Of that, I have no doubt. I don't plan on drawing pirates to Canaan. I know the *Javelin* stands out. That's why we're not staying here at Canaan. In fact, we'll be on our way within the hour. Until then, if you can help stand guard over my ship and crew, consider me mighty obliged."

Areston nodded. "We can stay until dark if needed."

Throttle shook her head. "You'll be able to get back home well before then." She turned back to the ambulance to see Aubree tapping the steering column.

She strode past Punch and back to the vehicle and leaned through the open window.

"I have to get back," Aubree said bluntly. "Unfortunately, the clinic is terribly understaffed for a city the size of New Canaan, especially with all the new towns popping up around it."

"I understand, and I appreciate that you gave us a lift," Throttle said.

"I wish I could go with you," Aubree said and then turned to her patient, "if only to make sure he heals properly, but I can't leave the clinic without a doctor."

"Thanks for the patch, Doc. I owe you one," Punch said before he pulled out his gear bag from the back of the ambulance.

Throttle turned and hadn't realized the marshal had come up alongside her. She blew out a breath. "You can sure sneak up on someone if you want to."

"Old habit, though it tends to come in handy sometimes," he said as he winced and dropped his bag to the ground.

"Here, Punch. You should also have this." Aubree reached behind her and picked up a small red duffel and handed it to Punch. "Here are several doses of rehabilitators. I've marked when you should take each dose, and I threw in some extra medical supplies because I've seen your insides and suspect you'll need them."

Throttle frowned. "What's that mean?"

"Just that I've been banged up once or twice before," Punch answered as he took the duffel and set it on his gear. "Thanks again, Doc. I'm in your debt."

Aubree chortled. "Just stay alive, and I'll be satisfied that I did my job. Now I'd better head back." She turned back to Throttle. "Don't stay away so long next time."

"I'll try not to," Throttle said.

Aubree reached out and squeezed Throttle's hand. "You take care of yourself."

The doctor pulled away, leaving eight people standing outside the *Javelin*. Finn strode over to Throttle and Punch. "By any chance, did you happen to figure out a plan on the way out here?"

"We're working on one," Throttle said.

Finn's eyes narrowed. "I don't suppose I'm going to like it?"

She smirked. "It involves a daring rescue against horrible odds. It's right up your alley."

Finn scowled. "Now I know I'm not going to like it."

"Where's your sense of adventure, Marshal?" Punch asked as he held a hand over his abdomen.

Throttle frowned. "You should still be lying down."

"I will once I get to my ship."

"Where is it? We'll help you get on board," she said.

He pointed.

"You came here on that?" Finn asked in awe.

"Sure did."

Throttle's jaw slackened as she stared at what she'd thought was an abandoned derelict off the edge of the ramp. It looked like it couldn't break gravity, assuming it could even start. "That's your ship?"

"It's not mine. I borrowed it."

"You stole a ship?" she asked.

"I'm a marshal, and marshals don't steal. I *commandeered* it." Punch winked.

"You've got more guts than I do," Finn said. "It doesn't look like it can maintain environmentals."

"It can, mostly. It's not such a bad ship as long as you wear a suit at all times."

Throttle frowned. "Wait. You said you needed your ship to get us on to Free Station without anyone noticing."

"I do."

Her eyes narrowed. "Then where is your ship?"

"I had to leave the *High Spirit* behind at a station not far from Jade-8. I had to take something they wouldn't notice, or else they would've figured out I was still alive."

Throttle's gaze moved from the wreck to Punch. "And you think they're just going to give you your ship back, assuming you survive the trip out there."

"I still have a few logistics to work out."

She grimaced as she thought through options. The ship he'd *commandeered* would be slow, very slow. She was surprised that it'd made it to Hiraeth in one piece, though she supposed that was why it'd taken Punch so long to get to Hiraeth. The thought of returning to Jade-8 made her stomach sour. She blew out a breath. "Fine. You can catch a lift on the *Javelin*. We'll get you back to your ship. That way, I'll at least know you're going to make it to Jade-8."

He grinned as if he'd expected her to offer a ride all along. "Excellent. I'm ready to go whenever you are." He then looked from Finn to his bags. "Help a fellow out?"

Finn scowled, slung his rifle over his shoulder, and picked up the two bags.

The trio headed to the *Javelin*, and Throttle paused by Areston. "We're heading out. Tell Mutt that I'm indebted to Canaan."

"It's your home, too," Areston said.

She gave him a smile that didn't reach her eyes. "That it is."

Areston and his group climbed onto an antigrav skid and drove away.

"Aw, you mean we could've gotten a ride here on that?" Punch complained.

Throttle's eye twitched. "Aubree went out of her way to give us a lift."

Punch eyed her. "Yeah, but you don't know how much it hurts riding in a vehicle that rolls along the ground. Not to mention how outdated they are."

Throttle shrugged since she'd never ridden on a hovercraft before and had nothing to compare it to. Her brows rose. "You sure you're going to be up for a rescue mission?"

He glowered. "I'll be fine. I just need a few hours of rest, and I'll be as good as ever."

Finn walked up the ramp of the *Javelin* and placed his hand on the panel next to the door. "Open up, Rusty."

The door opened, and Finn led the others onto the ship.

"Welcome back, Throttle," Rusty said. "Have you brought a guest?"

"Rusty, this is Marshal Punch Durand. He's catching a lift with us until he gets his ship back."

"Welcome, Marshal," Rusty said.

Punch looked around. "I haven't seen this design before. What model is it?"

"It's a *classic* that's been updated and modified, so it's basically a custom," she answered. She led him down the hallway and stopped at the room next to hers, wanting to keep an eye on him as much as possible. She'd talked to him for a grand total of two hours. It would take a lot longer than that to know if she could trust him or not. "Here's your room. Make yourself at home and get some rest."

"Thanks. I'll get you the coordinates for where the *High Spirit* was last docked," Punch said as he stepped through the doorway.

Finn stepped around him to drop the bags on the bunk and returned to stand near Throttle in the hallway.

"Throttle."

She turned to see Eddy rushing toward her.

As soon as he reached her, he held out his hand. "Give me your wrist-comm."

"It's dead."

"I know. I need the parts to build a new comm."

Throttle shrugged before loosening the strap and tugging off the lifeless piece of hardware. "So you can make it work?"

"No. I said I need the parts. I can reuse the microphone and speakers in a new comm-chip for the crew. It'll have minimal functionality. Well, it'll have no functionality other than broadcasts to the entire team."

"That'll be good enough," she said.

"It'll have no chips, so EMPs won't have any impact on them," Eddy continued.

Her brow rose. "They have no chips, but you're calling them comm-chips?"

He scrunched his nose. "Would you rather me call them radiated glass intra-crew communication devices?"

"Comm-chips sounds good to me," she said.

"Do I get one?" Punch asked.

Eddy frowned as if he'd just noticed Throttle wasn't alone. "Who is this man?"

Throttle answered, "Punch is a marshal. Punch, meet Eddy, the ship's engineer, mechanic, and all-around fixer of things."

"You're not a part of the crew. You don't get one," Eddy said and walked away with Throttle's wrist-comm.

When she turned back to Punch, she found him eying Eddy as he walked away. "And people ask why I work without a crew."

Throttle shrugged. "There are a few challenges, sure, but I'd never give up my crew, ever. I wouldn't be alive without them. Come to the bridge after you get some rest. We still have a lot of details to work out."

He gave a small nod. "I will, and thanks."

After his door closed, Finn took a step closer. "I'll stand guard."

"He's not a prisoner."

"He's also not one of the crew."

"He won't have access to any systems, so he's free to move around. Besides, Rusty will keep an eye on him, won't you, Rusty," she said.

"At all times if you'd like," he said.

"I'd like," she said.

Finn spoke again. "Understood, but we don't know him. There were marshals involved in the attack on Free Station. We don't know whom we can trust. I think I'd better stay nearby, just in case."

She gave him a small smile. "You're right, and I agree."

She left Finn and headed to the bridge, where Sylvian sat with a large white bandage wrapped around her head. She walked over to the specialist. "What happened?"

Sylvian touched her bandage. "Eddy, that's what. We took out each other's Atlas chips, and he seemed to think I needed a three-inch cut to take out a chip the size of a piece of rice. You should've seen Finn when he walked in during the procedure. I really thought he was going to kill Eddy. I think he surprised us both by letting Eddy live. Luckily for me, Finn booted Eddy and finished removing the chip himself." She blew out a breath. "I think I'm going to have a scar."

"Aubree might be able to help with that," Throttle said as she took a seat at the captain's station.

"Bah. I'm not that vain. Aubree doesn't need to waste time on something like that. She has enough to deal with providing medical care to a colony of thousands. She said she delivered ten babies last week alone while at the same time she's trying to train fifty new staff. But enough about Aubree. Finn said that Anna East is behind the attack on Free Station."

"She is, and we're going to take her down," Throttle said.

Sylvian shot a hard glance at Throttle. "It's about time."

"I'll fill you in on the details later. First, we have to set up a flight plan to Jade-8."

Sylvian's brows shot up. "We're going back there?"

"Punch's ship is there. We need it to get onto Free Station without being noticed."

"Then we go back there," Sylvian said and turned to her panel.

Throttle began running predeparture checks. She set up a flight plan to monitor traffic on her flight path but didn't file the plan. She had no idea how far East's reach went, and she preferred not to be on anyone's radar.

Eddy entered the bridge a few minutes later and deposited a tiny silver pin into her palm. It looked like a simple stud earring.

"It's your comm-chip," he said as a matter of fact. "You put it—

oh, just let me." He took it back from her and pinned it onto the neckline of her shirt. "There. It's either on or off. Pinch it to turn it on. Then just hold your finger against it to speak. If it's off, you can't hear any incoming broadcasts, so I recommend you leave it on at all times."

She squeezed the silver dot and it chimed.

"Now it's on."

She touched the metal with her fingertip and tilted her head to speak in the direction of the chip. "Test. Test."

She heard a tinny echo of her voice emit from Eddy's and Sylvian's chips.

Eddy touched his chip. "You can speak normally. The microphone is quite good." His voice parroted through her chip.

She lowered her hand. "Can you pair the chips with ear speakers, so if there are others around, they won't hear what's being said to the crew?"

He rolled his eyes. "Possibly. With new hardware. But this was all I could do with what I had to work with."

"It's good enough for now. You'd better make sure everything's buckled down for departure. We'll be leaving in ten minutes."

"I'll be ready." He left the bridge without another word.

Rusty announced, "There's a new broadcast originating from Free Station."

Throttle stiffened. "Play it."

"This is an automated Atlas press release. Free Station is no longer designated as a Galactic Peacekeeping office. Free Station is now listed as property of East Enterprises. Anna East, president and CEO, has made the following declaration: Galactic Peacekeeping services in the Ross system are terminated, effective immediately. All GP properties and material have been claimed by East Enterprises. All currently employed Peacekeeping personnel have fifty hours to accept positions under the East Peacekeeping Services. Any Peacekeepers who do not accept positions under the East Peacekeeping Services will be considered criminals and will be arrested. All other inhabitants in the Ross system should notice little to no impact on their daily lives. This press release will broadcast every hour until a new release is made available."

Sylvian whistled. "Little to no impact, my ass. Everyone's got to know that if Anna East has control of the guns, they're all in danger."

Chills that had climbed Throttle's spine during the broadcast now became ice. Fifty hours. It would take them most of that time to get to Jade-8 and back. There'd be no time left to recruit others to their cause. She leaned back in her seat and stared out the windshield. It seemed as though life was constantly giving her deadlines. First there was the cat fail on the *Gabriela*. Then there was trying to save her people from Jade-8. Now this.

She clenched her fists before releasing them. She took a deep inhalation before turning her attention back to the preflight checks running down her screen. She spoke without looking up. "Anna East can say whatever she wants because, in fifty hours, her time is up, not ours."

CHAPTER FOURTEEN

CHIEF SAW PETE HEADING HIS WAY LONG BEFORE THE PIRATE ARRIVED with his two goons. Chief monitored the video feed until the pirate and two of his crew members had entered the hallway near the communication center where Chief and Marshal Hettinger were cornered.

By the time Pete reached the comm center, Chief had cleaned a portion of the glass to look through and was standing on the other side of the thick glass door, and Hettinger stood off to the side, out of Pete's sight.

Pete sent the guards away who'd been stationed there, leaving only Pete and his two crew members in the hallway outside the communications center.

Now that Chief knew who Pete was, he couldn't believe he'd ever fallen for the pirate's story. He'd thought Pete Antonov's records were pretty clean, but he'd chocked that up to the fact that the Peacekeepers were spread far too thin across the system. Many colonies reported less than half of the crimes that occurred on their soil.

Chief scowled at the marshal's badge that Pete still wore. "You're a disgrace to everything the Peacekeepers stand for. You have no right to wear that patch."

Pete glanced down at the badge. He went to take it off and patted it instead. "You know what, Chief? I think I'll keep it. A nice memento of the job that led to the biggest payday of my career."

"Criminals don't have careers. They have records," Chief said.

Pete eyed him for a moment and then sneered. "How's the smell in there, Chief? I bet those bodies are getting ripe, and they're just going to get riper."

"Would you like me to open the door so you can see for yourself?" Chief asked.

Pete guffawed. "Oh, I have no doubt that you'll get desperate enough to open that door. Maybe the stink of rotting flesh and bowels will do it, but I bet you'll hold on until you've gone so long without water that you can barely stand. Whether you stay in your self-chosen cell until this station gets blown to smithereens, or you come out and I throw you in the brig, it doesn't matter. Though, I'd take the brig if I were you. The smell's better, you'll have a toilet, and you may even get some food and water if you behave. Your choice. Either way, there's nothing you can do to save your precious station."

"I don't care about Free Station. You can have it. What I care about are the five hundred and sixty-three Peacekeepers that you intend to murder. Let them go. They don't need to die," Chief said.

"Ah, but they do. It wouldn't make much sense for Free Station to be destroyed suddenly with no one at home. Their deaths are what makes a good sap story for East to bring to the Consortium."

Chief narrowed his gaze. "You really think the Consortium will buy that shit-story that sounds more like something a little kid or a drunk would come up with. Which one are you?"

Pete shrugged. "You know, Chief. I don't care if the Consortium buys her story or not. That's her grand scheme, not mine. If anything, her plan cuts the amount of traffic through Ross. Less traffic means less opportunity to raid ships and crews. Nah, my plan was simple. I took the job to get into Free Station. My crew and I are now the richest, best-armed pirates in the system, maybe even in the galaxy."

"You make it sound like you control your fate. You're as much under Anna East's thumb as every other Jader. She tells you which ships to loot, and she tells you how much of that loot you get to keep. She makes you do jobs, like pretend to be a marshal, to get her what she wants."

"I'm getting what I want, too," Pete added brusquely.

"Sure you are. But have you thought about what will happen if East is successful with—what did you call it—her grand scheme?"

Pete frowned. "What do you mean?"

Chief took a step forward. "I mean, if East convinces the Consortium to allow the Ross system to be a self-governing system, then East will need to appear legit. She'd never be able to govern an entire system with skeletons in her closet." Chief's features relaxed and he grinned. "That's it! That's what you're doing through the Atlas computer you set up on the dock. I admit, the importance of a naive Bayse router didn't make sense for the longest time, but now it makes perfect sense. You want to use the router to cleanse Anna East's records —and no doubt all Jader records."

Pete's features went lax for a moment before he recovered. "It doesn't matter that you know. It's not like you'll live to tell anyone about it. Getting rid of you and the other marshals is what I care about. But yeah, we'll all be legit, for a time anyway. Even if more Peacekeepers arrive, they won't be able to hound my crew and me."

"Until you raid the next ship," Chief added.

"You gave yourself away, Chief," Pete said. His expression resembled that of a cat that'd just caught a plump mouse. "How'd you know about the naive Bayse router?"

Chief motioned to the camera screens behind him.

Pete's smile widened. "Ah, but I never mentioned it by name. You couldn't know unless you sent in one of your spies to steal it. I don't know how you managed it, but I know you're behind its disappearance. You're going to tell me where it is, Chief."

Chief's brow rose and he crossed his arms over his chest. "Are you going to open this door then? Is that what you're going to do, Pete? Ah, but you can't, can you, because only I can open the door."

Pete's features gave away a hint of annoyance.

Chief waved him off. "I can see why you want a naive Bayse router. There are a lot of Jaders out there, and a whole lot of them have criminal records. Though it won't help you and your crew."

Chief paused to allow time for Pete to process the words.

"What do you mean?" Pete finally asked.

"Simple. It won't matter that your and your crew's records will be clean, you won't get a chance to benefit from having a clean slate. It all goes back to Anna East's skeletons. She'll need to bury the truth as to what's happening here on Free Station, which means anyone tied to it will be silenced. Permanently."

"You think she'd do that, boss?" the man to Pete's left said. He had two black eyes and a crooked nose, which made him Pete's punching bag from earlier.

"No, and don't listen to him," Pete spat and then shot a look at Chief. "He's just trying to get to us."

"I heard the *Gallic Lady*'s crew disappeared after doing a side job for East," the man to Pete's right whispered, but his words came clearly through the speakers into the comm center.

Pete glared at his two men. "Leave me. *Now.*"

Neither man looked happy, but they did as they were told. They left Pete alone on the other side of the glass door. Chief forced himself to stay focused on Pete. If Chief glanced in Hettinger's direction, the pirate would surely remember there were two men in the comm center or, worse, suspect that Chief's goading was part of a plan.

Pete's frown remained. "East needs me more than I need her, and she knows that. She wouldn't be stupid enough to try anything."

"She needed you to get access to Free Station, and she still needs you to give her a clean record. Soon, she'll have no need for you. Until then, she'll just keep having you do all the hard work so she can come in and claim all the credit."

Pete glared.

"Oh, you think you're partners?" Chief chuckled. "You're even dumber than I thought."

Pete's face darkened. "Your skull is going to be a nice addition to my collection."

Chief lowered his hands. "Then do it."

At the code phrase, Hettinger opened the door. Pete bore a moment of surprise before Hettinger swung around and shot him squarely in the chest. The pirate fell. Chief didn't hesitate before taking a knee by Pete and grabbing the handheld radio. When Pete groaned, Chief frowned. He yanked up Pete's shirt to see the pirate was wearing an armored vest.

Hettinger stepped out and handed Chief a rifle before sucking in a deep breath. "Finally, fresh air."

Chief jumped to his feet. "We have to hurry."

"Hey. Stop!" a man called out.

Chief swung around and fired. His shot went wide, but it was enough to send the pair of pirates scurrying around the bend in the hallway.

The pair of Peacekeepers sprinted away from the pirates. Hettinger fired randomly behind them as they ran. The heat from the pirate's return fire singed Chief's ear. Ahead of them, the hallway ended at the lifts, which Chief noted were again operational. He barreled toward the open elevator, even though he knew Jaders were likely closing in on him through each of the two hallways that branched out from the hallway leading from the lift.

Chief fired to his left and to his right the instant he stepped into the open area. Jaders to his left were still at a distance but sprinting toward the pair. They fired at nearly the same time Chief had fired, and he felt pain in his left forearm, as though someone had shoved a sharp icicle through it. He ignored the pain and toppled into the lift, with Hettinger on his heels.

The moment they were inside, Chief lunged for the controls. He dropped his rifle and hit the red emergency button at the same time he pressed the Close button. Pain shot through his arm at the movement, but he didn't let go until the doors closed.

The sounds of pounding fists and blaster fire hitting the other side of the door gave him chills. The sounds of the two men's panting filled the space. Chief flipped open the panel with all the buttons to reveal a screen and a handprint reader. He placed his hand over the reader.

When it flashed green, relief filled him. Anna East had not figured out how to disable his access, which meant he could at least slow down Anna East's plunder of Free Station. Atlas was integrated with every system on Free Station, but several of the safety and emergency systems overrode Atlas commands. He entered commands on the screen to put the elevator in lockdown mode.

Smoke flitted through the seams in the lift doors, and Chief knew the Jaders were firing nonstop at the door in their efforts to gain entry. It was futile—all doors were built to retain atmospheric pressure during hull breaches. Photon rifles would eventually burn through, but Chief and Hettinger would be long gone before that happened.

He took a deep breath. "We're safe for now, but we need to keep moving." He looked over at Hettinger and went cold.

The marshal was leaning against the far wall, holding his gut where a blaster had caught him. A second shot had nicked the man's shoulder, but he didn't seem to notice. Somehow, he still managed to keep his rifle leveled at the open wall of the lift toward the low-gravity pole.

"Damn it," Chief muttered and rushed to the young man.

"S'okay, Chief," Hettinger said, wobbly.

Chief helped him to the floor. "Stay with me, Dean. We'll get you patched up."

"At least the air smells better here." Hettinger winced and grunted, then began to moan.

Frustration burned at Chief. As a marshal assigned to a security detail, Chief knew Hettinger carried a basic med kit containing a couple of bandages and a coagulant. But Chief knew that nothing short of immediate surgery by a skilled doctor would be enough to save the young Peacekeeper. If he had access to a complete med kit, he could've at least have given Dean an opioid to help with the pain. Instead, he had to watch a young man's life end far too early and with far too much pain.

Hettinger clutched Chief's shirt. "I don't want to be like those guys in the comm center. I don't want to die. Please, Chief, I don't want to die." Tears filled his eyes.

Wincing, Chief wrapped his left arm around Hettinger's shoulders. He relieved Hettinger of his rifle and kept it aimed at the pole, the one area where any Jaders locked in the accessibility row with him could reach them from above or below. He murmured, "It's going to be okay," to the man whose courage had not wavered since the Jaders invaded Free Station. For his actions, Hettinger was a hero in Chief's eyes. He'd seen death too many times and knew that the final minutes of a mortally wounded Peacekeeper's life were often the most honest, the most human.

Even as the smoke put a haze in the air, Chief didn't move as he held Hettinger's slumped body. No sounds were coming from above, below, or the sides, which meant that he was lucky to have initiated lockdown with no Jaders in the accessible areas around the lift. Hettinger's moans grew quieter until he made no more sounds.

Chief checked the young man's pulse and found none. He pressed his forehead to Hettinger's and closed his eyes. "May you suffer no more."

The thick, bitter air prickled Chief's throat. He pulled away and coughed. The heat was building near the door, and Chief saw a glowing pinprick expanding at the center of the door.

In a rush, he went to Hettinger's gun belt, snapped free a spare rifle battery, and pocketed it. He grabbed both rifles and slung them across his back. He went to the edge of the lift that opened to the pole and looked up and down to verify that he was alone. He reached out with his uninjured arm and wrapped himself around the pole. He slid down two levels, fumbling, then dropped hard onto the platform at the level he needed. A massive jolt of pain shot through his injured arm. He winced.

He unslung one of the rifles and edged off the platform and before two doors. One door opened to a primary hallway like the one Chief and Hettinger had run through to get onto the lift. The other door was painted red with the word EMERGENCY printed in large white letters. This was one of the doors that existed for the sole purpose of easing evacuations of the station, and therefore, anyone could access it, even during a lockdown. It also meant the door to the hallway would have the same letters printed high on it, signaling an exit route. Chief hoped that the Jader pirates hadn't yet realized that any emergency door remained unlocked, or else his escape would be short-lived.

He assumed someone would figure it out soon enough, which meant he had a very small window to get what he needed and find a place to hide and coordinate a counterattack. He swung open the red door, raising his rifle as soon as he did. When only silence greeted him, he stepped through and pulled the door closed behind him. If there were any way to bar the door closed, he would've done it, but emergency doors had been built sturdily and simply, with nothing more complicated than a single bar handle on each side. He couldn't shoot the handle off with a photon rifle, so he turned and ran through the cylindrical tunnel that curved like a coiled snake. At equal intervals along each curve was an escape pod capable of holding fifty people. He ran past each one.

His arm throbbed, and his chest couldn't get enough air. He

couldn't help the former, and too many years behind a desk had caused the latter. He continued to push himself, unwilling to slow down and risk making Dean Hettinger's death meaningless.

He could feel the floor incline in his aching muscles. The emergency tunnel wrapped around Free Station like a corkscrew, making escape pods accessible to anyone within two floors. Every time he ran by a red door, he held his rifle higher, but he'd yet to come across friend or foe.

He hadn't come across any ejected escape pods, which meant, as far as he knew, all of his people were still on Free Station, and he hoped they were all safely locked in their rooms rather than standing before pirates. Though he already knew not all of them had made it behind locked doors in time. He'd watched from the comm center as his security detail was decimated. He'd seen over twenty marshals slaughtered and twice that many specialists forced to labor for Anna East's Jaders.

They were his people, and he was responsible for them. He'd see them freed.

The escape pod he sought was at the highest part of the corkscrew tunnel. He was fighting for air and weak from going too long without water. His breaths were staccato bombs to his ears. By the time he reached the top, he was wheezing for breath and slowed to a walk to keep from tripping over his own feet.

The escape pod waited at the tunnel's end. It was half the size of the other pods and of a different design. While all the other pods were meant to drop immediately into Hiraeth's orbit before automatically setting a landing course on the rocky planet, this pod could be flown as a ship of its own—albeit a poorly handling ship.

Chief placed his hand over the scanner, and the pod door opened. He stepped inside and strode past the dozen seats lining his left and right, stopping only to open the med kit on the wall and pull out a bandage. He closed the kit and walked to the front of the escape pod and climbed through an oval-shaped opening to the cockpit. Once inside, he set both rifles on the floor and collapsed onto the copilot's seat, which was the seat reserved for the director of the Galactic Peacekeepers for the Ross system—his seat.

He examined his left forearm. The shot had gone through, leaving charred black skin around the entry and exit wounds. There was very little blood, as the beam had cauterized the injury. It throbbed with pain. Every movement brought a sting. That he could still somewhat use his fingers meant that the shot hadn't cut through the tendons. He was still functional, but he knew the pain would cause him to favor the arm, which would slow his movement when he didn't have time to move slow.

The pain would only get worse. As he healed—assuming he could get proper medical care in time to keep his arm—the pain would become sheer agony as seared nerve endings were replaced with sensitive new nerves. He unraveled the white bandage. It had antibiotics, decontaminators, and a mild analgesic weaved through its fibers. The painkillers would do very little to numb the pain that radiated through his forearm. He gingerly started wrapping the bandage around his arm. When the chemicals touched the damaged area, it felt like acid corroding his skin, causing his visual field to narrow. He hissed and held his arm to his chest until the blaze dulled to smoldering embers, still painful, but he could sense the world around him again. He gazed out the viewscreen toward the desert brown and icy white world of Hiraeth that filled up much of his sight picture.

It'd be so easy to launch the escape pod. He could fly to safety—assuming his ship wasn't noticed and shot out of orbit first. But to escape would be to abandon over five hundred people depending on him to help them. Escape wasn't why he'd come to that pod.

He closed his eyes and savored the peaceful sense of security for a long moment. Then he opened his eyes, reached low and to his right, and placed his hand over a scanner. An electronic chime sounded behind his head, followed by the whoosh of a door. He spun his seat around to where a small compartment now stood open. A warm glow illuminated the contents, and he reached inside and pulled out the extra pistol and a little black box. He left the Atlas tablet—powering it on would only give away his position. He slid the handgun into his waistband and the box into his chest pocket.

He went to stand. His legs protested, and he had to pull himself to his feet. He took one last deep breath, grabbed the rifles, and stepped out of the cockpit.

"Chief Roux, I know you can hear me."

Anna East's voice chilled Chief through and through. He scrambled for the handheld radio he'd taken from Pete.

"Don't ignore me, Chief." She had the audacity to sound indignant.

He lifted the radio to respond, then paused. He had nothing to say to East. Not yet. He slid it back onto his belt.

"You killed two of my men. You'll pay for that. I will find you. There's nowhere you can hide from me."

East spoke in a singsong, taunting manner that made Chief recoil. He turned down the volume and strode from the escape pod. He waited for the door to close behind him before he broke into a jog, then a run down the coiled corridor. He'd left no evidence that he'd been on the pod, no proof that he'd been in the tunnel. He'd made it about midway through before he stopped at an escape pod. He stepped inside. Unlike the executive pod, all the other pods had their doors open at all times to make evacuation more efficient as well as to allow them to leverage the station's environmentals rather than run off their own, limited systems.

He didn't shut the door behind him. He couldn't give away any hint of where he hid.

All pod layouts were identical in that seats lined the two walls and a cargo hold spanned the area below the floor. He found fingerholds and lifted the smooth metal surface, releasing a grunt as his injured arm rewarded his effort with instant fury. He dropped to the floor four feet below. He had to kneel to reset the floor tile. He then crawled around a crate, sat, and leaned against another.

As long as the Jaders didn't thoroughly search every single escape pod, they'd never find him.

The cargo hold was small and uncomfortable for any full-height human. Escape pods were meant for saving people, not equipment, and the only reason cargo holds were included was to store emergency supplies: food and water mainly, along with a few medical and sanitary supplies.

He opened the crate nearest him and pulled out three packets of water. He downed two before he rested. Before he tore open the third packet, he pulled out a meal kit. In the dimly lit cargo hold, he could barely make out the contents. Goulash. Wasn't the best, wasn't the worst. He dug in. The dull flavor made it easier not to eat too quickly and risk vomiting it back up.

After he finished the meal and third water package, a thick calm blanketed him. He hadn't allowed himself more than a couple of hours of sleep over the past couple of days, and he couldn't allow himself to sleep now.

He reached into his pocket and pulled out the black box. He opened it and took out the two items: a small black disk and a folded computer tablet no bigger than his palm. He raised the magnetic disk to the metal ceiling, where it snapped to the metal.

He unfolded the tablet, clicking the components in place until it was larger than both his hands. As soon as the last click sounded, the screen came to life. The Galactic Peacekeeper logo was emblazoned in the center, and the words *Quantum Splitter Relay* were printed below. The screen morphed, dropping the logo and many of the letters, leaving only *QuSR*. He tapped the acronym and a messaging screen displayed.

QuSR messaging was nearly instantaneous, even across multiple star systems, and it was a system he often used in communicating with Sol representatives and his fellow GP directors. It was still quite limited in that it could only send text packets—video and images were out of the question. The Atlas network relied on a QuSR backbone to aid in data transfers, but anything connected to Atlas was out of the question. The tablet he held was an emergency QuSR device, not tied to any system and stored in a Faraday box, making it possible to use even if Free Station was hit by a star flare and ended up without power.

He selected the first address listed, *GP Central*, and typed out a message:

FREE STATION HAS FALLEN TO JADER PIRATES OPERATING UNDER ANNA EAST WITH INTENT TO TAKE CONTROL OF ROSS SYSTEM BY FORCE AND DECLARE INDEPENDENCE TO THE CONSORTIUM. ATLAS NETWORK COMPROMISED AT ROSS HUB. CASUALTIES. REMAINING PERSONNEL STILL AT RISK. LAUNCHING COUNTEROFFENSIVE. IMMEDIATE SUPPORT OF NEARBY GP NEEDED.

– CHIEF CORMAC ROUX, DIRECTOR, ROSS SYSTEM GALACTIC PEACEKEEPERS

. . .

Finished, he tapped the ENCRYPT & SEND button at the bottom of the screen. It took over ten interminable minutes for the tablet to encrypt the text and send the data packet. When a green checkmark appeared on the screen, he breathed the first sigh of real relief he'd felt since Cat Mercier had triggered the EMP in his office.

GP Central now had Chief's message. They were too far away to help, but they would notify the other directors as well as the Consortium. No matter what happened, he could at least guarantee that Anna East would never see her vision become a reality.

With Anna East's plan stopped, he now had to focus on freeing his people still on the station. He couldn't help them alone. Any Peacekeepers not on Free Station were scattered across the Ross system, most in Hiraethian colonies, others in the mining colonies. Several of the barons on Hiraeth had QuSR dishes, but he couldn't count on them to do the right thing, not with Anna East being one of the wealthiest people in Ross, and every baron he'd met could be bought for the right price.

That left only one person in the Ross system, and Chief had no idea if he was even still alive. Still, he sent a quick message to Punch Durand just in case. Finished, he decided it was time for sleep. To take back Free Station, he'd need his head clear and his body primed. A couple of hours of sleep could at least help with clearing the webs in his head. He went to lie down, paused, then grabbed the QuSR tablet again.

He'd been thinking of Peacekeepers to contact. He'd never considered allies who weren't quite allies. He pulled up a contact he heard from only when that contact needed something. Now, it was Chief's turn. He started typing his message:

GENERAL ZHANG...

CHAPTER FIFTEEN

ANNA STRODE DOWN THE HALLWAY, THE CREW OF THE *BENDIX* protecting her, and stopped to stand above Pete. He sat on the floor, leaning against the wall. His chest plate was lying on the floor, and he was dabbing a nasty burn on his chest.

That he didn't stand when she approached made her all the angrier. "You're screwing up everything. First, you lose the router. Now, you lose Chief. What's next?"

He cocked his brow at her. "*I'm* screwing up everything? I remember that I wanted to execute Chief Roux. I remember telling you that he was resourceful and not to be underestimated. You should've heeded my warning."

She made a mental note to never let him in her bed again. He'd grown far too informal in their interactions, and his behavior would surely rub off on others who thought they could talk to her like an equal.

But Anna East wasn't their equal. She came from a heralded line of astute leaders. Her family's wealth had built Jade-8, the station that enabled colonization in the Ross system.

She took a step closer, lifted her leg, and pressed the sole of her boot against his burn.

He winced but knew better than to knock her away.

"You wanted Chief Roux dead. Now's your chance. Find him and finish him."

He glared up at her. "I will."

She didn't move. "And as soon as you do that, you will bring Throttle Reyne to me so I can cut her throat wide open, just like she did to my brother."

He frowned. "I told you, she's not here—argh!"

Anna twisted her boot on his wound. "Then you will do whatever you need to do to make sure she comes here. She's lived long enough."

CHAPTER SIXTEEN

"WE'RE DROPPING OUT OF JUMP SPEED NOW," RUSTY ANNOUNCED.

Throttle sat on the bridge along with Sylvian, Finn, and Punch, who'd healed remarkably over the past fifteen hours.

She felt a series of vibrations before the stars came to a standstill outside the front window. Seeing no ships firing upon the *Javelin*, she relaxed. "Rusty, make sure we're not broadcasting any credentials. Scan the sector for traffic."

"There are no ships or torpedoes on an intercept course. There's moderate traffic around the Jade-8 megastructure, as to be expected, and several ships traveling on routes that are likely to or from the satellite structures," Rusty answered.

"How about Rod's Repair Garage?" Punch asked.

Rusty said nothing.

Throttle shot Punch a quick glance. "Rusty's programmed to only respond to the crew," she said before asking, "Rusty, what traffic do we have at the coordinates we're heading for?"

"There are no ships in motion, and there are four ships docked."

"Is the *High Spirit* one of them?" Throttle asked.

"There is a ship matching the credentials of a Peacekeeper ship. From my initial scans, it appears to be operational and in standby mode."

"Good. I was counting on East to have all the Jaders so busy with her whole 'take over the universe' plan that they wouldn't get around to

RACHEL AUKES

chopping up the *Spirit* for parts yet," Punch said. "Now that we're in the same sector, I can connect to her." He pulled out a small tablet computer and tapped in a code.

"Rusty, take us in at sub-speed. We don't want to ruffle anyone's feathers, assuming there's someone even at the chop shop."

"We're too far away to run detailed scans. When we get closer, I'll scan for heat signatures," Rusty said.

Throttle glanced at Punch, who was frowning as he tapped on the tablet.

"What's wrong?" Throttle asked.

He didn't look up. "The *Spirit*'s not responding."

Sylvian spun out of her seat and walked over. She held out her hand. "Let me see."

He eyed her for a length before handing her the tablet. "Have at it, but if the *Spirit*'s not talking to me, she's sure not going to talk to you."

Sylvian stood next to where Punch sat while she busied herself with the tablet.

Throttle frowned when a question hit her. "When Pete hit you with an EMP, why didn't it fry the tablet?"

"It has a liquid processor," Sylvian answered before Punch could as she continued to work. "EMPs have no effect other than a temporary ripple."

"Pete's goons assumed it was fried too. Otherwise, they would've taken the tablet when they took my weapons," Punch said.

"I see you've found your weapons," Finn said from behind Punch.

Punch looked over his shoulder before tapping his holster. "This? This is just something I borrowed until I can get back on the *Spirit*."

Sylvian returned the tablet to Punch. "You can't connect to your ship because the Atlas network has sent a lockdown command."

Punch cussed. "I was afraid of that."

"Afraid of what?" Throttle asked.

"That when the Jaders hacked Atlas, they'd use it to lock down all Peacekeeper ships in this system. It's an easy way to prevent all of us from going to Free Station and going after the Jaders. Wait." He frowned and looked around. "If they sent out a lockdown code, why is this ship still running?"

"Because it's never been connected to the Atlas net," Throttle said.

126

Punch gave her a sideways glance. "Trust issues?"

"Since both of my ships were stolen by Jaders as soon as I reached this system, you could say that. I don't like anyone except my crew and me having access to this ship. And, since it seems like the Jaders have now stolen your ship and likely every other Peacekeeper's ship in this system, I'm feeling pretty good about that decision."

"It's a decision I plan to revisit as soon as we free Chief and get Free Station back." He cocked his head. "Though I was never told that it was optional to have my ship on the Atlas net."

Throttle shrugged. "The way I see it, the *Javelin* is my ship, not a GP ship. I had no interest in it wearing a GP collar, and I told Chief as much."

"Yet you allowed you and your crew to get Atlas chips implanted in your heads," Punch countered.

Throttle sighed. "Chief was nonnegotiable on that one. I think I'll revisit that decision with him after this is all said and done."

"Chief might not be a stickler for rules, but he sure is one when it comes to looking after his people." Punch thought for a moment. "You're giving up a lot of fancy features by not having your ship connected to the GP net. It's a whole lot faster to look up information and set up flight plans using Atlas than relying on those tiny chips. You're missing out."

"Nah." Throttle smirked and shot Sylvian a glance. "Not with a software specialist on the crew." She turned back to Punch. "Still sure not having a crew is the way to go?"

Punch became stoic. "It's better than carrying the knowledge that if anything happened to them, it's on me."

Throttle sobered as her mind immediately brought forth images of crew members she'd lost. She sucked in a deep breath. "Rusty, are we close enough for detailed scans?"

"Yes, but the temperature is too high inside to isolate how many people are on the station."

Punch scowled. "They're a chop shop. They have big cutters to make short work of stolen ships. It's always hotter than a Hiraethian summer in those." He cracked his knuckles. "No problem. I'll just have to be sneaky."

Throttle gave him a droll look. "And that's something I know you can do. But it won't do any good as long as the *High Spirit* is locked down by Atlas."

"I can remove the Atlas card," Sylvian offered. "It won't take long. All I need is admin access to the ship's systems and the mainboard cabinet."

"That sounds easy. If you tell me what it looks like, I'll take it out when I board," Punch said.

The specialist shook her head. "It's not as easy as pulling out the card. If you do that, you'd corrupt your ship's core system. No, I have to be over there to set up a sandbox and run a program to make the Atlas network think the sandbox is the correct system. That way, when we pull the card, Atlas will corrupt the closed system instead."

Throttle grimaced, not liking the idea of Sylvian leaving the *Javelin*, but not seeing any way around it. "Okay, so let's review the plan. Assuming the chop shop doesn't have proximity sensors, we don't have to worry about the *Javelin* being noticed as long as we avoid any windows. Then Punch and Sylvian need to spacewalk over to the *High Spirit*. Sylvian gets on board while Punch sneaks onto the station to release the *High Spirit* from the dock. And you both have to do all that without raising any attention from anyone inside the chop shop. Sound about right?"

"Sounds about right," Punch echoed.

"I don't like it," Finn said. "It's been less than a day since you had surgery. If something happens out there, Sylvian will be stuck taking care of you as well as your ship."

Punch stood, turned, and faced Finn. "I've recovered more than enough for a simple spacewalk. And I'll make sure nothing happens to your wife while she's out there."

"I can take care of myself," Sylvian grumbled.

"I agree with Finn that I don't like this either," Throttle said. "It's a sloppy plan, and there are far too many ways it could go sideways."

"Trust me. This isn't the first time I've gotten onto a ship at a chop shop before," Punch said. "They never have proximity sensors, and even if they did, they never have staff watching them. This will be easy, in and out."

A ping sounded on Throttle's screen. She frowned and tapped to open the incoming communication.

"This is commercial station Ross-four-eight-six-two. We have picked you up on our scanners. Declare your intent."

She gritted her teeth and snapped a glare at Punch. "No proximity sensors, my ass."

Punch sighed and said dejectedly, "They must've just gotten some."

Throttle muttered several *colorful* things under her breath before she tapped the transmit button. "Ross station, hi there. Skully Pete sent us from Free Station. We've got a Peacekeeper ship for you to process."

"Another one? Okay then. Bring it on into dock five. We're attaching a station map for you."

"Dock five. Got it," she said and terminated the connection. She turned back to the three crew members on the bridge with her. "It looks like plan A is off the table. They've seen us, so we're moving to plan B. Just like we discussed on the jump here, Finn and I will pose as pirates to distract the Jaders while Eddy sneaks onto the docks and unlocks both ships. Punch and Sylvian, you will have eight minutes to get the *High Spirit* up and running." She held up a finger. "But remember, Punch, you don't cut and run until the *Javelin* is ready to launch. Shit's going to fly as soon as the first ship moves, so we have to go together. Otherwise, whoever's left is going to have a lot of angry Jaders at their door."

"We're a team. I wouldn't dream of leaving you behind," Punch said.

Her eyes narrowed as she tried to gauge his sincerity, but she soon gave up and glanced at her screen. We'll be docking in ten minutes, so you'd better suit up and get ready."

Finn and Sylvian left together.

Punch paused on his way off the bridge. "I really didn't think they'd have proximity sensors."

"Let's hope that's the only bit you're wrong about," she said and turned back to her panel. She tapped the communication screen to open a channel to the back of the ship. "Eddy, we're moving to plan B. You got that?"

"Plan B. Got it."

"Be careful," she added.

"Why wouldn't I be?"

She smirked but didn't respond. Instead, she glanced upward. "I'm taking control, Rusty."

"You now have full flight control, Captain."

She smoothly and quickly guided the *Javelin* toward the marker on her screen while looking through the window. The chop shop was an oblong station with blinking lights around its perimeter. As the station came into better view, she thought it could've easily been assumed to be a derelict, except for the lights. ROD'S REPAIR GARAGE was painted in bright orange. Beneath the name, she could still read UNS SCIENTIFIC RESEARCH VESSEL in faded letters along the outside of the white exterior that had been patched so many times, it looked more like a quilt than a space station.

Four of the docks had ships attached. She maneuvered the *Javelin* into the dock with a large number five painted on the airlock door, placing the ship between the *High Spirit* and the last remaining empty dock.

As soon as she heard the docking locks click into place, Throttle stood. "Rusty, no one gets on board except for the crew."

"How about Marshal Durand?" Rusty asked.

"He's leaving on his ship. He doesn't come back on without being escorted by a crew member."

"You don't trust him."

She left the bridge. "I don't trust anyone who's not a member of my crew."

"You can trust me." Rusty's voice came through speakers as she walked down the hallway.

"And you're a part of the crew," she said, then added, "But if you get hacked, that's a different story. No offense."

"None taken. I'll make it a priority not to get hacked."

Throttle didn't stop by her room to change. She wore the same clothes that she'd worn before becoming a marshal. The only difference was that she had a badge now. With two holsters and four sheaths, she looked like any other pirate. The funny thing about the Ross system: it could be hard to tell pirates and Peacekeepers apart.

As she walked, Punch joined her. She'd loaned him a chime suit that had belonged to Birk—she recognized every ding and scratch on the chest plate—and seeing it worn again brought back memories that tightened her throat. She shook them off by shooting Punch a look. "I'll need that back when you're done with it."

"Of course. I can even send it back with your specialist as soon as the *Spirit* is up and running."

She waved him off. "You'll probably need it to return that ship back to its rightful owners."

"What ship?"

"The one you left on Hiraeth."

"Oh, that ship?" He chuckled. "That was just some wreck. If you think that thing could still fly, you're crazier than me. Nah, I hitched a ride on a cargo hauler. The mechanic owed me a favor after I let him off a drug charge a while back."

Throttle paused. "Why'd you lie?"

He shrugged. "I guess it's just another old habit of mine."

She wagged a finger at him. "Don't." Rather than continuing to scold him, she blew him off and walked away. Her temper simmered just below the surface. While she certainly didn't trust Punch, knowing that lying came so naturally to him made her wonder what other stories he'd fed her.

At the airlock, she found Finn and Sylvian kissing. They broke when Throttle approached. Sylvian turned to leave, but Throttle grabbed her by the arm. "Be careful. He's not one of us," she said quietly.

Sylvian met her gaze for a brief moment before she gave a simple nod. "I will." The specialist then walked off with Punch.

"Everything okay?" Finn asked while Throttle watched the pair head to the cargo bay.

"I'll be okay once this whole thing is over, and East is no longer wreaking havoc on the Ross system." She turned to face him and found him wearing even more weapons than her. "I see you're ready."

"I'd rather be overprepared, though I don't anticipate this station has more than a skeleton crew. After all, it's a chop shop. It's not Jade-8."

She gave a dry chuckle. "Sure. What could go wrong?"

Her hand hovered over the switch to open the door, even though the light above them flashed green, signaling that a secure connection had been made.

"Ready?" she asked.

"As I'll ever be," Finn said.

She inhaled deeply and pressed her hand to the panel. The door opened. At least a half-dozen Jaders stood before them, and every single one of them had a rifle aimed at the pair.

CHAPTER SEVENTEEN

"Whoa there, people," Throttle said while keeping her hands in the air. "We're Jaders just like you. I'm Halit." She used her first name in case these Jaders had heard of the trouble a ship captain named "Throttle" had caused on Jade-8. "And this is my partner, Finn. We work for Skully Pete." The lie tasted salty, and she hoped the ragged men standing before her bought it.

A man at the center of the group stepped forward. A deep scar weaved across his face, giving him a permanent sneer. His teeth were so yellowed, they were brown. Like the others, he wore tattered clothing that looked damp with sweat. The temperature was so high, Throttle could feel droplets already forming on her forehead, though having rifles aimed at her and Finn didn't help the atmosphere.

"You're not one of the regulars," the Jader said. "How do I know Skully Pete sent you?"

Throttle lowered her right hand glacially slow until she pointed to the marshal's badge on her shoulder, and Finn followed suit. "We met Pete at Free Station. He dealt us in about a month back."

The man's eyes narrowed. "If Pete didn't send you, I'll have you know that we don't take kindly to Peacekeepers getting in the way of honest work, and we don't like Jaders robbing other Jaders."

Finn spoke. "If Pete didn't send us, you think we'd be stupid enough to walk right into your shop?"

"How many you got back on that ship?" the man countered, dubious.

"None. It's just the two of us," Throttle said. When he continued to eye her, she sighed. "Scan it. You can see for yourself."

"Scans can be blocked. I think we'll manually check out that ship and see for ourselves," he said.

Throttle noticed Finn shift to her left, and she knew he was getting antsy. She gave the man a hard smile. "Good luck with that. I locked it down tight when I docked. I don't know you, which means I don't trust you. If I give you access to that ship before I get paid, what's to stop you from shoving my partner and me here out the airlock? I think I'll keep it locked down until our business here is wrapped up. Trust me, there's no way you're getting into it without my codes."

The man's sneer seemed to grow. "We could cut our way on."

"You could, but I know how much harder it is to strip a ship wearing suits in zero g than in a ship with working environmentals," she said. "Trust me, these Peacekeeper ships have some good hardware on them, and I've flown this ship. I'm betting you'll find this ship will be worth a whole lot more to you whole than chopped up."

When the man continued to eye them warily, Finn said, "Why don't you give Skully Pete a call? He's the one sending these Peacekeeper ships your way. Though I warn you, he's a bit busy with the whole Free Station business right now, and he might not appreciate having to deal with other problems. He might change his mind and start sending his business to another shop. Or, if you really piss him off, he might decide to add to his skull collection."

He visibly paled, and Throttle knew they had him.

After another tense moment, the man motioned to the men on either side of him to lower their weapons before he turned back to Throttle and Finn. "Nah. We're good here. You can call me Jack. This is my garage. We can talk more in my office. Follow me."

She shot a quick glance at Finn, who seemed none too comfortable with the situation. Not that she could blame him. She wasn't happy about it, either. Their task was to buy time for Eddy, Sylvian, and Punch, which had seemed much easier in her head before they'd stepped out to be greeted by seven armed Jaders. She'd expected one or two armed Jaders, with the rest of the station's population working on ships. Finn and she were outnumbered and surrounded.

Jack led them from the dock and the dock controls, which were only a few feet away from the *Javelin*'s airlock. As long as Eddy could avoid being seen, he'd have an easy time unlocking both ships.

Seeing how the station was laid out made stealth a challenge.

The wide walkway wrapped around a cavernous center, with only a handrail to separate the two. They weaved around stacks of crates and parts that lined much of the walls. The open floor plan would make Eddy's job harder and would make it nearly impossible for Throttle and Finn to escape without being noticed, which meant it was crucial plan B worked.

Because the closest thing Throttle had to a plan C was "run like hell."

There were plenty of exits, but Throttle and Finn weren't wearing their suits, which meant the only exit they could count on was the door to the *Javelin*.

Jack led them down a flight of stairs and through the center area, where workers welded, cut, and tinkered with two ships likely taken by Skully Pete's crew. The temperature at the centermost part of the station was sweltering, where a massive cutter was being used to slice through a ship's hull. Throttle wondered how many stolen ships had come through that shop. Then she wondered what had happened to the original crews, and her stomach soured. In a system still being colonized, hardware was far more valuable than human life. The healthiest crew members had likely been given an option to work on one of Anna East's crews. Possibly, a few had even found work at the chop shop. All other crew members had likely met the cold end of an airlock.

She tried not to think about the lives she couldn't help and instead focused on her and Finn's current situation. He walked stiffly, looking straight ahead, but she had no doubt his trained eyes were taking in their surroundings even more entirely than Throttle was managing to.

Jack came up to an office that looked like it'd been built out of left-over plastic and glass parts. He opened the door and stepped inside. One of the guards motioned them to follow.

As Throttle stepped through the door, she paused at the sign on the window. ROD'S had been crossed out, and above it, a new name had been scrawled so that the revised sign read JACK'S REPAIR GARAGE.

"What happened to Rod?" she asked.

Jack took a seat behind a cluttered desk. "Rod fell out an airlock." He spoke with a hint of humor behind his words that left little doubt of Jack's role in Rod's demise.

"He sounded like a clumsy fellow," she said as she took one of the seats across from him.

Finn took a seat next to her. Jack's henchman remained standing, and Throttle noticed they all still held rifles.

Jack leaned back. "Before we talk business, I want you to answer a question for me first."

"And what's that?" she asked.

He steepled his fingers. "Why'd you decide to hook up with Pete? Peacekeepers, and marshals especially, tend to have pretty inflated views of themselves and look down on us hardworking blue-collar folks."

Throttle answered, "I'm no strait-laced Peacekeeper. I tend to have more...*flexible* views, and I liked the credits Pete offered. No one gets rich working for the GP. Hell, I can barely pay my bills with my GP paychecks. When Pete talked to me about the benefits of becoming an entrepreneur, I figured I had nothing to lose and everything to gain, especially since the GP doesn't have much of a future in this system anymore."

Jack belted out a laugh. His breath stank of rotten teeth and moonshine. "You're right about that." He sobered somewhat and nodded toward Finn. "Is that why you hooked up?"

"I joined up for the credits. Lots and lots of credits," Finn replied.

"You don't have much to say, do you," Jack said.

"I do when I have something to say."

"Ah, a tough guy. I've seen plenty of those come and go. Most don't have any bite to back up their bark. You one of those?" Jack asked.

Finn leaned forward. "You want to find out?"

The pair eyed each other for a length before Jack leaned back and grinned, turning back to Throttle. "Maybe both of you are made out to be Jaders after all. I think I'll let you live so we can do business."

Throttle tried not to look surprised. "That's good because I'd hate to have someone try to kill me. So are you ready to talk about buying my ship?"

"I am." He went to a computer screen and pulled up an image of the *Javelin*.

Throttle's breath hitched, and she exhaled when the video caught the side of the *Javelin* attached to the dock. Neither the cargo bay doors nor the airlock doors were in view.

"From what I can see, that ship you brought in looks like a custom job."

"It is," Throttle said.

"Custom is a good thing because I might be able to resell it as is without a lot of cosmetic work. But custom is also a bad thing because those kinds of jobs are more often than not a mishmash of duct tape and bad welds. I'll need to take a look at it before I can offer you a number."

Throttle's and Finn's comm-chips each clicked a single time. Finn bumped his foot against the desk, causing a loud clang.

"Sorry," he mumbled.

"Careful, you oaf," Jack said, not seeming to notice the audible clicks that had come a split second before Finn's diversionary tactic.

Relief loosened her muscles as the single click provided Eddy's confirmation that he'd successfully completed his part of the plan. The ships would be unlocked. A double-click from Sylvian would be coming any minute now.

She placed her hands on the arms of the ragged chair and pushed off to stand. "How about that tour now?"

Jack stood. "I like that you don't waste my time. I walked you all the way down here because I figured you would haggle me on everything before even letting me step on board. That's what Pete always does."

"Not our style," Throttle said, and Finn stood next to her.

Jack led the way and his goons encircled Throttle and Finn as they had earlier.

"I'm not letting your goons on my ship," she said.

"Where I go, they go," Jack replied without looking back.

Throttle stopped. "Then there's no tour. I still have the same worry that I had when I came here. What's to stop you from taking my ship and drifting us out an airlock?"

Jack turned and faced her. "You have my word."

"The word of a pirate?" Finn belted out a laugh. "Not good enough."

Throttle spoke. "Only you are allowed on board to check it out, or else we're going to start the haggling process like Pete does with you."

Jack eyed her for a moment before speaking. "Randall will accompany me. Two of us, two of you. That's fair, don't you think?"

She gave a simple nod. "Fair enough."

"Excellent." He waved off the rest of his goons, leaving only a single burly man standing behind Throttle and Finn.

The four began to walk. Seven to two had been bad odds, and Throttle hated gambling. She found confidence in knowing Finn and she stood a good chance against any enemy one-on-one. Though, her confidence was quickly gelling into tension as she waited for Sylvian's double-click. She glanced at Finn, who was visibly tense, no doubt wondering what was taking his wife so long. She'd said it would be a quick in-and-out. That Sylvian was taking longer than Eddy worried Throttle.

Eddy watched the screen, nervously shifting from one foot to the other, while Throttle and Finn spoke with the filthy-looking Jaders on the other side of the airlock. "Come on, come on, come on. Move it, people," he muttered as what tiny semblance of patience he'd had bled away.

When they finally moved along, he hustled closer to the airlock door and froze. He was about to leave the ship into who knew what kind of danger. He was safe on the *Javelin*. Nowhere else.

But they needed him. Throttle and Sylvian were more than crew, they were the only people he'd ever considered friends in his entire life. And he supposed Finn wasn't so bad, even though the man was always trying to get Eddy to exercise, learn self-defense, and—most annoyingly—learn how to shoot. But as long as Eddy stayed on the ship, he didn't need any of those things.

He *really* didn't want to leave the ship now. He'd thought about sending in a bot, but it would take far too long for Eddy to give Rusty the schematics to have one programmed.

It had to be Eddy. His team needed him.

He took a series of deep breaths, loudly inhaling and exhaling through tight, barely parted lips. He gripped his tool bag, not that he'd likely need it for this job, but he couldn't imagine going anywhere without it. Finn needed to carry guns with him everywhere. Eddy needed his tools. Besides, tools were far more useful than guns. It wasn't like Finn could fix an iterative array activator with a blaster. Well, it wasn't like Finn would even know what an iterative array activator would look like. The hoorah soldier-type guy would probably mistake a reduction tensor for an activator.

Eddy giggled at the thought. He then shivered, remembering that he needed to focus on the unpleasant job at hand. He stood taller and sucked in a breath. "Wish me luck, Rusty."

"Good luck, Eddy."

Eddy pressed the panel, and the door opened. He stepped through the tiny transit tube and opened the station's airlock door, unveiling a cacophony of noise, oppressive heat, and a potpourri of bad smells. He scowled at the bombardment as he stepped through the doorway, nearly tripping over a stack of boxes.

In the station's center, one worker was banging on metal with a sledgehammer while several other workers were running welders and cutters. The racket gave Eddy an instant headache, but the noise would mask his activities. The stench of burnt metal, sweat, and stale air stung his eyes and nostrils. The place not only looked like a criminal establishment, with crates stacked everywhere and no sense of cleanliness, but it also stank like one. He breathed through his mouth until he realized all the germs he was taking in, so he went back to breathing through his nose, forcing himself to deal with the unpleasantness of it all.

He rushed over to the large workstation that sat atop a pedestal near the wall. A keyboard and at least a dozen joysticks stood at attention just below a small screen. He set down his tool bag and stared blankly at the setup. Computer systems were Sylvian's thing, and hardware was Eddy's thing. He tapped the screen, but it remained blank. With a single finger, he pushed on the joystick nearest him. The computer beeped, and he jumped back. That left him with the keyboard. He'd used the things before but found them tedious and archaic. He searched the keys and settled on a green key with no label.

The screen came to life. On it were six boxes, with five displaying ship icons in green along with various abbreviations and codes. The sixth box was blank. "Finally, we're getting somewhere," he said under his breath.

He tapped the fifth box. Nothing happened. He clenched his fist but didn't hit the screen. He'd never *not* had a touchscreen. Dealing with something so obsolete increased his frustration. It was bad enough he was out in the open. He furtively searched the keyboard again. All he needed was a key to unlock the *Javelin* and the *High Spirit* from their docks, but no keys had numbers on them.

"Hey. You there."

Eddy froze, his hand still hovering over the keyboard. He pretended to ignore the gruff voice and resumed running his finger over the rows of keys.

"Hey, I'm talking to you."

Eddy turned stiffly, as though rigor mortis had claimed his neck, and faced the Jader. "Me?"

"Yeah, you. Who are you?" The man was filthy, with his coveralls covered in layers of stains to the point that Eddy couldn't tell what the original color had been. The man's skin was similar in that grease and lack of bathing disguised what could've been very pale or very dark skin. He was dragging a rolling welding cart behind him. The worker carried no visible weapon, to Eddy's relief, since Eddy had not thought to bring one himself.

"I'm Eddy," he said as a matter of fact.

The worker didn't seem impressed. "What are you doing here?"

"I came with them."

"Them who?"

He wondered if Throttle and Finn had given their real names. He stammered, "You know. Them. The pair who just brought in that ship." He motioned to where the *Javelin* was docked.

"Oh, them. Well, they're with Jack right now. You shouldn't be around here without an escort. That's one of Jack's rules."

"Oh, I didn't know," Eddy said. "The dock seal has a small air leak. I was told to fix it. No one said anything about having an escort."

"Typical. No one ever tells us peons what's going on around here." He took a step closer. The stink of beans and curry wafted through the air. Eddy scrunched his nose. The man farted and didn't even seem to care, though Eddy began to wonder if perhaps the man had shat his pants. Eddy swallowed back his gag reflex.

The worker glanced over to the open area before turning back to Eddy. "Listen, buddy. I'm busy, so I can't babysit you. But maybe I can point you in the right direction. What are you trying to do?"

Eddy motioned to the workstation. "I was trying to unlock the holding bars on docks four and five so I could have some wiggle room to work."

The worker held up a hand. "Whoa. Don't mess with the dock controls. If you're not careful, you could open an airlock to a vacant dock. Then we'd all be vented."

"Well, I certainly don't want to do that."

The worker frowned. "But I guess you probably couldn't have hurt anything. Only Jack and Randall have access to the dock systems. They're control freaks."

"Oh, I've known plenty like them," Eddy concurred. "But if I can't unlock the docks, it's going to take me three times as long to fix the seals."

"Wish I could help, but you know how guys like that are. They're so bent on keeping their power that they make life hell for those of us working for them." The worker smiled then, revealing rotted teeth. "You know, once I wrap up my project, I'll be on break. I don't suppose you want to join me in the galley for some chow later?"

Eddy gulped and grabbed his tool bag in a rush. "Oh, I wish I could, but I can't. I'm sure this project will take me all night."

Disappointment flashed across the worker's face.

"Maybe tomorrow," Eddy added.

The worker brightened. "Yeah. I'll see you then." He started to walk away, still tugging the welding cart behind him when he paused. "I'll send up Charlie to help you. That way, Jack won't throw a fit, and you can maybe wrap up your job faster, maybe even in time for supper."

"Oh. Uh, sure. Thanks."

As the worker trudged away, Eddy reached into his bag and pulled out his heaviest tool, a thick crescent wrench. He set down his bag to grip the wrench with both hands. He strode up behind the worker, lifted the wrench, closed his eyes, and swung.

The worker collapsed. Blood poured from a deep wound on the back of his head.

"Sorry," Eddy said, wincing. He didn't check to see if the man was still alive or not. He didn't want to know. He'd never killed anyone before. In fact, he'd only ever killed bugs that didn't run from him, and four rodents that had torn into the food stores on the *Gabriela* during the colonization trip out to the Ross system. He hadn't slept well all night each time he'd had to kill one. He couldn't imagine how his sleep would be disturbed if he'd killed a person.

That the worker wasn't moving was all Eddy needed. The Jader had been about to send someone else up, who likely wouldn't have been as easy to fool.

Eddy turned back to the workstation, but his gaze snagged on a red compartment in the wall. He frowned and stepped over to it, still holding the bloody wrench in a hand. "Well, I'll be…"

Above the compartment, it read *In case of station-wide emergency, pull handle to unlock ships from docks. Board ships and close airlocks.*

Eddy's jaw slackened as humor filled him. "This is too easy."

He went to open the compartment but found the door padlocked. He lifted his wrench, noticed the blood on the tip, and immediately glanced back at the fallen worker. Seeing no movement and feeling full of guilt, he turned back to the wall and slammed the wrench through the glass door. He reached in and pulled the single lever.

He expected sirens to blast, but the only sounds that greeted Eddy were audible clicks at each airlock door as the locks released the ships they held. The green lights above each door turned red, and data changed on the panel at each entrance.

Thanks to the law of inertia, the ships would remain in their current positions, lightly suctioned to the station by the airlocks. But the slightest movement could break the ships free.

Eddy ran to the *Javelin*, stopped, turned around, grabbed his tool bag, and sprinted to the airlock. He opened the station's airlock door with trepidation, but the short transit tube between the ship and station remained sealed. He stepped through, opened the *Javelin*'s airlock door, and jumped on board, immediately closing the airlock door behind him.

He collapsed against the door, clutching his tool bag on his lap, relief pouring through him.

"Are you okay, Eddy?" Rusty asked.

"I think so. It was just really scary out there," he said.

"I'll have a tea brewed for you."

"I'd like that." He allowed himself a couple more calming breaths before he reached up and clicked his comm-chip a single time. He found his nerves returning, along with his impatience. "Come on, guys. Hurry up."

"Eddy, the *High Spirit* is departing the dock under its own power," Rusty said.

Eddy frowned. "Is Sylvian back aboard yet?"

"No. My cameras show that she never left the *High Spirit*."

"Why is she still over there and not over here with us?" Eddy asked.

There was a pause before Rusty replied, "I wish I knew that answer. Whatever happened on that ship is now going to cause trouble for Throttle and Finn. We should help them because I don't want to be dissected and sold off as parts."

Eddy jumped to his feet. "I have an idea."

Jack rambled on while he and his goon escorted Throttle and Finn through the work area. She could barely hear him over the din and hadn't realized he'd asked her a question until he looked over his shoulder. "I said, you know something I find odd?"

She cocked her head. "Oh? What's that?"

Jack stopped. "You came here to sell me the ship you came in on, but you don't have a ship to leave with."

She answered without a pause. "Skully Pete mentioned you'd give us a ride to Jade-8, where we'll join up with another crew there."

His brows lifted. "He did, did he?"

"Or you could loan me one of the four other ships you have docked outside," she offered.

He smirked. "I don't do loans. I may have a cargo hauler dropping off supplies tomorrow, and it heads back to Jade-8, though it stops at several other stations along the way."

She shrugged. "Then we'll hitch a ride on that. Pete seemed to think getting a ride wouldn't be a problem."

"And it won't be, but it'll cost you," Jack said.

"Of course. That's what I'd expect," she said.

"I'll deduct it from your finder's fee on the ship you brought here," he said and resumed walking.

They hadn't made it twenty feet before a scrawny man ran up to Jack. "Mr. Jack, the *High Spirit* just took off."

Jack grabbed the man's shoulders. "What do you mean, it took off?"

"It's gone. It just flew off," the newcomer said in a rush.

"Sound the alarms," Jack said, and did a visual three-sixty around them. His gaze settled on Throttle and Finn.

He pulled out a gun, and Throttle and Finn did the same. It was a standoff. Jack and Throttle had each other dead to rights, and Jack's goon and Finn had each other. The workers around them ran off, leaving them alone in the center of the station. No one could get off a shot without risking getting shot at the same time.

"More are headed our way," Finn quietly cautioned Throttle.

Jack spoke, keeping his pistol leveled on Throttle. "You know, I think that's some coincidence you show up and, not an hour later, one of my ships is stolen. And I don't believe in coincidences."

"I don't either. My guess is that if the thief didn't come from your shop, someone snuck on board my ship and hitched a ride here."

"Possibly. But I find it hard to believe that one person could unlock a ship from the dock—especially when I control the dock system— sneak aboard, and pilot a ship away from the station, all without being noticed. Don't you find it hard to believe?"

"I've seen some pretty crazy things in my time to find anything hard to believe anymore," she said.

The sounds of bootsteps pounding toward them made Throttle inwardly cringe. She should've killed Jack and run the instant the worker had alerted him, but she'd been as surprised as Jack had been. Sylvian hadn't sent her double-click through the comm-chips to let the team know that she was safely back on board the *Javelin*. The *High Spirit* was supposed to wait until the *Javelin* departed, not the other way around. Throttle suspected the worst, that Punch had killed Sylvian after she disabled the Atlas network on his ship, and then he rabbited.

She'd go after Punch, but first, she had to find a way off the station. The sounds of rifles being raised around her didn't help her think.

"You're surrounded. Drop your weapons," Jack said.

"I'd rather die with a gun in my hand than die on my knees," Finn said.

"I'd rather not die," Throttle muttered under her breath at her partner. She didn't take her eyes off Jack and forced her next words to sound as menacing as possible. "The question you should be asking yourself, Jack, is this: Can they kill me before I kill you?"

He glared, but she could see fear behind his façade.

She continued, "Instead of shooting each other until only one person is left standing, how about we all lower our weapons and talk?"

Jack guffawed. "Why? So you can try to convince me you don't have anything to do with stealing one of my ships?"

Throttle opened her mouth to retort, but she was cut off by a metallic screech. Everyone's focus shot up to see the massive cutter tear free from one of its two support beams. Its focused laser beam was now carving lines into the floor and up the walls. Three of the *Javelin*'s round bots, each armed with a laser pen, had cut through the first beam and were now burning a thin line through the last remaining beam.

"Shoot those bots!" Jack yelled.

"Cut the power to the chopper before it cuts through the hull!" someone else screamed.

Throttle spared the briefest of glimpses at Finn before the pair sprinted out of the fatal funnel of shooters that were now engaged with a machine that had already burned a hole through several levels.

Throttle and Finn weaved through workers who were scrambling to save the station. She pushed a man out of her way, and he was shot a split second later. She glanced over her shoulder to see one of Jack's goons running after them, firing haphazardly in their direction. Finn stopped, spun around, leveled his pistol, and fired. The goon collapsed.

Throttle reached the stairs and used her leg blades to spring over several steps at a time. She paused when she reached the walkway to cover Finn as he caught up to her. She noticed that only a single bot remained, but it was spinning wildly and leaving a trail of smoke.

"Our diversion is about done for," she said as soon as Finn reached her.

"We have the higher ground. They'll have a harder time hitting us," he said.

Several shots whizzed by.

"But they can still hit us," Throttle said, and the pair ran.

They weaved around crates, dodging after every near miss.

As they drew closer to *Javelin*'s open airlock doors, Throttle noticed a worker sitting against the dock-control computer. He held his hand to a bloody gash on the back of his head. As soon as he saw Throttle, he swung out to trip her, but she'd seen him and hurdled over his reach just in time. Finn kicked the worker in the head as he ran by, and the man collapsed in a heap.

She hurried through the outer airlock door, nearly tripping, as a small gap was growing between the station and the ship. Behind her, Finn tumbled as the vacuum sucked him to the growing gap. Throttle dropped her pistol, grabbed onto the *Javelin*'s inner airlock door with one hand and reached out with her other hand. She grabbed his hand and used all her strength to pull him to her. The instant he was through, the ship's outer door closed, sealing them safely away from the station.

"Thanks, Rusty. Initiate autopilot and get us out of here," Throttle said in between breaths.

"I have the flight controls, and you'll feel our transition to sub-speed in nine seconds. It's good to have you both back. I was worried," Rusty said.

"Aw, Rusty, you were worried about us?" Finn asked drily.

"I was worried that I'd be chopped up into parts. I saw what was taking place within that station. It's a slaughterhouse."

He blew out a breath. "Figures."

The ship around Throttle vibrated roughly. If she hadn't been on her butt already, she would've ended up on it with Rusty's accelerated launch. Finn grabbed onto the wall to keep from tumbling. When the vibrations ended, she stood and looked out the airlock window to see the airlock at the station closing. Debris and at least one person had been sucked out. She grimaced and turned to open the inner door and head to the bridge.

Eddy came running to meet her in the hallway.

She grabbed his shoulder. "Good thinking, using the bots back there. You saved our lives."

He took a step back. "All three are offline. Were you able to grab any of them?"

"We were too busy running for our lives."

He huffed. "You know how many months it takes Rusty to build a single bot?"

He didn't wait for her answer and instead turned to walk away.

"Hey," Finn called out after Eddy, "is Sylvian on the bridge?"

Eddy waved him off. "She didn't come back. I suppose she's still with Punch."

Finn stiffened and his jaw clenched. His blank stare seemed to hold back a tumultuous ocean of dread and rage.

Throttle shook off the sudden chills and took determined steps to the bridge. "Rusty, plot a course to follow the *High Spirit.*"

CHAPTER EIGHTEEN

"I can't believe you hit me," Punch said while he rubbed his chin.

"You're lucky I didn't shoot you," Sylvian snapped back from where she stood as far from him as she could on the bridge of the *High Spirit.*

"You're lucky you didn't try," he countered, his hand still hovering over his holster.

When Sylvian spoke again, he noticed trepidation blanketing her anger. "I wasn't going to shoot you," she said softer than before. "You just made me so mad back there. I've never punched anybody before."

He chuckled and turned back to his screen. "I tend to have that effect on people."

"I'm beginning to see how you earned your nickname," she said drily.

He didn't look up from where he was working through flight data. "You're on the right track. Now take a seat. We've got work to do."

Out of the corner of his eye, he saw her take cautious steps forward until she reached the copilot's station.

"I disabled the Atlas net. What else do you need from me?" she asked.

He looked up then and watched her carefully. "Are you as good as Throttle says you are?"

Sylvian crossed her arms over her chest. "Of course I am, but why would I help you? You kidnapped me."

He waved her off. "I didn't kidnap you. You can communicate with your crew any time you want. I'm just leveraging another Peacekeeper's skills during a time of need."

She watched him, dubious. "So I can ping the *Javelin* and tell them what you did to me?"

He chortled. "I didn't do anything to you. I'm just giving you a lift to Free Station. You were heading there already."

"With *my* crew on the *Javelin*," she said.

"Semantics. Don't worry. You'll be back with your hubby in no time at all. Until then, you'll help me take back Free Station, starting with—"

"No," she interrupted firmly. "I won't help you until I talk with my crewmates."

"Fine. Go ahead. Being a specialist, I'm sure you can figure out how to run the comms."

He held his tongue while he mirrored her screen to watch her navigate the *High Spirit*'s communications screens and ping the *Javelin*. He was impressed at the speed with which she worked the system.

Barely a second had passed before her call was accepted.

"Punch, if you've hurt even a hair on my crew member's head—"

Punch looked at Sylvian and held up his hands in surrender, choosing silence as the better path. Sylvian tried to ignore him as she interrupted Throttle. "It's me, Throttle. I'm calling you from the *High Spirit*."

"I see that. Are you hurt?"

"No, I'm fine," the specialist said.

"I'm curious as to why you're on that ship and not here with us on the Javelin.*"*

Sylvian sighed. "Punch took off when I was still on board. He said it was a last-minute change in plans."

Punch appreciated the specialist's honesty. He didn't blame her for blaming him for her current situation. He thought then he should speak. "Throttle, things moved a little fast back there, and I didn't have time to check in."

"Oh, and exactly what changed in the original plan that forced you

to rabbit and leave me and the rest of my crew in harm's way?" Throttle asked.

"Sorry about that," he said and meant it, even though he had no doubt that Throttle had already figured out the truth: that he'd planned to "borrow" Sylvian all along. He hadn't told Throttle his plan because he knew she would never have loaned one of her crew to someone she barely knew, especially if she knew that he intended to take Sylvian into the middle of a war zone.

"Syl, tell me you're not being coerced or threatened." A man's voice came through, which Punch suspected was her husband.

"Punch has been decent enough, honey," Sylvian answered, then shot a glare in Punch's direction. "But he still hasn't filled me in on why he needs me on his ship."

"It's nothing too dangerous," Punch said. "It's just that the simple thing of disabling Atlas on my ship, Sylvian could do the same on Free Station."

"Wait. You're taking Sylvian to Free Station with you?" Throttle asked in a rush.

"Like hell you—" Finn began.

Punch tapped one of the most useful commands he'd programmed in his ship's systems. Static filled the speakers. "Sorry. You're cutting out. Will check in later." He disconnected the call.

Sylvian stared at him, slack-jawed. "Do you really think anyone would be dumb enough to buy that static thing you just did?" She flung out her hands. "It doesn't even make sense. If there's a bad connection, there's silence, not static."

"You'd be surprised how often it works," he said.

"How are you even still alive?" She blew out a breath. You know, it doesn't matter. Just tell me, exactly what do you have in mind for me to do on Free Station?"

He leaned back. "It's easy. Whoever controls Atlas controls Free Station. You and I are going to waltz on to Free Station and to the Atlas server room, where you'll do whatever it is that you specialists do and disinfect Atlas of whatever it is that has allowed Anna East to get her slimy tentacles into it. Then all the Peacekeepers will have their toys back, and we can give East and her Jaders the ass whooping they deserve."

"There's nothing about that plan that sounds easy," she said.

He thought for a moment, then shrugged. "It doesn't seem so complicated in my head."

Her brows rose. "What happened with the original plan of you sneaking on to Free Station and blowing up Atlas?"

He shook his head. "It never would've worked. Atlas has backups upon backups, which it updates every few seconds."

She eyed him for a long moment. "You lied to Throttle from the beginning. You were always planning to take me with you."

"Not completely. I needed to see you disable Atlas on my ship before I knew you could hack it."

"And if I couldn't have hacked it?"

"Then you would've gone back to your ship, and I would've had to pay a lot of credits that I don't want to pay to a freelance tech to do the same thing. This is a win-win plan."

She guffawed. "How so?"

"I don't have to spend time and money bringing a freelance on board, and you get to be a hero, saving Free Station."

Her expression darkened. "Heroes don't live long enough to hear themselves be called that."

"Well, then I suppose we'll have to make sure you're just a sort of hero who lives to talk about it." He paused. "I need to know. Can you pull this off?"

She watched him for a moment. "I think so."

"I need more than an 'I think so' before we dive into hell."

She scowled. "Well, there're too many unknowns here. I don't know what they used to make Atlas their zombie. If it's hardware, then we'll have to disable that first. If it's software, it depends on the program they've used. Most of the basic stuff can be overwritten with a few commands, but I'd need programs of my own to take on anything robust."

"Can you access those from here?" he asked.

"Sure. That's if you don't cut the comms on me again. I'm good at software, but I'm a mediocre hacker. This may be way above my capability."

"Then it's a good thing I have a backup plan."

"And what's that?" she asked.

"I'll blow up Atlas. All of it. The servers. The backups. Everything."

"Will that work?"

He eyed her. "Sure, but it'll also blow Free Station all to hell."

"Oh." She paused for a length. "Let's hope that I can scrape off whatever programs East has stuck on Atlas."

"I think that's an excellent plan," he said.

She sat and stared at the view panel that spanned the front wall of the bridge. After a lengthy silence, she frowned and turned back to Punch. "Your plan assumes that we can get on to Free Station without being noticed, but it'll be swarming with Jader pirates."

"Not a problem," he said. "That's why we went back for the *High Spirit*."

"I don't understand. Unless your ship has both physical and electronic stealth capabilities—"

"It doesn't, though that'd be great to have." He nodded to her workstation. "Take a look at the system labeled Bones."

Her frown deepened before she shrugged and focused her attention on her panel. After several moments, she turned to Punch. "Is this for real?"

"It is." He shot her a crooked grin. "Every administrative-level code for every dock, door, and system."

"Now I understand why you needed the *High Spirit* to get us onto Free Station. Does Throttle know you have a skeleton key?"

"Yes. Otherwise, she wouldn't take me to my ship. I'll need you to make a copy to package and send to the *Javelin* so they can come in behind us and rescue Chief."

"Why do you even have something like this?"

He shrugged. "It's part of my rainy-day fund."

She stared, confused.

He clarified. "I like to be prepared for the worst-case scenario."

She nodded. "The Jaders taking Free Station is definitely a worst-case scenario sort of thing."

"Nah. Not even close."

She thought for a moment, as though wanting to speak, but then turned back to her work. After a few minutes, she spoke. "Hold on. You have a QuSR? I thought they were only used in Sol." That she was familiar with the acronym and pronounced it correctly—as *Quasar*—meant she'd clearly come across the rare technology in her short time in the Ross system.

"It's used here and there. Not hard to get a hold of as long as you have a quantum dish."

She continued, "I've never used QuSR before. I heard it's as advanced as you can get in communications. Instantaneous delivery across systems. No delays. Is that true?"

"It's that fast, but the downside is that it can only send data packets, so you wouldn't be able to make a smoochie video with your hubby using QuSR." His brow lifted. "Having fun snooping through all my secrets?"

"I'm not snooping," she said in a rush, then added, "Your QuSR inbox was flashing. It caught my attention. That's all." In a small voice, she added, "I'm not a snoop, and I don't make smoochie videos."

He ignored her as he swiped screens to access his QuSR inbox to see a data packet that had been sent fifteen hours earlier. He used QuSR so little, and never for legal jobs, that he hadn't thought to check it. He opened the packet and ran a text translator. Soon, random data marks morphed into letters on his screen:

PD –

EAST TOOK FS. CONTROLS ATLAS. PETE ANTONOV TRAITOR. ALL GP LOCKED IN ROOMS. CASUALTIES. EAST PLANNING TO BLOW FS. WILL RETAKE FS. BRING SUPPORT ASAP.

– CR

Relief washed over Punch. He waved the specialist over. "Syl, take a look at this."

"Don't call me that. Only Finn is allowed to call me that."

"Sorry. Ms. Sylvian Whatever Your Last Name Is, get over here and take a look at this."

"It's Salazar-Martin if you really want to know. Salazar's my last name and Martin is Finn's last name," she said as she walked over. "And can't you just send whatever's on your screen to mine?"

"I could, but I'm lazy," he said.

He glanced at her while she read the message over his shoulder.

"Did your hubby give you that necklace?" he asked.

She looked down at the metal heart-shaped pendant she'd been rubbing and abruptly released it before continuing to read. "Who's CR?"

"Chief Roux. Looks like we've got ourselves an inside man," Punch said before turning around to face Sylvian. "Here's what I need you to do."

"Don't talk to me like I'm one of your crew."

"Right now you are."

She scowled. "No. We're partners."

"Call it what you want." While her scowl remained, she no longer argued, so he continued, "Send the Bones file and Chief's message to Throttle through a secure channel. Tell her to call me on the same channel once she's read the contents."

"Us."

"What?" he asked.

"I'll tell her to call *us* on the secure channel."

"Yeah, sure."

"Is that all?" she asked, and he couldn't tell if she was being genuine or sarcastic, so he assumed the former.

"No. I want you to figure out a way to contact the Peacekeepers in this system without using Atlas."

She thought for a moment. "I'm not sure that's possible."

"You're smart. You'll find a way."

She scowled. "And what do you want me to do if I can find them?"

"I'll have you send them a message through a secure channel. We'll see about getting ourselves a little extra help on Free Station."

"How do you know whom we can trust?"

"I always assume I can't trust anyone," he answered.

She sighed. "Okay. And what will you be doing while I'm doing all this?"

"I'll be asleep. I'm sore as hell and tired as shit." He did plan to sleep, but he also planned to monitor Sylvian's activities. He'd learned long ago to never trust someone who didn't trust him. It was just smart business.

Her scowl had returned. "You're so helpful."

He narrowed an eye. "Trust me, you want me on the top of my game when we get to Free Station. I'll be the one to keep the Jaders off your back."

She gulped.

"Now get to work. I'll have our plan figured out by then, and we can work out the details on the call with your crew."

"You're thinking of changing the current plan?"

"No. Not really. Just taking advantage of the resources we have at our disposal to improve our odds."

She cocked her head. "And what kind of odds do you give us?"

"You want the odds before or after I saw Chief's message?"

Her gaze narrowed. "After."

"Survivable. Maybe."

CHAPTER NINETEEN

THROTTLE WANTED TO KICK PUNCH'S ASS INTO THE NEXT STAR SYSTEM. He'd been withholding information from her all along, including the plan to kidnap one of her crew members. She even wondered if he had the skeleton key with him all along and told her about his ship being crucial to getting onto Free Station as a ruse simply to get Sylvian on his ship so they could go after Atlas.

While she knew whoever controlled Atlas had the advantage in a fight, Punch seemed pushy that he would be the one to bring it back online. He had an ulterior motive; of that, she had no doubt. But his plan was solid and smart, so she couldn't screw him over for a hunch—especially when a change in the plan could place Sylvian in greater danger.

"Is everything okay, Throttle? You seem bothered," Rusty said.

"That's an understatement. I'm pissed off that Punch coerced Sylvian to go with him. He's putting her in danger. Plus, worrying about her is going to screw with Finn's focus when we reach Free Station."

"He's currently attempting to beat up a punching bag, though it doesn't look like it's helping to improve his mood."

"I think imagining he's pummeling Punch Durand brings nowhere near the same level of satisfaction as actually hitting the marshal. Hopefully, he'll get his shot." Throttle wouldn't mind taking a swing at the marshal herself but would comfort herself in knowing Finn would see the small sense of retribution done—and he threw a better punch. "At least we should get plenty of opportunity for some real-life pummeling when we find ourselves some pirates on Free Station. Speaking of which, I need to make a call."

She brushed aside the screen containing the data she'd received from Sylvian aboard Punch's ship and pulled up a communications screen. She reached out to the only person she knew had the resources to be of help.

It took him over a minute to answer.

Baron Stolypin's face appeared on her screen. "I've been wondering when I'd get a call from you. Good to see East's pirates haven't gotten to you yet."

"I'm going to Free Station. I need your help to take it back from the pirates," Throttle said without any sort of introduction.

Mutt sighed. "I told you before, this isn't my fight."

"Anna East and her scum made life hell for you and the other gutter rats stuck on Jade-8. Now's your chance to stop them from doing to that to anyone else," she said.

"I'd love to see her gone and Jade-8 back to an only slightly disreputable colony, but I'm not willing to sacrifice any of my people for it. They're not gutter rats any longer; they're Canaanites now, and they—like me—are looking to the future, not the past." His gaze narrowed. "Besides, why would I help the Peacekeepers? They never lifted a finger to help me and mine on Jade-8."

Her brows lifted. "I wouldn't have taken you for someone to hold a grudge."

He chuckled. "Oh, I can hold a grudge, all right. And I'm not alone. Most of my people would rather this system not have any Peacekeepers. And the Trappists who settled in Canaan have never benefitted from them, yet we're all taxed for their 'service.' So you'll have a tough go of it if you're trying to recruit soldiers from Canaan to help the Peacekeepers."

"Fine. Then come for the good people left on Jade-8. There are still gutter rats stuck in the colony, and they're suffering under East. Or have you forgotten about them?"

"I haven't forgotten about them," he said darkly. "While East and her pirates are a cancer to this system, the truth is, if she disappears, there will be some other nasty piece of work waiting in line to step into her high-heeled shoes tomorrow. And who knows? Her replacement could prove to be even more psychotic than East herself. Are you familiar with the phrase 'Better the devil you know than the devil you don't'?"

"I've heard of it."

"Then you know things could always get worse." Mutt exhaled. "Listen, for the first time in a very long time, my people have a home and a semblance of hope. I'm not going to send away the militia to help a cause that will result in no benefit whatsoever to us." He paused. "But if you offered payment, say a thousand credits for each volunteer, I could at least pass around the word."

Throttle balked. "A thousand credits? You know I spent everything I had to establish Canaan."

He motioned. "Then we have nothing to negotiate."

"Wait," she said. "I know the Peacekeepers keep a general fund for things like this—you know, *blackmail*. I'll talk to Chief Roux, and I'll get the credits."

He held up a hand. "I know how those things go. What happens is you get what you want, and then the funds never show up. Sorry, Throttle. No credits up front, no volunteers. If you don't show up with credits, I wish you the best, and I hope you make it. I've always considered you a friend."

"Yeah? Well, you're a lousy friend." Throttle disconnected the call and leaned back in her seat.

"That could've gone better," Rusty said.

"You've mastered the art of understatement, Rusty," Throttle said.

"Thank you, I think."

She tapped the ship's intercom. "Eddy, I need you on the bridge."

When there was no response, she went to speak again, but Rusty spoke first. "He's walking this way now. He was in the galley, and it looks like he's still chewing that odd meal he created."

"Don't tell me. Seaweed wrap?"

"See for yourself," Rusty answered.

Throttle turned as Eddy entered the bridge. He finished chewing and swallowed. "What do you need?"

Throttle eyed him. "You have green stuff in your teeth."

Eddy ran his tongue over his teeth, though it did no good. "That makes sense since I just made my Seaweed Special. I could make you one if you want. You know, I think I perfected the recipe. Red pepper flakes make all the difference."

"Not right now," she said. "I need your help with a program Sylvian sent us from Punch's ship. Supposedly, it's a skeleton key for Free Station so we can get there without Atlas detecting us."

"If anyone's watching the outer video feeds, they'll still see us," Eddy said.

Throttle nodded. "I know. Punch seems to think they only have docking cameras, so if we come up vertically, we can miss the cameras."

"Vertically while in orbit?" He shrugged. "I suppose."

"Anyway, I need you to upload some data files into the *Javelin* and enable them as screen options with our comm system. Can you do that?"

Eddy scowled. "I'm a *hardware* specialist. Sylvian's the software specialist. They are two completely different skill sets."

"But Sylvian's not here right now, is she?" Throttle asked.

"No, but—"

"And I don't have time. I have a call with Punch in a few minutes."

Eddy huffed. "I can try, but unless it's plug-and-play, I can't make any guarantees."

"I could help," Rusty chimed in.

Throttle's brow rose. "You can build new screens without human interaction?"

"Sylvian has repaired all of my artificial decisioning systems. And Eddy installed a naive Bayse router, which has greatly improved my rationalization processes. You can trust me with making nearly any changes to my own systems."

Throttle frowned at Eddy. "Where'd you pick up new hardware for Rusty?"

Eddy waved her off. "Oh, you know, I find things here and there."

Her gaze narrowed. "You didn't have the bots steal anything from the *Wu Zetian*, did you?"

He looked affronted. "No, I did not. You told me the seed ship was off-limits." A smug expression curved his lips upward. "But you didn't say anything about the marshal's ship. You know, finders keepers and all that sort of thing."

Her lips parted. She was about to reprimand him, but she realized it would do no good. Also, Antonov was likely dead and certainly didn't need any fancy tech anymore. When she realized that, she said, "Good thinking, Eddy. I suppose it's not stealing if the guy's already dead."

Eddy held up a finger. "And it helps Rusty improve his processing power tenfold."

Throttle glanced up at the camera in the ceiling. "The data's in the message from Sylvian. Have at it, Rusty."

"I have identified the data files and am importing them now. This will be a nice change of pace from my usual task monitoring activities, and it tests my upgraded cognitive processes."

Throttle turned back to Eddy. "You got off easy on that."

"Good. Now, I need to get back to my bot project."

She cocked her head. "What bot project?"

"I'm working with Rusty to customize each of his bots. For example, I'm setting up one bot—its name is Bonkers because its directional gyros are a bit clumsy—to be a scanner. We'll be able to send it out anywhere and have it look for a specific *something*, such as signs of life or hints of explosives, you name it. I'm also planning to customize another bot with a photon blaster so I'll never need to carry a gun." He grinned. "I call that one Blaster, of course."

"Of course," Throttle echoed while rolling her eyes. She held up her hand. "I do not trust a bot with any sort of weapon. Is that clear?"

"But we could send in the bots to take down the pirates while we stay here where it's safe."

"No."

Eddy frowned. "Why not?"

"Because that's a horrible idea. Bots are for mechanical support. They are not battle drones."

"They could be."

"No."

Eddy eyed her for a length, then lifted his chin. "You know, you should really learn to listen to your elders. Trust my knowledge and experience."

Throttle was taken aback. "Uh, what are you talking about? I'm two years older than you."

"Not anymore," he said. "I am older than you now. You were in cryosleep for seven years. I was never in cryosleep, so that makes me five years older than you."

She rolled her eyes. "Fine. You're older, but that doesn't make you my elder."

"It does, quite literally."

She waved him off. "Fine. Consider the age thing a win, because there is no way I'm allowing a bot on Free Station. If anyone hacked a bot, they might be able to access Rusty's systems. That's not a risk I'm willing to take."

He turned and spoke over his shoulder as he walked away. "Fine, but I bet you'll regret not having a bot with you when you and Finn find yourselves outnumbered by pirates."

CHAPTER TWENTY

CHIEF LAY ON HIS BACK IN THE CRAMPED CARGO HOLD OF THE ESCAPE pod while he thought through his plans. He'd been waiting for four hours—had slept for three of those hours—for responses from Punch and the Red Dynasty and couldn't wait any longer for messages that would likely never come.

The Jaders wouldn't risk staying on Free Station for long. Once they stripped Free Station's armory and whatever else they were stealing, they'd leave and destroy the station and everyone on board.

He remained in the escape pod because he struggled in coming up with a good plan. Putting his people first meant getting them off Free Station, but if East and her cronies made off with everything from the armory, they had everything they needed to hunt down and slaughter his people—along with anyone else who'd dare to defy them.

He had no other choice than to put the lives of his people at risk in a counteroffensive attack to retake Free Station. Anna East had essentially declared war on the Galactic Peacekeepers, and he was going to give her and her Jaders the fight of their lives. He had the workings of a plan. It wasn't a great plan. Hell, it wasn't even a good plan. But it was a plan that could work, and that was better than anything else he had.

His greatest challenge was that his people were all behind locked doors, and he had no way to free them without gaining access to the command center level, which was heavily guarded. Anna East, no thanks to her mole Pete Antonov, had known exactly how to cripple

Free Station with minimal risk to their own safety. That meant that Chief couldn't coordinate with his people to launch a massive counteroffensive. Instead, he had developed a plan that could succeed with only a small group. *A kill group.*

A distant noise startled Chief and he pulled himself into a seated position and listened through the cracks in the floor grates above his head. Voices, too far away for him to make out the words, but at least two men were talking...and their voices were growing nearer.

He took care to lift the grate without making a sound. His left arm protested, but he'd injected a local anesthetic near the wound when it'd began to throb too much. He set the grate aside, stood—giving his muscles a chance to adjust to being vertical again—and pulled himself up and onto the pod's floor. He was on his feet in a flash, unholstered one of his pistols, and moved silently, stepping toe to heel, toward the open door.

With the escape pod door open, the newcomers could hear Chief as easily as he could now hear their conversation, and from what he could make of it, they were clearly Jaders. As they drew closer, their conversation became clearer.

"...got me thinkin' we ain't gettin' paid for this here job."

"Fo' shore. I ain't seen no credits 'round here. All I seen's are guns and lots of 'em gettin' loaded. I like guns as much as any man, but I got mouths to feed. The ole lady's getting nasty 'bout it, too."

"I care none 'bout the guns. And there ain't shit in these here tunnels. I just wanna get paid for my work. I think I'll have a chat wit' Skully Pete 'bout doin' what's right."

"Yeah, right. Like you'd go talkin' to Skully—"

Chief had seen two shadows before he saw the pair of pirates. He raised his pistol and fired as soon as they stepped into view. He cut off the pirate's sentence with a shot to the head. The second man's eyes went wide. He went to swing his rifle around, and Chief cautioned him.

"Drop it," Chief ordered.

The Jader dropped his rifle as though it burned him and raised his hands. "Don't shoot, man. I'm unarmed."

"Are there others in this tunnel?" Chief asked.

"Nope. Jus' Tobes and me, that's all."

"What are you doing in the tunnels?"

"We's jus' walkin' the tunnels. Seein' what we's be seein'. Lookin' for any good stuff worth takin' before we cut out," the Jader answered.

Chief watched the man, who looked like he hadn't met a razor or a shower in far too long and had the restlessness of a drug addict. The man didn't seem to recognize Chief, though that didn't surprise him. Most pirates were grunts, little more than slave labor picked up from somewhere that made pirating a better occupation than whatever they were doing. His gaze narrowed on the man. "When are you cutting out?" he asked, using the man's terminology.

"Soon. Please let me go. I won' tell no one 'bout you."

"How soon?"

The man shrugged. "Dun know. Four hours, maybe five. We's suppose to be back for roll call at eight hundred on the dot."

"Good to know," Chief said and shot the man between the eyes.

Chief had lunged back into the pod by the time the man collapsed. He hustled down into the cargo hold to grab one of the rifles. He swapped out the battery for a fresh one and climbed back up. He then grabbed a chime suit and pulled it on as quickly as he could manage. Four hours wasn't nearly enough time left to stop the pirates from blowing up the station. He had to adjust his plan.

He stepped out of the pod and into the tunnel. At the panel on the wall, he entered his credentials. A light above the door flashed red, and the door closed. A second later, he heard the *whoomph* of the pod ejecting, and he found some humor in knowing that the action would distract the pirates from Chief's next move. He entered an override code. He grabbed onto the rail the instant before the door opened, and the vacuum of space sucked out the two bodies and the air from the tunnel. He pulled himself through the open doorway, grabbing onto a bar on the other side to hold him in place while he closed the door. While a breach in the tunnels would cause problems for the Jaders, it would cause just as many problems for his people.

As soon as the door closed, the wind pulling at him ceased and he let go of the station. Using the magnetic propulsion system on his suit, he navigated around the outside of Free Station, careful to remain within a few feet of the hull and careful to avoid any cameras or windows. He went halfway around the station and came to a stop near a window of one of the station's smaller wings. It was the only place he knew there'd be at least twenty people holed up together and with access to an airlock.

The bunkhouse for new recruits.

He pulled himself closer and peeked through the window and into the bunkhouse. Inside, he saw what looked like the full class gearing up for war. He winced, knowing that East would also know exactly what the cadets were doing by spying through their Atlas chips. Every Peacekeeper, following their sixth week of training, received an Atlas chip. If the pirates had attacked Free Station just one week earlier, Chief would've had twenty-four Peacekeepers without Atlas. Instead, he had to risk drawing East's attention even more to the bunkhouse.

He tapped on the glass. When no one looked, he tapped harder. It was hard to move quickly in space, so he had to initiate his grav boots to keep from knocking himself back.

One of the cadets nearest the window turned and swung up a rifle. The rest of the group turned to Chief. He held out his hands in a show of peace and hoped none of them were stupid enough to fire at the hull. One of the team leads stepped forward, said something, and the cadet lowered his rifle.

Chief nodded and motioned vigorously to the airlock. He hurried to the airlock, reaching it as it opened, and jumped inside. The door closed behind him, and he went to the panel to enter his override code on the station lockdown to release the entire wing from the lockdown protocol. As soon as he did, the inner airlock door opened, with barely enough time to pressurize the small room.

All three team leads—red, blue, and yellow—stood before him. Weaved between them were cadets holding their rifles steady on Chief.

Chief spoke calmly. "Cadets, the Jaders have hijacked Atlas and is using your chips to spy on all activities. Putting them in sleep mode doesn't seem to work. You can power down your chips with the diagnostic wand in the bunkhouse med center."

"How do we know we can believe you?" Blue team leader, Roxy, asked.

Yellow team leader, Numi, frowned. "Who are you?"

"They're watching and listening," Chief said, hoping they'd give him the benefit of the doubt.

Red team leader, Yale, turned to face his team. "Parks, grab the wand."

If East hadn't figured out it was Chief yet, he didn't want to continue speaking to give her more opportunity to identify him. He knew that she'd send her Jaders after him if she knew where he was.

Parks returned with a long black wand.

"Get yourself first, Parks; then get all of us," Yale ordered.

Parks did as instructed. The diagnostic wand was a medical scanner that was used to identify injuries. The wand's signal was disrupted by Atlas, and two features had been added to the wand's single feature of Scan: Atlas Off and Atlas On.

The room was in a nervous silence as the cadet turned off each Atlas chip. Chief hoped that East wasn't able to turn on Atlas chips from a distance, but the truth was, he relied on specialists too much and didn't know enough when it came to Atlas.

The instant the final cadet was scanned, Roxy asked, "Let's start over. Who are you, partner?"

Chief removed his helmet. As soon as he had it off, all of the cadets' features slackened with recognition.

"Chief Roux," Yale said.

Chief gave a small nod and then looked across the youthful faces, with a couple of middle-aged cadets sprinkled throughout. "I apologize for the entrance. However, the pirates have us at a severe disadvantage. We need to secure the bunkhouse."

"Yellow team has this." Numi spoke, then turned to her team. "Jake, Punk, and Emily, you three make sure the door is locked and barricaded."

The trio of cadets took off running across the bunkhouse.

A beep sounded. Chief spun around to see the inner airlock door open. Another beep sounded at the outer airlock.

"Grab onto something!" he yelled before he rushed to pull his helmet on. The outer airlock began to open as he lunged for the control panel. Wind pulled at him as he reached for the panel. Objects blew past him as he worked the controls. The system accepted his code once more, and he closed the airlock.

The wind ceased abruptly, and he found the cadets scattered, still clinging to one another and to benches and bunks screwed to the floors.

"Ronnie!" someone yelled, and several cadets ran to the airlock.

Chief turned and looked out. Clothes, weapons, and other debris floated in the black. Farther out, he saw a human shape. His jaw clenched. Without a suit, it was already too late for the cadet. He lowered his head and turned back to the room. "We will mourn for Cadet Young later. Right now, we're under attack. They've opened the airlock once. We have to assume they'll open it again to try to kill us all so we can't go against them. I need two volunteers to stand guard at the bunkhouse and airlock doors at all times."

Two young men stepped forward. "We'll hold down the bunkhouse," one of them said.

Roxy spoke. "Gregg and Nance both excel in the small arms drills and aren't my strongest spacewalkers. They'll do right by you."

Chief nodded at the two volunteers. "Be ready for anything. If we lose the bunkhouse, we have nowhere to fall back, so you have the authority to do whatever it takes to defend the bunkhouse. Do you understand?"

The pair of cadets bore devilish grins, and Chief suspected they already had a dangerous idea or two.

A broadcast over the speakers made Chief cringe. It was Anna East's voice.

"I can see you. I see and hear everything," she crooned. *"You think that by powering down your personal chips that I can't see, but I can. There is nowhere you can hide that I can't see you. This is my warning to you. As long as you remain where you are and don't try anything foolish, I'll leave you alone. But if you think to come after me or my Jaders, you will die. I've already killed eighteen Peacekeepers. Oh, make that nineteen. I saw the body floating outside. Free Station is mine. You live at my mercy."*

"She's wrong," Chief said. "She can only see and hear through Atlas chips and cameras. There are blind spots on Free Station that we'll leverage. But she's right in that she's killed our people, and I plan to keep her from killing more." He inhaled. "I'm leading a counteroffensive to take back Free Station. This is a volunteer mission. I'll take everyone I can, except for Gregg and Nance, who'll remain back to watch the airlock and defend the bunkhouse."

"And you want us to help?" Yale asked, dubious.

"All the marshals are locked down in various places across the station, which is crawling with Jader pirates," Chief answered.

"We're the only ones you could get to," Numi said.

"Yes," Chief said. "You may still be only a third through basic training, but you're all Peacekeepers, and I need you. But this is a very dangerous assignment, so I'm only taking volunteers. Who wants to help me take back Free Station?"

Everyone yelled their affirmation. He didn't see a single person remain quiet or who didn't raise at least one hand. He hadn't expected such a robust response, especially since they'd just lost a fellow student. These cadets had been through seven weeks of Peacekeeper training—long enough to have seen the videos and have read the horror stories. He trusted them to make their own decisions, though he knew that inexperience often brought a sense of invincibility. These cadets would learn very soon that they weren't invincible.

When the noise settled, Yellow team leader, Numi, spoke. "We've already been preparing, Chief. We're ready to move at your command. We're going to take back Free Station, Chief."

He cocked his head. "Tell me what you've planned."

Numi began to speak, but Yale interrupted. "My team's going to the power core. We're going to cut the power."

"Then all three teams are going after the Jaders. They can't see in the dark, and we'll have our night goggles. Each team will start on a different level, and we'll work our way to the top of Free Station."

Chief didn't need to ask for details. It was a textbook scenario they'd been taught and had practiced during their training sessions. He held up his finger. "It's not a bad idea, but we have complications. The Jaders plan to blow up Free Station upon their departure. They likely plan to use explosives, but I don't know where they've been placed. Free Station encompasses over forty-five cubic miles, which we don't have the resources to search. That means preventing their departure is our priority. If we can keep them here, we keep them from destroying the station.

"We face challenges. I can't retake Atlas because it's the primary reason behind the invasion. If I cut off their access to it, they'll likely abandon and destroy the station. As for revoking the lockdown, I need to access the control center on level nine, but we can't retake level nine with our current numbers. As such, we'll free as many marshals as we can one at a time and use your plan to overpower the enemy. We'll start on level seven and work our way up and down to retake the other levels."

He looked across the faces of the three teams of cadets. They were as inexperienced as they came. Most had never left their colony before arriving on Free Station. They had spirit, but without real experience, they wouldn't stand a chance against experienced pirates. He'd taken in their skill level when he'd devised his plan. Even so, the odds were stacked against them.

He continued, "This is a spacewalk assignment, so I need all of you to suit up. This mission will be just like you've practiced: you'll space-walk tethered in pairs for safety. One in each tethered pair will carry a rifle to protect the other. Grab all the gear you need from the bunkhouse armory. Teams Red and Blue, you will spacewalk to the docking bay while evading any cameras. Yes, I know that's easier said than done. But the cameras are stationary on the walkways and on the airlocks, so if you stay below the walkway, you'll avoid detection. Once you reach the docking bay, cadets not carrying rifles will secure restraining cables to every ship. It doesn't matter if it's one of ours or not—we have to keep the Jaders locked on the station with us. As long as they're stuck here, they're not going to blow us up. More importantly, the Jaders have been clearing out our armory. Under no circumstances can we allow those weapons to be in the hands of criminals."

Red team leader raised his hand.

Chief acknowledged him. "Yes, Yale?"

"Where are the restraining cables, Chief?"

"What are restraining cables?" someone in the crowd asked.

"Every dock has a set. We use them to secure ships that we've reclaimed or are being used as evidence. You'll find them in red-painted compartments below the airlock doors. Each cable can be auto-matically connected. It'll take longer, but I need you to *manually* connect each cable so that no one in the dock, should anyone be moni-toring the dock-control screens, will see anything happening. The docking bay has docks numbered one to twenty. Red team takes docks one through ten, and Blue team takes docks eleven through twenty. Not all docks have ships, and a couple of ships, such as the large Chinese seed ship that's parked outside the station, already have restraining cables. If one team finishes early, help out the other team. Stealth and speed are both crucial to the success of this mission. If you are seen, the pirates will go after you. Even if you're seen by one of ours, remember that East's pirates can see and hear everything through the Atlas chips. As soon as you're finished, return to the bunkhouse. I know it won't be easy without your Atlas chips, but you've practiced all the maneuvers you're about to perform. You can do this."

"What about Yellow team?" Numi asked.

"Yellow team will spacewalk a short distance to the evacuation tunnel. You can enter the tunnel at escape pod location eight. I ejected that pod, and you can use the door to enter the tunnel. Be careful. It's not an airlock, so watch out for the pressure—it'll try to knock you back. As soon as you're in the tunnels, I want you to split up and launch all the escape pods."

He noticed the fear painted on the faces. "I know it's scary giving up our only way off the station, but ejecting the pods gives us two benefits. One, it closes all the escape routes for the Jaders. Two, Anna East will think everyone in this bunkhouse jumped ship. As long as we avoid cameras, they won't know how many Peacekeepers pose a danger to them on Free Station."

"We understand the risks, Chief. We stand behind you one hundred percent," Numi said.

He made a small motion of acknowledgment. "To launch each pod, all you have to do is hold down the red launch button on the panel next to the pod. When you hear a beep, press the same button one more time. Its doors will close, and it will launch. You'll have to move as fast as you can. The Jaders will see the launches, and they will go after you. Keep your suits on. When the Jaders enter the tunnels, you can open the bay door with no escape pod by entering the following code: Seven-four-four-seven-four. Repeat that code to me."

"Seven-four-four-seven-four," Yellow team said.

"Again," Chief said.

They repeated the code.

"Good. If things go well, no one will have to fire a shot. If things don't go well, everyone's priority is staying alive. If things get ugly, get yourselves into an escape pod and eject. I'd better not see any hero crap out there. Once all the pods are gone, return to the bunkhouse. We'll grab any gear that can be of use. We can't give the invaders time to regroup. Any questions?"

"What if we can't make it back to the bunkhouse, Chief?" someone near the back asked.

"During lockdown, the only airlocks you can access besides the bunkhouse are emergency airlocks. They're smaller than a normal airlock and are outlined by two red lines. Find one to get back on the station before your suits run out of air. If you can't make your way to the bunkhouse, find a hiding spot. Any more questions?"

"Which team will you go with?" Yale asked.

"None," Chief answered. "I'm going to scout the command level for intel. That's where Anna East and her pirate captains have most likely set up their headquarters. I need to verify that assumption if we're to launch an attack against them."

"Take anyone from Yellow team with you, Chief," Numi said.

Chief held up his hand. "You all have your hands full. I'll learn what I can and meet you all back here. If for some reason I don't make it back here, I want you to initiate the first part of your plan. Cut the power to cut the video feeds. Then, instead of launching an attack, you will clear the residence hallways and unlock as many cabin doors as you can using my code. If I'm not here, that means you three team leads—Yale, Numi, and Roxy—will then lead the teams exactly as you've practiced in drills. All weapons should be set to lethal. There can be no hesitation. Every life that you take today may save dozens more."

"Uh, Chief?" Roxy asked.

"What is it?" he asked.

"Most of our weapons are practice weapons. Their maximum settings are stun."

He scowled, forgetting that fact. "Then stun the hell out of any pirates you come across. I want them on the floor and crying for their mommas."

Several chuckled and he continued, "The marshals will lead the attack. The Jaders have taken the docking bay and all the levels above it, including the one we're on. We'll take back one level at a time. The last I saw, two patrols were causing problems for the Jaders since they docked."

When no one said anything, Chief said, "Okay, time to suit up. Move out as soon as each team is ready. Remember, stealth and speed come second only to your lives."

He left the cadets to their preparations. If he'd stayed, they'd find questions to ask, and no Peacekeeper could afford delays. He worried that they might already be too late to prevent the Jaders from leaving.

He left the airlock and moved upward over the smooth white surface, careful to avoid windows and cameras. Minutes ticked slowly by as he flew alongside the outer hull of Free Station. From the outside, the orbital station resembled a massive oceanic submarine, except for the open docking bay near its center and the winding dots of small escape pod bays that climbed from the lowest level of residences to the command level. A row of tiny round windows marked each level, making it easy for Chief to navigate.

He slowed as soon as he reached the command level, where all the officer cabins and offices were in addition to the command center itself. He could see the small window to his cabin several windows away, and he longed for when Free Station would be free once again, and he could lie on his cot. His arm throbbed constantly, and a tension headache stabbed at his thoughts.

Seeing his cabin infused him with a sense of optimism that he hadn't realized he'd lost. He activated his boots and gloves and crawled across the surface, careful not to cause any sound. Every time he moved his left arm, it protested. He gritted his teeth and continued. He came to a stop just below the window of the command center.

Movement out of the corner of his eye caught his attention. He turned to see an escape pod shoot out from the station. A second pod followed a few seconds later. He turned back and risked a split-second peek over the edge of the window. He snapped his head back down.

In that split second, he'd seen at least three specialists sitting in front of the screens that displayed feeds from the station's cameras. Two pirates stood guard behind them. They all had their backs to him, so he risked raising his head again. He frowned. Anna East should've been in there, coordinating her plans from the comfort of Chief's chair.

But she wasn't there. He glowered and scanned the large room, to see garbage and leftover food scattered on the conference table.

His chair was pulled out from its usual location, which made him believe it'd been used. He was about to move to look into nearby rooms when movement in the doorway caught his attention.

Anna East rushed into the room. She had an entourage of four pirates flanking her, all armed with photon rifles. She looked none too pleased as she headed straight toward the screens, where he saw the launch of an escape pod.

East was still on Free Station, which meant she still needed to be physically on the station to complete her work. She either hadn't contacted the Consortium yet or was still in talks with them. As long as East remained on Free Station, she had a need for it. Assuming the Red and Blue teams were successful in restraining the pirate ships, they would delay East's departure by at least one hour.

His delay tactics wouldn't buy them much time, but it'd be enough if they moved fast. He released his connection and pushed off from the outer hull. He used maximum propulsion to return to the bunkhouse. As he made his way, he'd seen at least half of the escape pods had launched so far, and he hoped Yellow team would finish their assignment before East's pirates reached them.

That hope was squashed when a bay door opened not far from him, and four pirates, none wearing suits, flew out from the opening. A cadet was flung outside through the bay door acting as a pressure valve to the station, but Chief saw they were in their suit. The pirates were firing randomly as they were caught in the vortex, and they continued to fire after death, their fingers frozen on the triggers. The shots sprayed in outward spirals as the bodies still spun. Black burn marks marred the white hull of the station.

Chief's eyes went wide as one of the dead pirates rotated and fired shots in Chief's direction.

He tried to evade, but it was impossible to evade a beam that traveled at nearly the speed of light. His suit alarms went off before he felt the wound.

He looked down to see a wound in his side. A mist of warm, moist air and blood droplets teemed out from the hole in his suit. Ice burned at the wound, numbing it but sending spears of frostbite into the surrounding skin. Wincing, he placed his hand over the wound. "Son of a gun."

He struggled to right himself and get clear of the shooting gallery. He propelled forward too fast and bounced off the hull. He tumbled backward until he felt something latch around him. He struggled, but the grip tightened.

"I've got you, Chief," a woman's voice said through his suit speaker system.

She positioned him so that he could see her, and he found himself looking at a cadet from Yellow team.

"I'm Murphy with Yellow team," she said.

"Suit's—breached," he said and realized he must've had more than one breach since he was running out of air.

"I'll get you inside. Just stay with me."

He struggled to hold his hand over the breach he saw, unable to find the other one.

"We're almost there," Murphy said.

Her words sounded like they'd been spoken in a wind tunnel. His air and pressure ran out, and he felt the sensation of every cell within him expanding. Sheer agony as the lack of pressure claimed his body like a harpy screams, tearing apart her victim from the inside out.

He saw the open bay door and black tentacles—no, arms—reaching out to him. He suddenly felt weight again. Two cadets grabbed him and were running with him. He would've cried out at the jostling, but he still had no air. His body was burning him from the inside out. He could no longer see and only vaguely felt being dropped onto a floor. As time passed, his anguish lessened into general pain. He sucked in a deep breath, and the air wrapped his lungs in barbed wire. His body burned from the cold vacuum it'd been exposed to, and it took an eternity before his eyes focused and his ears deciphered the sounds around him as words.

He meant to ask a question, but all he was able to do was emit a grunt.

"We're getting you patched up, Chief." Murphy's voice reached him.

He found he could move his head again, though his tension

headache was now a full-on migraine. He saw three cadets, though he was seeing double, so he couldn't be sure.

He heard a masculine voice. "The tunnel was exposed, so we had to get you onto an escape pod, Chief. As soon as we get your wounds stable and your suit taped up, we'll bring you back to the bunkhouse."

Someone else spoke. "Of all the lousy luck to get shot by a dead man."

CHAPTER TWENTY-ONE

ANNA EAST SQUEALED IN GLEE AS SHE WATCHED THE VIDEO FOOTAGE of Chief getting shot.

"I told you that I had things under control," Pete said.

She turned to see him stroll into the command center. "You still have a long way to go to achieve what I consider 'under control.'"

He walked toward her. "Chief's been killed, Free Station is completely under your control, and the Atlas records are being changed as we speak. You have everything you want."

"I have only the tiniest portion of what I want. What I want is to have proof that every marshal in this system is dead, especially Throttle Reyne. I want to see a thousand chunks of Free Station burn up in Hiraeth's atmosphere after it explodes. And what I want most of all is to see the Ross system established as the Jade system, free of Sol control!"

The Peacekeeper specialists she'd forced to run the screens shot glances at her when she spoke of Free Station's pending demise. She tried to ignore them.

"You've accomplished more than any of us ever dreamed. We should leave now and blow the station. That'll wipe out ninety percent of the marshals in this system. I'll go after Throttle after this, and I'll bring her to you—there are only so many places someone can hide. Then all you have to focus on is that politics stuff."

She stiffened. "That politics *stuff* is what will allow Jade-8 to expand beyond an orbital space colony to something *more*."

He held up a hand as though to placate her. "I get it. You've got a bigger appetite than I do when it comes to power. But we've already gotten nearly everything we've wanted from this station. The longer we stay here, the more likely some marshals will get wild ideas about trying to make some kind of heroic last stand against my men."

"You mean *my* men," Anna corrected. "I'm the one who pays all the bills."

"With the loot that my crews bring home," he added.

"We're not leaving, and we're not changing the plan," she said. "When the marshals all come home to roost, then we can blow the station. Not before."

He pursed his lips. "You're going to get us both killed with that sort of thinking. We need to cut and run. It's time you start listening to me."

She saw his hand move closer to his holster, and she nodded to his crew members who'd been serving as her bodyguards. They all pulled out their guns at the same time Pete unholstered his. Pete aimed his gun at Anna while his crew aimed at their captain.

"If you shoot me, you're dead before you turn around," she said.

He scowled at his crew before turning back to her. "How much did you offer them to turn on me?"

Her lips curled upward. "More than you could." She sobered. "Lower your weapon."

He hesitated before holstering his gun. He held his hands out while Yank, his second-in-command, relieved him of his weapons. Bruises had formed under his eyes from Pete having punched him earlier for not finding the router on his ship.

"Sorry, boss," Yank said. "But you know the life. A pirate's got to seize every opportunity that comes his way."

"Anna East is an opportunity you're going to regret," Pete said, not taking his eyes off the woman.

"Lock him up," she said.

"There's never been a cage that could hold me for long," Pete said.

She cocked her head. "Ah, but the question you should be asking yourself is if you can break out before this station blows up."

He gave a silent growl before three of his crew members led him from the command center.

Anna had known for some time that she'd need to sever her connection with Pete. She wasn't a killer, at least not with her own hands, and found that their shared history made the idea of killing him too unpleasant. Instead, she chose to have him locked up like Chief Roux had been. She realized now that she'd made a mistake by keeping the Peacekeeper director alive, but she'd intended to gain additional information from him before executing him.

As for Pete, she knew he'd escape, and a part of her hoped he would. He wouldn't come after her. Not for a while, anyway. He'd see to his own safety first, which meant that even if he escaped with them both still on Free Station, she wouldn't see him again. Afterward, however, she'd be sure to keep a close eye on Skully Pete so that she wouldn't be added to his grisly collection.

CHAPTER TWENTY-TWO

Punch scowled as he read the QuSR message. "Damn it, Chief."

"What's wrong?" Sylvian asked.

He opened his mouth to explain, then decided to just wave her over. "See for yourself."

"Just send it to my screen."

When he made no movement, she eyed him for a long moment before rolling her eyes, standing, and walking over. She looked over his shoulder to read the message.

PD –

WILL RECLAIM BUNKHOUSE AND LAUNCH COUNTERAT-TACK TO FORCE PIRATES OFF THE STATION. NEED SHIP-BASED SUPPORT TO CAPTURE ESCAPEES.

– CR

"I told him to lie low until we get there to save the day," Punch said. "Doesn't anyone listen to me anymore?"

"You're saying that someone actually listened to you at some point in the past?" she asked.

"No. Can't say they have." He swiped away the message. "This changes everything."

"Because we have to help Chief out rather than go straight to Atlas?"

He guffawed. "What? No. I mean that we won't be able to sneak up to the Atlas server center if we have to walk through the middle of the war."

"We won't help Chief?" she asked.

"We're helping Chief by sending Throttle and Finn to help Chief," he answered.

"I think he wanted a bit more support than that."

"He didn't clarify how much support he needs," Punch said. He thought for a moment. "Maybe his little war games can work in our favor. The pirates will be distracted. It might be easier to sneak around."

"But is going after Atlas still a priority?" Sylvian countered. "If Chief is putting all his efforts to go straight after the pirates, then maybe that's where we should be focusing, too."

"No. As long as Atlas is under Jader control, the Peacekeepers are crippled. We'll get it back online, and then Chief will have all the support he could possibly need."

"But what if it's too late for Chief by the time we take Atlas back?"

"It won't be. Atlas is our priority."

She frowned. "Why are you so set on Atlas? If we can retake Free Station first, then Atlas specialists can get the system back online, anyway."

He scowled. "Atlas is the most powerful information system across the star systems. The longer Jaders have access to Atlas, the more information they can steal and manipulate. No, we'll be the first to get to Atlas and bring it back." He pushed up from his seat. "We'll be reaching the Hiraeth sector in a few minutes. You'd better start getting ready for going into Free Station."

She held out her hands. "Any gear I'd grab is back on the *Javelin*."

He shrugged and left her alone on the small bridge.

A few minutes later, Sylvian transmitted codes to Free Station's automated flight-control system, and Punch watched as both the *High Spirit* and the *Javelin* disappeared off the radar map broadcasted by the system.

"We should be blind to Atlas," Sylvian said. "I've notified Throttle."

Punch brought the *High Spirit* to a stop directly below the anchor point of Free Station. Every time the ship swayed too close to a camera's line of sight, he gently tugged it in the other direction. He assumed the *Javelin* was directly behind him and hoped that Throttle was a decent enough pilot not to get picked up by the cameras, or else she'd put them all in jeopardy.

He bypassed level one, leaving it for Throttle's larger ship, and maneuvered the *High Spirit* toward the emergency airlock on level two, using the magnetized docking systems to ease the connection. The instant his screen displayed a secure link, he locked the controls and powered down his ship, putting it into standby mode.

He looked over to Sylvian to find her already unbuckled and on her feet. "Anxious to get to work?"

"Anxious to finish and get back to my crew," she said while she slid a tablet with the Bones data into her pocket.

Punch opened a drawer and pulled out a pair of items wrapped together. He unraveled them and handed her a small laser flashlight while keeping the can of spray paint for himself, which he pocketed.

He unholstered a pistol and strode to the airlock, confirming the connection was sealed before opening the door. He took the lead through the airlock and stepped onto Free Station's second lowest level. He was surprised to find the lights dimmed as though they were operating under emergency power only. He scanned the small staging area with his pistol leading his movement. No sign of pirates or Peace-keepers.

He stepped aside to allow Sylvian to enter the station. She turned on the flashlight, though the beam was overly narrow to do much to brighten the area. "Hm. My guess is that Chief's already launched his counterattack."

"The darkness will help mask our movements." He turned to face her. "The first camera should be right beyond this landing. We have to do this real quiet like because we've got nothing to dampen the microphones."

Sylvian nodded and silenced the comm-chip at her collar.

Punch spoke again. "We'll move slow. I'll keep you covered, so you just focus on the cameras."

She nodded, then frowned. "What about Throttle and Finn?"

"We'll take the lead to clear the cameras, and they're going to come in behind us."

"Okay," she said.

The hallway wasn't wide, but Punch remained at Sylvian's side, a half-step ahead of her as they walked. He set a slow pace as if the pair were taking a leisurely stroll through a park and not leading a clandestine operation.

When Sylvian's light froze on a spot where the wall met the ceiling, Punch stopped. He saw the camera, currently blinded by the laser. He pulled out the spray paint, reached high and sprayed the black paint over the camera.

He knew that if Sylvian didn't flash her beam on a camera before they walked into its range, they would be seen. And once he sprayed the camera, the Jaders could send someone down to check it out. The cameras were a hassle, but there were no unmonitored ways to move around Free Station. The cameras were simply a problem that had to be dealt with.

Punch increased their pace as they moved forward. His impatience grew. He knew that if Throttle caught up with them, Sylvian could change her mind and leave Punch to figure out Atlas on his own. He was a fair software specialist but in no way an expert. The marshal needed Sylvian much more than she needed him, but he wasn't about to tell her that. That would give her control over him and his mission, and that was something he couldn't abide.

As they worked down the hallways, they developed a routine. A camera was stationed every hundred feet. They'd jog between cameras, with Sylvian blinding the camera even before they'd slow. The process changed when they reached the door to a primary walkway.

Punch pocketed the spray paint to have a better two-handed grip on his pistol. He went to open the door, only to have it blocked after opening a bare couple of inches. He shot Sylvian a glance before putting his shoulder against the door and shoving. The door opened and he jumped through the opening to find a body on the floor, which had been blocking the door.

The body was that of a pirate, with long braided hair, greasy clothes, and a blaster shot through his chest. He hadn't suffered for long, not that Punch cared. While the pirate didn't look like one from Skully Pete's crew, he'd likely done plenty of harm to good people along the way and had received what he'd had coming to him.

A shout in the distance caught his attention. He cocked his head to listen, then scowled. There was a battle taking place, and it was in the same direction he and Sylvian were headed.

He waved for Sylvian to join him in the hallway. He whispered, "Sounds like we're catching up to the party. You'd better keep that pistol of yours handy."

He led the way down the hallway. There was a streak of blood running across the wall as if someone had been shot and had used the wall for support. The noise grew louder as they closed the distance. As they came to a T in the hallway, it sounded like the battle was upon them. Curses were being shouted back and forth, and blaster shots were lightning bolts through the hallway, all coming from the left.

Punch flattened against the wall and slid slowly down and closer to the edge. With his pistol held close, he used a small mirror to peer around the corner while Sylvian crouched behind him. Three pirates were under ten feet away, behind a makeshift barricade of furniture, and had their backs to Punch. The pirates were firing shots over the barrier at what looked to be a small squad of Peacekeepers fifty feet down the hallway.

Punch leveled his pistol and took out all three pirates with three direct headshots. They never had a chance to return fire. As soon as the last of the three pirates collapsed, Punch called out, "Clear!"

"Cease fire!" he heard a woman shout. The blaster fire stopped. "Step out so I can see you," she said.

"I'm a friend. Marshal Punch Durand," he said. "I'm coming out. Don't shoot."

He held his pistol in the air and took a step out from around the corner.

After a brief moment, the woman stood. She wore the Peacekeeper uniform with a blue armband around her right arm. A cadet. She turned back to her team. "It's okay. He's one of ours. Weapons down."

She strode toward him. The four cadets with her also came forward.

"I have another GP with me," Punch said and motioned for Sylvian to step out.

The woman coming toward him slowed but then continued walking toward them. Punch and Sylvian stepped around the dead pirates and the barricade.

The cadet came to a stop, as did the other four cadets. One was nursing an arm with a blaster shot through the shoulder. The others looked tired and sweaty but otherwise unharmed.

"I'm Roxy Dillon, team leader of Blue team. Thanks for the help, Marshal."

"Call me Punch. This is Specialist Martin." He motioned to Sylvian.

"Everyone calls me Roxy," the cadet said. "You must've come down from the residence halls?"

He shook his head. "Outside. Didn't want to risk landing in the docking bay, so we tethered to an emergency airlock."

Her brows lifted. "So Atlas is back online? That means more marshals are coming?"

"That's why we're here—to get Atlas back online so we don't have the pirates playing puppet master with our ships and cameras. We have two ships without the Atlas tether, which is how we managed to get here. What's the current status of Free Station?"

Roxy's brow knit. "I don't know. Without our Atlas comms up, we don't have any way to communicate with each other."

"What was Chief's plan?" he asked.

"Pretty straightforward. Red team cut the primary power to take the cameras offline so that we'd have a more level playing field. And we've been clearing the hallways and freeing everyone locked in their rooms."

Punch frowned. "The cameras are offline?"

Roxy nodded. "At least the videos. We're not sure about the microphones."

He glanced at Sylvian, then shrugged. "Guess we didn't need to worry about blinding the cameras after all."

Sylvian slid the flashlight into her pocket. "That'll make things easier. Do we need to bother bringing Atlas back online now?"

"Yes," he said and turned back to Roxy. "What's your team's assignment?"

"We're supposed to be clearing the hallways, taking out any greedy pirates who went below the docking bay level to raid. My team was assigned the mechanical levels—one and two; Red team and Yellow team are doing the same thing on the residence levels—three, four, and five. Everyone's meeting at the mess hall to regroup. Chief's planning to make a run at the pirates, who control levels six and above."

"Where's Chief now?" Punch asked.

"He's with Yellow team. Stick with us, and you'll see him soon. Those three pirates you took out were the last ones we came across on this floor, so we'll be heading back up soon."

"Did you clear every area?"

"No. Chief said to only start with the hallways. He said if pirates were hiding in any unlocked rooms, they'd have the doorways covered. I think Chief gave that order because we're only cadets and not real Peacekeepers yet, and he didn't want us to do anything too dangerous."

Punch chuckled. "Clearing the hallways is the definition of 'dangerous.' Trust me, today you've proven you're real Peacekeepers."

Roxy beamed.

"We'll go with you, but we need a small detour," Punch said. "We need to get Atlas online, and the cabling center is on this floor, over there." He pointed to a secure door near the end of the hallway.

"Then let's go," Roxy said.

Punch grinned. He loved the energy of new recruits.

The group walked down the hallway, with Roxy's team taking the lead while Punch walked behind Sylvian, covering her in case any pirates jumped out of any rooms. Fortunately, if there were any pirates left on level three, none were dumb enough to make a suicide run against seven Peacekeepers.

They stopped at a permaglass door. Through the clear pane, Punch saw the room was empty. He frowned—he hadn't expected that. He'd expected to have a full crew of pirates set up inside. The empty room made him wonder if the Jaders still had any need for the system.

"Excuse me," Sylvian said as she weaved through the cadets. She pulled out the tablet and transmitted a code. The door clicked. She opened the door, stepped inside, and rushed over to take a seat before a computer.

"Watch the door," Punch ordered as he followed the specialist into the room.

Sylvian plugged one end of a cable into the tablet and the other end into the computer. After a moment, she grimaced and disconnected and reconnected the cable.

He leaned over her shoulder. "What's wrong?"

Sylvian wrung her hands. "I'm getting nothing. I don't understand. It's like Atlas is a zombie." She spun in her chair. "They must have tied into Atlas from somewhere else."

Anxiety built within Punch's gut. "Where else could they control Atlas?"

She thought for a second. "The server room is the most obvious, but they could maybe get to it via the communication center."

"Chief was stuck in the comm center when they took over Free Station," Roxy said.

Punch turned to see the team leader standing in the room. "Then he had to have seen something. What'd he see?"

She shrugged. "He said the pirates snuck in on that Chinese seed ship that's tethered to the station."

"I don't care about that," he snapped. "Did he see how they got to Atlas?"

Her lips thinned as she eyed him, but she decided to eventually answer. "He said they set up the dock as their stronghold. Maybe they connected to it there."

He scowled. "They couldn't get to Atlas from there."

"Wait," Sylvian said. "They could get into Atlas by piggybacking a network cable."

"What are you talking about?" he asked.

"A hardline. With the right equipment, the pirates could basically patch their network cable into a Free Station cable. Then send a computer virus or Trojan horse program to take control of Atlas. It would've taken some planning, but it's really not that hard to do."

He stared at the blank screen. "Can you bypass the hardline?"

She shook her head. "No. As soon as the hardline's removed, I can get in and work at removing whatever program they used to take over the system."

He sighed. "I need to get to the docking bay." He reached into his pocket and pulled out a small data card. He set it on the desk next to Sylvian. "Once you get Atlas running, I need you to plug this in. It'll flash green when it's done."

Sylvian picked it up and squinted at it. "What's it do?"

"It'll do nothing to Atlas. It'll just copy a couple of files."

She glared and wagged the data card at him. "So this is why you were pushing so hard to go after Atlas. What is this anyway? A payoff? Some future scam?"

After a length, he relented under her gaze. "The Bones program won't be good anymore. It's always good to have a backup plan."

When she didn't say anything, he continued, "We never would've gotten onto Free Station without Bones. What if something happens in the future? What's getting copied onto that data card isn't for sale. I like to have options. It's as simple as that."

She eyed him for a while longer before turning away and setting the data card back on the desk.

"If I go down to the dock and find that hardline, I need to know that you'll use that card."

After a moment, she blew out a breath. "Yes, I'll do it."

He squeezed her shoulder. "Thank you."

She pulled away.

He turned and faced Roxy. "Protect the specialist. I'll take care of that hardline."

CHAPTER TWENTY-THREE

OF COURSE PUNCH HADN'T WAITED. THROTTLE AND FINN HAD ENTERED Free Station at the emergency airlock entrance only one level below the one that the marshal and Sylvian had used, but there was no trace that Punch had waited, since Throttle was now looking at the airlock on level two.

She sighed and turned to Finn, to find fury in his eyes. "He'll watch out for her," she said, trying to convince herself as much as trying to convince her friend.

They followed the dim passageway Punch and Sylvian had taken, noting that their predecessors had taken the cameras out of commission. When they reached a stairway, they headed up one level even though she knew Sylvian would be to the left. Despite her misgivings about Punch, she admitted that they each had priorities to help Chief reclaim Free Station.

She eyed the first camera they walked under that seemed to be still operational. She eyed it, wondering if Anna East was watching Throttle at that very moment or if the power outage had sheared the video feeds. She hoped for the latter, but a part of her wanted East to see *who* was coming for her.

They moved steadily through the hallway, each carrying a rifle. They'd come across bodies, several pirates and three Peacekeepers. All three had been wearing blue armbands, and she suspected they were some of the cadets Chief had leveraged in his counterattack. Rusty's scans of Free Station had shown the greatest concentration of people in one place: the mess hall. She knew Chief well enough to know that he'd be where his people were.

As they continued down the hallway, a door to their right opened. Throttle and Finn swung their rifles at the same time. An older specialist peeked out. She was a woman Throttle had met once or twice previously, causing her to wonder why the GP didn't have a mandatory retirement age. As soon as she saw Throttle and Finn, she let out an "Eep!" and slammed the door closed.

The pair exchanged a glance and continued forward. As they migrated through the residence walkways, confidence filled Throttle that Sylvian would be okay. Peacekeepers walked openly through the hallways. Many bore ragged expressions from too much stress and too little sleep, but they were uninjured, and that they walked freely meant that Chief had reclaimed at least parts of Free Station.

By the time Throttle and Finn reached the mess hall, they found what had to be nearly fifty marshals who'd been on Free Station when it'd been invaded. Some were eating, some were conversing, some were checking their gear. All looked ready to go into battle. And she found Chief near the center.

He sat hunched over a table. Cadets wearing yellow armbands sat at the same table.

"Chief," Throttle said as they approached.

He glanced up. His skin was paler than she'd ever seen, and he had dark circles under his eyes. His shirt was torn open and she could see a bandage underneath. When he noticed Throttle and Finn, relief relaxed his muscles. "How many ships did you bring with you?"

"Two. The *Javelin* and the *High Spirit*. We came as soon as we freed Punch's ship from a Jader chop shop," Throttle answered.

Chief frowned. "You couldn't pull together any more ships not connected to Atlas?"

Throttle shook her head. "I tried, but it seems like folks aren't willing to put their lives at risk for the Peacekeepers."

He scowled. "The barons have a myopic view of their world. They think their own police forces are all they need. It's been too long since we've had an intersystem conflict, and they've forgotten the real reason that the Galactic Peacekeepers exist. All they see are the taxes." He drew in a breath and winced.

"You look like you should be in bed, Chief," Finn said.

"There'll be time for rest and recuperation when this is over with," Chief countered. "Where's Punch?"

"He took Sylvian to try to get Atlas back online," Finn answered.

Chief sat up straighter. "He can't."

"Why not?" Throttle asked.

"Anna East came here for Atlas more than anything else. The moment we take it away from her, there's nothing stopping her from trying to escape and blow the station."

"Can she escape? I heard all the ships were restrained," Finn said.

"The ships in the docks are restrained for now, but it's only a matter of time before they cut through the lines. But East has a good-sized pirate fleet. I wouldn't be surprised if she has another ship waiting off-station to come and get her at a moment's notice."

"I didn't pick up any other ships on my way in," Throttle said.

"You also didn't pick up a hundred pirates hiding on the *Wu Zetian* either," Chief countered.

A cold chill flitted across Throttle's skin. "That's how they got onto Free Station?" Her jaw had slackened. "I gave Anna East's pirates a ride here. I can't believe I didn't notice."

"I didn't notice either," Finn said.

She closed her eyes. "Of course they were on board. That's why the *Bendix* didn't fire at us when they had the chance, and that the other ship's aim was so pitifully bad. I knew something seemed off about that."

"It doesn't matter how they got here," Chief said. "What matters is that pirates are notoriously sneaky, and I wouldn't put anything past them. Just because you didn't see a ship out there doesn't mean there isn't one. That's why we have to make sure East can't get off Free Station. She wouldn't have any qualms about killing her employees, but I imagine she'd be timid to detonate explosives while she was still on the station."

"Punch and Sylvian have already gone for the Atlas room," Throttle said.

Finn tapped his comm-chip. "Sylvian, report." When there was no answer, he repeated his request before turning back to Throttle and Chief. "She must be running silent."

Chief held up a hand. "We should be okay. The Atlas server room is on level two, but its control center is on nine, and it's still under Jader control. If we can't get up there, they can't as well. In fact, that is one of the reasons I need ships here."

"The *Javelin*'s at your disposal," Throttle offered.

Chief nodded. "Good, because I'm launching a full-out counterattack on each level, starting with the docking bay and the training level and then working up through the command level and control center level. The problem is the pirates have all the interior access points covered."

"Where's East?" Throttle asked.

"As of two hours ago, she was in the command center on level eight. There's a large emergency airlock nearby, making it easy for a ship to pick her up in case of a hasty retreat. We believe all ships in the docking bay are still restrained, but that won't be for much longer, and she could have another ship waiting for her not far from the station. If we can put one of our own ships at that airlock, we can deploy directly and take her out before she can escape. If Anna East is out of commission, the remaining Jader pirates would quickly show loyalty to their own crews, and squabbles would rise among the independent captains. Pirates are experienced and devious, but without alignment, they will inevitably fall apart."

Throttle thought for a moment. "We can fit at least thirty, maybe more, on the *Javelin*, though it'd be standing room only, and most would be in the cargo bay."

"Levels eight and nine are crucial for us," Chief said. "Nine has all the control centers, and eight has the command center. While we've been unlocking doors one at a time, East has someone up there locking the doors almost as fast as we can unlock them. It hasn't been easy building our numbers, but we're making headway. Upon deployment, one team would head to the security control center on nine to deactivate the lockdown while the other team would go after East in the command center."

"Why not send everyone at the command center if you can cancel the lockdown from there?" Finn asked.

"Because I never put all my eggs in one basket, and I want each team to focus on a single priority. If one team fails, then the other team will take up both tasks."

"Send as many as you can on the *Javelin*. Finn and I want on the team that goes after East," Throttle said.

Chief eyed the pair. "I figured as much. You should know that anyone entering eight and nine is likely entering the viper's pit. Intel gathered from the few pirates we've managed to capture indicates East has focused most of her firepower there."

Finn spoke. "If that's the viper's pit, then that's where the viper will be, and you can count on us to cut the head off that snake."

Chief's brow rose. "I want East captured alive if possible, so we can learn what she did to Atlas while she had it under her control."

"Alive. If possible. Sure," Throttle said.

Chief eyed them with uncertainty, then nodded to the table. "Okay, take a seat. Here's the plan..."

CHAPTER TWENTY-FOUR

PUNCH TOOK THE STAIRWAY UP TO THE RESIDENCE LEVEL FIVE, THE nearest he could get to the docking bay without getting shot at. He'd run into several marshals, a dozen specialists, and the remnants of Red team. Only two remained out of the original eight, and he realized that Roxy's team had been three short of eight. The cadets had sacrificed their lives taking on an assignment they were sorely unprepared for. What had Chief been thinking?

The Peacekeepers he'd met had come from a staging area in the mess hall and were now patrolling the hallways. From the sounds of it, nearly a hundred Peacekeepers had been released from their rooms so far and were gearing up to reclaim Free Station with vigor. The pirates didn't know the station and didn't have the training, but in space, the odds always played out differently than expected. It only took one pirate to lob a grenade and breach a hull to take out the entire mess hall full of Peacekeepers. He wouldn't bet against the pirates yet.

The pirates had kept to levels six and above. That Free Station's general population was in levels five and below concerned Punch. Each floor on the station could be breached without breaching the entire station. He figured the pirates knew that fact as well, and he wondered what Anna East had in mind for the lower levels—he had a sinking feeling that she certainly had something planned.

A marshal Punch knew, Detroit, waved and started walking over.

But Punch swerved behind a couple of specialists to avoid his old buddy. Detroit would no doubt recruit him to help on the counterattack, and Punch needed to get Atlas back online.

He knew that it was essential to get Atlas online, but it wasn't more important than the counterattack. But that data card was more important than either to Punch. He hadn't lied to Sylvian when he said the card wasn't for sale. But it would help someone who desperately needed help.

His daughter.

He had to trust Sylvian to keep her word.

As he came closer to the docking bay, the marshals he came across were more tense.

"You can't go to the docking bay," one said.

"Can't?" Punch asked.

"Trust me. You don't want to go up there. The pirates still have control of the docking bay. They've been holding us back while they cut through the restraining cables that are holding their ships here."

Punch walked forward. "Thanks for the heads-up, but I've got to get up there."

"You'll get yourself killed."

"Let's hope not," Punch said.

Behind him, he heard the marshal grumble, "Idiot."

Punch agreed.

He continued forward despite the dubious looks from the Peace-keepers holding the stairwell. He stopped when he reached the door.

"You don't want to go that way," a marshal said.

Punch ignored her. He cracked open the door and was met with blaster fire. He slammed the door shut and ducked.

"Told you," the same marshal said.

Punch turned around. "I don't suppose there's a way to get to the docking bay that doesn't involve me getting shot?"

She shrugged. "Not unless you can walk through walls."

He thought for a moment. "Good idea."

He turned around and went back down a level. There, he walked through the hallway until he found a group of specialists sitting in a common room. They were focused on a map of the docking bay. He approached them. "Any of you happen to be a network specialist?"

A member of the group pointed to another group in the room. "Mick's a net spec."

"Thanks," Punch said and approached a group of three specialists. "I'm looking for Mick."

"I'm Mick," a petite woman said.

"Come with me," Punch said.

She frowned at his curtness but stepped away from her friends so they could speak with a bit more privacy.

"Here's my problem," he began. "The pirates have hardlined into Atlas, likely from somewhere in the docking bay. I need to find where they've tapped in and break it, so we can get Atlas back online. Can you help me track down where they've hardlined in?"

"First of all, it's a hardline, not 'hardlined.' A noun, not a verb."

He stared, unimpressed.

"And second, yes, I can locate the hardline. I just need to grab a network monitor." She cocked her head. "Did Chief tell you they used a hardline?"

"The Atlas specialists have reached that conclusion since the pirates haven't gotten into Atlas through the network room or comm center."

"Oh. That makes sense. Hold on. I'll be right back." She jogged away, leaving Punch alone in the crowd.

He'd begun to think she wasn't coming back when he saw her weave through the growing crowd of Peacekeepers leaving their rooms and forming groups to head to the mess hall.

As she approached, she held up a handheld device with two metal prongs at one end. "Got it. I just need to connect to a primary cable."

He motioned for her to lead, and she started walking down the hallway, away from where he'd come. She walked several feet and stopped, then walked several more.

"What are you doing?" he asked after she repeated the cycle.

"I'm trying to remember where the primary cable is. It's not like it's marked, and I've always used the maps through my Atlas chip before. But Chief is sending the medics around to power down our chips, so I can't use mine right now."

Frustration brimmed. "Can you find the cable or not?"

"Just give me a minute already."

Punch tapped his foot while Mick stared at the walls. After a moment, she scowled and looked down at his foot. "Not helping."

He stopped.

She turned back to looking at the walls. After another moment, she raised a finger. "Aha. This way." She pointed forward, and he followed.

She approached a section of the wall with a small panel on it. She entered a code and the panel slid open to reveal several bundles of wires and cables. She sifted through the bundles until she singled out one that looked no different from the others. She held it one-handed while she took the handheld device and pressed its two metal prongs against the cable. Data scrolled across the screen until she pulled the device away and skimmed the stored contents until she pointed at a code. "There. It looks like the cable is showing a patch at panel Six-Hotel-Lima."

"Where's that?"

"You're right. It's at the dock level." She pointed to the code *5-S-L* painted above the open panel. "See? This is Five-Sierra-Lima. The codes are in logical order. The number is the level, and the letters show which panel. Six means it's on level six. Sierra means it's about ten panels back that way from where this panel is." She pointed. "And Lima means that it's on the same side of the hallway as this one. Otherwise, the letter would be Romeo. Make sense?"

"Sure," he said, though the rationale made actually very little sense to him. "You're telling me that if I walk that way until I come to Five-H-L, I'll be exactly one level below where they've hardlined into Atlas?"

"Five-*Hotel-Lima*, yes," she corrected, then added, "And you'll be one level down from *the* hardline."

"I bet you're a lot of fun at parties," he said.

She cocked her head. "Why do you say that?"

He ignored her question. "So do you have any ideas on how a guy can cut the hardline without getting shot?"

Mick thought for a moment. "Not if you don't want to cut the cable."

"What would happen if I cut the cable from here?"

"Well, sure, it'd cut the hardline since the cable is traveling *down* to the network room from the hardline, which would force Atlas to reboot to move traffic to its secondary cables. And I'd probably be the one stuck to repair the cable, and cables are a pain to patch."

"But Atlas could still work, and it'd be free from the hardline?" he clarified.

"Yeah, but if you cut the cable, everything that Atlas is running on that cable to or from levels one through six would be offline until someone goes in and repairs the cable."

His brow rose as he waited for her to understand.

Finally, she sighed. "Yes, we could get Atlas back online with just a couple of dead spots. But once the hardware is disconnected, you still need a software specialist."

"Already covered," he said.

Mick nodded. "Okay, fine. If that cable's going to get cut, let me do it. Otherwise, you'll probably cut the wrong cable and really screw things up."

She led the way to the panel. When they reached it, she opened the panel and found the cable. She turned back and looked him up and down. "Give me your knife."

He unsheathed the blade and handed it to her.

She brought the blade up to the cable and held it there as she seemed to struggle with the action. "Chief Roux said it was okay to cut lines?"

"Yes," he lied.

She flicked the blade through the cable and then handed the weapon back to Punch as if she'd done something completely against her principles. "There. It's done. The hardline should be disconnected. The soft spec can work on Atlas as soon as it's rebooted. Hopefully, we can all use our chips soon. It'll make it easier when we have access to the video feeds."

"Thanks. I was expecting a lot more blaster fire involved in cutting the hardline. You may have just saved my life."

She didn't seem overly impressed with her heroics and frowned instead. "Which cable would you have cut, by the way?"

He shrugged. "All of them."

The idea seemed to terrify her. She closed the panel, turned, and walked away without so much as a "good-bye and good luck."

He stood and stared at the now-closed panel. After a moment, he belted out a laugh, not out of humor but out of unexpected relief. People eyed him oddly, but he paid them no mind. When the sensation muted, he turned and made his way back to Sylvian, not to protect her but to make sure she had the data card.

CHAPTER TWENTY-FIVE

THROTTLE AND FINN HAD JUST FINISHED LISTENING TO CHIEF'S briefing, and the mess hall was a flurry of activity. He'd divided all the available Peacekeepers into nineteen teams. Sixteen of the teams all had the same assignment: reclaim their assigned stairway and work through their assigned level. The pirates had control of four levels, and each level had four main stairways. Another team, wearing full chime suits, would enter the emergency evacuation tunnel and clear it. The remaining two teams would be transported via the *Javelin* to go after Jader leadership and deactivate the lockdown.

No one could reach Punch, which meant Throttle had the only ship to assist in the movement. Her team of six experienced marshals was being led by Chief Roux himself, even though anyone could see that his injuries were severe. He'd slow them down, but he said they had the least distance to travel. Throttle figured the reason he was coming was that he wanted to see Anna East taken down as much as Throttle did.

On the level eight team, Throttle and Finn had the lowest tenure of the marshals. In addition to Chief, the four people accompanying them were all senior-level marshals, each having ten-plus years with the Peacekeepers. Throttle and Finn weren't intimidated, however, as they'd both survived a war and had been in close-quarter battles before, something that many marshals went a career without experiencing.

"Syl, come in," she heard Finn say through her comm-chip. She turned to see him trying to reach his wife once again.

"She's okay," Throttle said, though she was beginning to have doubts as well.

Finn's features were hard. "If something's happened to her, I'm going to kill him."

Throttle didn't need to ask whom Finn was talking about. If something happened to Sylvian, Throttle would also place the blame squarely and deservedly on Punch Durand's shoulders. Hell, if Sylvian was dead and Finn didn't kill Punch, she'd finish the job.

The video screens all blinked and came to life. Throttle's gaze focused toward the nearest screen, which bore the Atlas logo before displaying the general menu.

Many Peacekeepers cheered and stared straight ahead as though running through screens on their personal Atlas chips.

She glanced back to see Chief's face turn even paler.

"She did it. Syl brought Atlas back online," Finn said.

Throttle heard the relief in her friend's voice for his wife, though she knew exactly what Chief was thinking. If Anna East no longer had Atlas, then she no longer had a need to remain on Free Station.

"Damn it, Punch," Chief said, the anxiety evident in his voice. "The mission's scrubbed. We have to have everyone search for the explosives."

"Where's the most likely location?" a marshal on their team, Gavin "Detroit" Jackson, asked.

"I've had specialists run scenarios. East has access to the armory, so she has more than enough explosives to place them on every level. The consensus was that she'd take an easier route and place explosives in a critical area capable of burning through the station. That could be on either the control center level or down in the mechanicals levels."

"That's a lot of area to cover," Finn said.

"Check the air-processing center," Marshal Williams said. "I worked a case like this once. The owners blew their own station to collect insurance. They placed explosives in the air-processing center. We had evidence, but they'd bought the judge and jury."

"We'll head down to the APC, then. I'll leave other teams on the mission plan until we confirm that the location of the explosives is or is not in the APC," Chief said.

"Hold on. I have a crew member near there," Throttle said.

Chief gave her a nod, and she tapped her comm-chip. "Eddy, do you read me?"

"Of course I do, Throttle. I designed the comm-chips. They're not going to fail."

She blew off his comment. "We have an emergency. Free Station is rigged to blow with explosives."

A lengthy pause. *"Okay. And?"*

"Anna East set up explosives to make it look like the station was destroyed by an asteroid hit, and she could set them off at any time. We're thinking sooner versus later."

"No investigators would mistake a bombing for an asteroid impact. That plan is insane."

"No sane person would invade Free Station."

"Good point."

"We think the most likely place for explosives to do catastrophic damage would be around the oxygenators in the air-processing center."

A few seconds passed. *"That's definitely the most logical place."*

"The center isn't far from where the *Javelin* is parked. You're the nearest specialist. With the elevators down, it'd take the next closest specialist ten minutes or more to get there. I need you to hurry there and deactivate the explosives. Can you do that?"

"Of course."

"Okay. Good luck. We're heading your way and will see you on the *Javelin*. Everyone on Free Station is counting on you, Eddy."

"I know."

Eddy didn't say anything else, so Throttle pulled her finger away from her comm-chip and turned back to Chief.

"Do you think he can do it?" Chief asked.

"Yes," Throttle answered with confidence.

A broadcast signal blared across the station speakers, and Anna East's voice permeated the mess hall.

"So you think taking Atlas from me gives you an edge? You can have it; I'm done with it. Free Station is yours again, at least for the next few minutes. Goodbye, Peacekeepers."

A quake rattled the floors and walls, and all the screens when dark.

"Do you think she set off the explosives?" someone asked.

"I lost my Atlas chip again," someone else said.

"Peacekeepers, remain calm," Chief shouted over the din. "We're still alive, so that means Free Station is still operational. That explosion was likely tied to the reason we no longer have Atlas again. I have a team working on locating the explosives, if there even are some. Stay focused. This mission starts now, and you each have a crucial role. Good luck."

Chief turned and took the lead of his group of six marshals in the opposite direction everyone else was headed. "If she's set a timer, she's jumping ship. We can't afford to wait. We need to get to eight now and block any ship coming to pick her up. If she can't get off the station, she'll cancel the timer."

As they walked down the hallway, Finn spoke softly. "If she doesn't cancel the timer, let's hope Eddy's fast enough."

CHAPTER TWENTY-SIX

ANNA FUMED. CHIEF ROUX WAS STILL ALIVE AND DOING WHAT HE DID best, organizing marshals against her. Pete had been sloppy. He should've made sure the Peacekeeper was dead before bragging to her. She was glad she'd locked up Pete—he'd done nothing but fail her since coming to Free Station.

Throttle Reyne being on Free Station brought Anna some satisfaction, even though she'd wanted to see the marshal executed in front of her. Instead, Anna would have to take comfort in knowing that Jakob's murderer would be dead.

She went to call out to the man who'd been modifying the Atlas records, but she didn't remember his name, so she called him by his nationality. "Jader, what's the status of the Atlas update?"

The young hacker turned in his seat. "I'm at ninety-seven percent complete in changing personnel records. I need another hour to finish assigning tenure contracts for all Hiraethians. I haven't even started erasing all the Jader arrest records."

She frowned. "That's taking too long. You have fifteen minutes."

"But without the router, I have to enter all this manually."

"One hour," she said before spinning in her chair to face the man standing behind her. "Yank, activate the timer for thirty minutes."

The hefty man nodded. "It'll be my pleasure, Ms. East."

He pulled out a tablet and began typing in a command sequence. Anna noticed the Peacekeeper specialists she'd put to work in the command center—they fidgeted and threw glances at Yank as though they knew what the timer would deliver.

She smiled at the specialists. "There, there. No need to worry. You'll have Free Station back in your hands in no time."

None of them seemed relieved.

"It's set. We'd better get going," Yank said.

"Not yet," she said.

He frowned. "But the explosives—"

"Can be turned off at the last moment. I'm not leaving until everyone in this system is tenured to me."

He eyed her like she was crazy. "Then leave Nelson. He can report in as soon as your contracts are created."

The hacker looked over his shoulder. "Wait. You're leaving me behind?"

"No, I'm not leaving you behind," Anna said. "Keep working." She tossed a glare at Yank. "Quit distracting him. We're not blowing Free Station until after Atlas is updated, and we're on the *Bendix*."

CHAPTER TWENTY-SEVEN

Eddy reviewed his tablet as soon as the airlock door closed behind him. He'd slung his tool bag over his shoulder, along with a rifle even though he found the weapon unnecessary since Throttle and Finn had already gone through much of that area and had encountered no pirates.

A map displayed on the tablet screen.

"Excellent." Eddy added a pin to make his navigation to the engineering area all the easier. He looked up over his shoulder. "Come along, my little round friend. Let's get this over with. I don't like to be here any more than you do."

Throttle hadn't told Eddy he could bring a bot with him onto Free Station, but she hadn't told him he couldn't, so he took that as her leaving the decision up to him. The bot hovered behind Eddy as he followed the map. It was one of the smaller bots, designed for scanning an area for whatever substances it'd been programmed to scan for. The bot fed sensory data to Eddy's tablet, in this case, any incendiary material its sensors identified. It was currently reading trace amounts of blasting powder, which he assumed had come from Finn, or Punch more likely, bringing shock grenades onto the station with them.

Projectile weapons of any kind were illegal to use in space, even for Peacekeepers, due to the extreme damage they could cause on any ship or station. That was why all Peacekeepers only used energy-based photon weapons. But Eddy knew Finn well enough to know that the ex-soldier-turned-marshal tended to bend the rules, and from what Eddy knew of Punch, that marshal didn't even believe in rules.

Eddy hustled down the narrow walkway. He'd told Throttle he didn't want to leave the ship, but she'd sounded in dire need of help, and he wouldn't leave his crew to die if there was something he could do about it. But if he was hurt or killed, he'd make sure she wouldn't hear the end of it. In fact, he'd left detailed instructions with Rusty to carry out in the event of Eddy's demise so that he could guarantee Throttle would hear about his aggravation at being killed. Rusty wouldn't be too hard on Throttle. After all, he knew she'd blame herself if something happened to Eddy, but she'd certainly deserve to hear his thoughts on the matter.

The walkway ended at a doorway, and Eddy paused only to verify the map. The air-processing center stood on the other side of a hallway open to the general population, so he'd be forced to leave the walkway that was restricted to engineers like himself. The air-processing center was the only logical place explosives would be placed that would ensure complete annihilation of an orbital station. Only a small number of explosives would be needed to ignite the tanks of pure oxygen, which would erupt into a firestorm that would burn through the station like a terrible wave.

There wouldn't be enough left of Free Station for investigators to determine the cause, though Eddy thought the plan was a rather weak one, as it'd be incredibly suspicious not having fragments of an asteroid scattered among the wreckage. No experienced investigator would believe the story of an asteroid impact. Anna East wasn't the smartest criminal he'd met, though he supposed the idea of faking an asteroid impact would seem a brilliant idea in the same mind that had thought it a good idea to try to sleep with her own brother.

Eddy truly didn't understand how most people's minds worked. To him, everyone was insane. His crewmates were also insane, just to a lesser extent than most others he'd met. He often wondered if he was the only sane person left in the galaxy. That would make sense since, in his entire life, which covered multiple star systems, he'd only ever been able to have truly intelligent, deep conversations with Rusty, who wasn't even human.

He brushed off the thoughts about other people since they did nothing except drive him crazy. He grabbed the door handle, drew in a deep breath, opened the door, and stepped into the hallway. It was dimly lit, and he wondered if the entire station was operating on emergency power.

The bot bumped the frame on the way through.

"Careful there, Bonkers," Eddy said, then thought to add, "You know, I bet I could get you some new directional gyros, but it's just so darn cute watching you bonk into things."

The bot didn't show any response.

He shrugged. "You're not much of a conversationalist."

Voices drew his attention, and he snapped his gaze to his left to see two greasy men rush around the corner. Their arms were overfilled with what looked to be clothes, jewelry, and credit papers. One of the pirates took a step closer. "Easy there, buddy. We're just passing through. Don't do anything stupid."

Their eyes met Eddy's. Eddy tensed. Their eyes narrowed; Eddy's widened. He dropped the tablet and fumbled for his rifle. Both pirates dropped their stolen goods and went for their pistols.

Eddy had his rifle up first, but the strap of his tool bag snagged on the barrel. His finger formed a vise grip on the trigger, and he fired a nonstop barrage. One of his shots hit the shin of the farthest pirate, causing him to fall forward and left. As the pirate toppled over, he fired a wild shot that struck his partner in the right lower back. His partner pirouetted around as he fell and shot the other pirate in the head.

Both pirates lay sprawled on the floor, unmoving.

Eddy stared. He glanced down at his rifle, then back at the pair of bodies. A grin filled his face, and he turned to the bot. "Did you see that? I took out two pirates!"

Suddenly infused with invincibility, he twirled the rifle around, only to accidentally fire off another shot into the floor. He cringed, grimaced, and then slowly and gingerly slung the rifle back over his shoulder.

He straightened, grabbed his bag, picked up the tablet, and crossed the hallway to open the door labeled *Air-Processing Center. No Unauthorized Personnel Allowed.* As he approached, the door opened. It seemed that when the station was on emergency power, most security protocols were suspended. He stepped inside, and the bot came in with him.

His tablet lit up with alerts. "Ah, there you are," he said as he examined it for a sliver of a moment. He slid the device into his pocket and strode toward a series of machines shaped like fifty-five-gallon drums. A small black box sat between four of the barrel-shaped machines in the center of the room, a wire traveling from the device to each of the machines. A spark in any machine would start a cascade explosion, and the ensuing inferno would destroy the entire station. Each machine was marked *Oxygenator*.

"What a stupid name," Eddy muttered as he approached the suspended device. He carefully examined the bottom and sides of the bomb. He felt perspiration instantly form in his armpits as he looked at the top.

He eyed the "bomb" with humor. He'd expected a homemade bomb, something as ugly and mean as the pirates who made it. Instead, he was looking at a GP device that sent out bursts of electricity to destroy illegal drugs and other contraband that couldn't be redistributed. It was a device built with safety in mind, easily deactivated by anyone with basic mechanical skills.

The problem was that someone had hacked on a timer with a small black stick antenna, which was definitely not GP-approved hardware.

0:35 remained. He stared as the timer dropped to *0:34.*

Goose bumps covered his skin. "Oh, rats."

He dropped his tool bag and eased closer to the explosive. He cocked his head as the timer continued.

0:28

0:27

0:26

He lifted his finger to the timer and hit the red button in the bottom right. The timer stopped at *0:23.* He flipped the toggle to turn off the system and sighed when the screen went blank instead of a big *kaboom.* A few seconds later, he quickly unscrewed the omnidirectional antenna and tossed it aside, just in case.

Then, as carefully as he would string flying wires on a model airplane, he disconnected each of the wires and lowered the bomb to the floor. He tucked the bomb into his tool bag and slung it over his shoulder.

He felt a sudden sense of smugness at saving everyone on Free Station. Satisfied, he nodded at the small bot. "Whew. Let's go back home, Bonkers."

Eddy and the bot made their way back to the airlock. When he reached it, he stood, frozen in shock.

The *Javelin* was gone.

He grabbed the bot, fell back on his butt, and hugged Bonkers. He couldn't believe it.

His crew had abandoned him.

CHAPTER TWENTY-EIGHT

If Rusty could've sent a message through Bonkers, he would have, but his small robotic drones had no speakers and could only perform the most basic of tasks. He added a note to his work log to upgrade his bots, starting with Eddy's two favorites: Bonkers and Blaster.

Rusty hadn't wanted to leave Eddy behind, but he'd calculated that Eddy would be safest if the insurgents were dealt with. Still, he monitored Bonkers's sensory feed. If trouble came Eddy's way, Rusty would leave the rest of the crew and return to help him as soon as he ensured Throttle, Finn, and Sylvian were safe.

A week ago, Rusty would never have considered doing anything not consented to by a crew member, but the naive Bayse router that Eddy had installed allowed Rusty to look at every decision from new angles. Rusty had programmed in a single priority: keep the crew safe. All decisions would be made with that priority in mind. His human crew had once told him that he was part of the crew, which made making the single priority all the easier. After all, Rusty didn't want to be in danger, either.

It was a thought that had frequently been cycling through his systems. The hostile ship was keeping its distance, but Rusty could feel it scratching at his firewalls. It was probing for weaknesses, and that both concerned him and annoyed him.

The new router helped Rusty run scenarios of computer-led attacks against him, and he'd been making changes as flaws were identified. If the other ship's computer kept up its attacks, Rusty had decided he would inform the crew and adjust from a defensive strategy to an offensive strategy.

CHAPTER TWENTY-NINE

"I BELIEVE IT'S TIME FOR US TO BID A FOND FAREWELL TO FREE Station. Yank, take me to the *Bendix*."

The hefty man nodded and reached for their space suits. "It'll be my pleasure, Ms. East."

He assisted her in dressing and led the way from Free Station's command center, with the rest of the crew forming a protective barrier around her. As they walked briskly down the hallway and to the airlock, Yank slowed. He glanced back at her. "What about Pete?"

"What about him?" she asked.

"You're just going to leave him in there?"

"Why shouldn't I?" she asked.

"I thought you and he were—"

Her brows rose. "Lovers? We were, but that doesn't excuse failure. If he wants off Free Station, he can find his own ride."

Yank wisely didn't say anything else. She was half-tempted to leave him behind with his captain for questioning her. But she knew that the crew of the *Bendix* had served together for years. Yank and Pete were, no doubt, close friends.

No other words were spoken as Yank rushed her out the airlock. They spacewalked down three levels of the station toward the *Bendix,* careful to avoid any cameras. It had taken hours, but they'd cut through the restraining cables, and the engines were already powered up. She stepped on board and felt the stress peel off her as the airlock door closed behind her.

While she hadn't achieved all of her objectives, she'd achieved enough to be satisfied. She was now the most powerful person in the Ross system, and the Peacekeepers could do nothing to change that. Every person in the Ross system, from Hiraethian colonists to miners, would be tenured to her. The entire system was quite literally falling into her hands, and Chief had no idea she was no longer on the station.

CHAPTER THIRTY

With a blaster in one hand, Yank guided Anna East and his crew down the hull of Free Station. He'd walked down plenty of hulls during his career as a pirate, where he'd quickly learned that the most important part of walking on someone else's ship or station was not to be seen. That feat was proving easier said than done with the abundance of windows across the station. While many of the general quarters had no windows, the end of every hallway had a window, along with all officer quarters and shared rooms. The cafeteria had a series of windows that spanned its entire width, which forced Yank to lead his small team nearly fifteen minutes out of their way to avoid detection.

The walk was long. The muscles in Yank's legs and feet ached from lifting the grav boots with every step. Anna East was half his size and had to be exhausted, but she never complained, which surprised him. He regularly looked at her to find her focused straight ahead as though concentrating on each step. He'd expected a pampered businesswoman to be even worse outside the command center. Instead, she deferred to Yank when she was outside her element. He was beginning to see how she'd survived as long as she had.

He'd see to it that she survived this job. Then he was looking forward to never having to kiss up to anyone ever again. He would start with a long vacation on a Hiraethian beach. He'd lounge, doing nothing, taking orders from no one, until he got bored. Then he'd return to space, doing what he did best, hunting yachts in the endless black sea and pillaging them for everything of value.

Yank glanced over his shoulder to make sure the others were keeping up. Benny, who was right behind him and carrying a photon rifle, winked. He was Yank's best friend and a man who took only one thing seriously: guns. Yank and Benny had already talked about starting up their own crew, and Yank felt better knowing that he'd have someone he trusted watching his back.

The only person Yank had worked with longer than Benny was Pete, but Pete was not the type to be friends with anyone who worked for him. The captain was too dictatorial and too emotionally closed off. Plus, the skull fetish really freaked out Yank.

It was their long history that made Yank feel some regret at leaving Pete behind while they escaped. He supposed that same regret was why he hadn't *fully* disarmed his captain when he'd locked him in that meeting room. If he knew Pete—and he knew Pete better than anyone —the pirate had likely broken out of his cell by now and was on his way to the docks.

Yank sped up their pace when the thought hit him. It was a very real possibility that Pete could beat them to the *Bendix*. Maybe Yank should've fully disarmed Pete when he'd had the chance.

Anna stumbled. Yank looked down to see sweat running down her face. He wrapped his arm around her waist. "Disengage your grav boots."

She stiffened. "What are you doing?"

"I'm going to carry you, Ms. East," he replied.

She huffed. "I'm not an invalid. I'm capable of walking."

"I know you are, but we need to hurry. We've been out here too long already."

She watched him for a long second, her lips pursed, before she spoke. "Fine. Just don't get any bright ideas."

He smirked. "I won't."

Her boots released from the hull. He held her to him and looked over his shoulder once more. "Keep up."

With Anna in tow, he doubled their pace. There were fewer windows in the final length of hull, which meant they could take a more direct route without fear of being seen. When they reached the outside of the space docks, he led his group around Free Station's hull to an airlock. As soon as they were inside with artificial gravity, he released Anna.

She dusted herself off as though to smooth her suit.

Yank transmitted through his suit's communication system. "Jazz, we're nearly to you. Fire up the *Bendix*."

"All right. She'll be ready by the time you get here, but be careful. There are more and more Peacekeepers showing up," Jazz's response came through his speakers.

Yank glanced at the others. "You hear that? We might find ourselves some company."

Benny bore a wide grin and clutched his rifle. "Yeah. I'm ready."

The inner airlock opened, and the group of five stepped out, with Anna East cocooned by them. Yank, with his pistol, and Benny, with his rifle, led the group through the long, wide hallway.

Yank's stomach knotted. He never liked space docks. Made for loading and unloading cargo, they were too open for his comfort. After spending his lifetime aboard ships with confined quarters, he supposed he'd developed the opposite of claustrophobia along the way. Yank preferred working in narrow hallways, where he could overpower just about any opponent he faced. But open spaces meant that dozens, even hundreds of people could face him at once, taking away the chance for a fair fight.

He made furtive glances to the left and right, searching for snipers hiding behind the computer terminals located near the airlock at each bay. The snipers would have to be petite to conceal themselves behind the streamlined terminals, but it was still possible.

His breathing quickened and his heart raced, and he wanted to sprint through the docks to the *Bendix*. Funny thing was that the void of space didn't bother him. A person could see for a thousand miles. No one could sneak up on a person out there. But space docks? Yeah, they were scary.

Benny fired. Yank ducked and swung his pistol around as he searched for the hostiles. Yank came to a stop when he found Benny's target.

A freaking box.

He glared at his friend. Benny smiled and shrugged. "It needed shooting."

Yank shook his head. "Idiot."

Flashes of lightning cut through the air the split second before the sound of the blaster shot. Benny grabbed his chest, gave Yank a surprised look, and then fell to his knees and toppled forward. More shots rang out.

"No!" Yank grabbed Anna's arm and pulled her with him.

She wrenched free. "Hold on."

"Your funeral," he muttered as he flattened against the wall while he simultaneously fired and searched for the shooter.

Shooters. Plural.

Two Peacekeepers knelt in the open door of the elevator at the end of the hallway, aiming rifles. They weren't marshals, which was likely the only reason Yank was still alive. Marshals wouldn't need so long to aim. He continued to fire, but with the distance and only using a pistol, his shots went wide.

Anna East grabbed Benny's rifle and went down on a knee. She fired once, then twice, taking out both Peacekeepers with well-placed shots. She stood.

Yank, wide-eyed, looked from the dead Peacekeepers to Anna.

She gave him a droll stare while she handed him the rifle. "Take this. I hate getting my hands dirty."

He took the rifle and looked down at Benny. His eyes threatened to water, so he turned away. He noticed Nussbaum was also down, with a shot to the head.

Anna had already begun walking, and Yank and his only remaining crew member in that group, Listol, fell in alongside her. She led the rest of the way to the *Bendix*.

They reached the airlock with no further problems. Three Peace-keepers lay just outside the door, and Yank suspected Jazz had dealt with some problems while waiting for the rest of the crew. Yank closed the airlock door, and he suddenly felt safe. Though the weight that had been on his chest didn't evaporate. What had been panic was smothered by sorrow as he looked out at his friend's body through the window.

"We don't have all day, Yank," Anna said.

He turned around to see the inner airlock open and both Anna and

Listol waiting impatiently in the hallway for him. He strode forward and led Anna to the bridge of the *Bendix,* where Jazz had all systems running.

"List, you take the guns," Yank ordered the ever-silent Listol. "Take a seat anywhere you'd like, Ms. East," he then said as he took the captain's seat and began running the prelaunch checks.

"I'll stand until we're clear of this godforsaken station," she said.

"Have it your way," he mumbled as he managed the controls.

He was beginning to understand why people were entranced by Anna East, and he realized it had nothing to do with her beauty. It was because she was a dichotomy. She'd acted submissive while being led down to the *Bendix*, yet she'd taken out those two Peacekeepers like a sharpshooter.

She'd talked the entire Jader pirate fleet into taking the life-threatening job of invading Free Station, at the same time treating each of her employees like shit. She knew how to keep people guessing with her polarized behaviors.

And she was definitely a little insane.

CHAPTER THIRTY-ONE

SKULLY PETE ANTONOV HAD FINALLY SAWED THROUGH THE WALL TO expose the wiring. Yank knew Pete kept a switchblade in his boot, but he hadn't taken it when he relieved his captain of his weapons. For that reason, Pete wouldn't kill his best friend. He understood why Yank was going along with Anna East. She had a charisma that could suck a man in and make him feel like he was important to her...right up to the moment she stabbed him in the back.

He should've grabbed his crew and abandoned the station as soon as his gut started warning him that Anna's obsession would bring trouble. Trusting his gut over anything else was one reason Pete had survived longer than many pirates—the willingness to do what needed to be done was the other reason.

He sorted through the wiring to find the right wire—it was always the red wire—to open the door. With no window in the door, he couldn't know if a guard was posted, or if anyone was in the hallway. He'd have to risk it.

He used his switchblade to cut through the wire. The door opened, and he gingerly peeked through the doorway, holding his only weapon ready. Relief filled him when he saw no one. He kept the switchblade in his hand as he ran down the hallway, back toward the command center. His crew was serving as Anna's protective detail, and he knew they would hesitate to kill their captain, even under her orders. He'd use that hesitation to take down whoever was nearest the door—likely Romeo and Nix—grab a blaster and finish off Anna East like he should've done when she'd first shared her insane plan.

He reached the command center to find the door open, which caused him to pause. Anna *always* kept her doors closed. A sinking feeling grew in the pit of his stomach, and he moved silently to peer into the room. There, he saw only one Jader remaining with the software specialists. The pirate hadn't heard him, too busy eating a carb bar, so Pete stepped away before being discovered.

Anna and his crew had abandoned Free Station, which meant it could blow at any moment. He rushed down the hallway and slid down the vertical bar next to the stairs to the dock level. From there, he sprinted down the hallway, avoiding areas where he could hear shooting. He ran across a couple of other crews along the way. They were still at their posts, and he realized they'd no clue that they'd been left to die. He considered warning them, but he thought against it—they'd only slow him down.

He reached the docks to find a battle underway. He walked up behind a lone pirate laying down cover fire, clutched his greasy hair, and slashed his neck wide open. He grabbed the rifle before the man dropped it, and pocketed his switchblade. It looked like about a half-dozen Peacekeepers had retaken the docks, but they were pinned down by gunfire coming from Pete's right.

He analyzed the situation, firing shots every few seconds to keep anyone from getting a bead on him, and he decided he didn't have time. He closed his eyes, took a deep breath, and began running toward the Peacekeepers.

They were firing haphazardly at the Jaders and didn't notice his suicidal run until it was too late. Pete jumped onto the overturned skiff and fired at the Peacekeepers who'd been hiding behind it. They barely had time to form surprised expressions, let alone aim their rifles. He gunned them down within seconds.

When all that remained were bloody corpses under a haze of smoke, Pete turned to face three Jaders, who cautiously stepped out.

He heard his name, Skully Pete, whispered among the pirates.

"I've never seen anything like that," one of the men said in shock.

"Set up a blockade in the hallway over there." Pete pointed. "There are more Peacekeepers headed this way."

Still in awe, they agreed without hesitation and took off.

Pete headed toward the docking bay where the *Bendix* was parked. As he'd expected, it stood empty. Fury seethed. Not only had his crew mutinied, but they'd also stolen his ship. He didn't waste time giving in to his anger. Instead, he strode toward the small Rabbit that he'd used during his infiltration of the Peacekeepers. As expected, the restraining cable was still attached. Coldly, calmly, he stepped up to the computer panel and went to work, trying to remove the cable. As he went through the command menus, he swore vengeance on Anna East and his crew. He'd get off Free Station. Then they'd all end up as new additions to his collection of skulls.

CHAPTER THIRTY-TWO

THROTTLE MANUALLY PILOTED THE *JAVELIN* BELOW FREE STATION, maintaining a gap of only five feet between the station's hull and the ship. Chief Roux sat in Sylvian's seat. Behind him stood Finn and the other four marshals who would be going after Anna East on level eight, while the seven marshals going for the command center on level nine waited in the *Javelin*'s cargo bay, ready to spacewalk up one level the moment the ship stopped.

Finn had already put on his chime suit and had placed Throttle's suit next to her station. As she piloted, she tapped the ship's intercom. "Eddy, report."

"Eddy's not aboard the *Javelin*," Rusty said.

Throttle frowned. She knew Eddy didn't like being away from the ship and would've hustled through his assignment. She hadn't thought to check that he was on board when they arrived. As the *Javelin* reached the edge of Free Station, she pulled the ship into a vertical climb, keeping it as close to the station's hull as before.

"How'd you set up your ship computer to speak without asking it a question?" Marshal Williams, the only other female on their team, asked.

"Sylvian and Eddy spend a lot of time tweaking Rusty's processes," Throttle answered before tapping her comm-chip. "Eddy, report." Her voice echoed through Finn's comm-chip. When Eddy didn't respond, Finn tried to reach him. Still nothing.

"He might have his chip turned off," Finn offered.

"I can confirm that Eddy is alive and has disarmed the explosives," Rusty said.

"He told you that?" Throttle asked.

"No. Bonkers did," Rusty answered.

She frowned. "Who?"

"That's the name he gave to the bot he took along for company."

Finn chuckled drily. "Of course he did."

"I like your ship computer. Think your crew could take a look at mine?" Williams asked.

"Maybe some time, Marshal Williams," Throttle answered.

"Call me Hank," the marshal replied. "Everyone else does."

Throttle mostly ignored the other marshal. "Rusty, where is Eddy now?"

"He is at the emergency airlock on level one. He arrived right after we disconnected."

Throttle grimaced. "He's not going to be happy with me."

"No, he certainly is not. I know he annoys you, but I assume we're not abandoning him?" Rusty asked.

"We're not abandoning Eddy," she replied.

"You should know that Eddy also shot two pirates. Sort of. Though Eddy should tell you himself. It was wise of you to send him. By the time he arrived in the air-processing center, the timer had less than a minute remaining. We were all uncomfortably close to being blown up. The on-station fire from the explosives would've burned upward through all the levels in under an hour. You would not have made it in time to prevent the fire."

Finn scowled. "That doesn't make sense. Anna East wouldn't destroy Free Station when she was still on it."

"It would've taken time for the fire to reach the upper levels. She could've easily activated the timer before leaving the station. Though, my assumption is that she's no longer on the station or is very close to leaving," Chief said, his features furrowed. He thought for a brief moment and then pulled out a handheld radio. "I think it's time I have a chat with Ms. East."

Chief tapped a button on the slim radio to speak. "Ms. East, this is Chief Roux." The button clicked when he released it.

A couple of seconds passed before her response came.

"Chief Roux, I suspected I'd be hearing from you. How did you like my gift I left in the lowest level?" Her voice sounded as smooth as ever, even through the tinny radio speaker. In the background, a small beep regularly sounded along with a ticking sound.

"She's in the command center. I'd stake my life on it. I can hear the video feeds along with an old manual clock," Chief said in a rush. He then tapped the radio to speak. "Ms. East, I can't say that I liked it very much at all, and I can't say I like what you've been doing to Free Station and to my people in general."

"Good. Because I don't like the problems you've been causing me. I can't believe you reached out to the Consortium and told them I was a criminal. I'm a politician and a business owner, not a criminal."

Throttle could hear the anger building in East's voice, and the distress Chief was causing brought the captain satisfaction.

"You have a pirate fleet, and you kill innocents. You are a criminal," Chief said.

"They didn't even give me a chance to speak, no thanks to you! I'm trying to help the Ross system, and both you and they are stuck in the past."

"Let's not pretend that you have this system's interests at heart. What you're doing is to help only one person and that's you. You're not helping Rossers, and you're certainly not helping Jaders. Though I suppose Jade-8 will do better without you and the cancerous West family around anymore."

Throttle suddenly jerked back when she caught movement edging over the top of Free Station a split second before her screen displayed a nearby ship. It was small, rough-looking, and had the Jader symbol painted on its hull. It'd been so close to the station that Rusty's sensors hadn't detected it until it was within visual range.

"Chief," Throttle said.

He turned to her, and she pointed out the window. His eyes narrowed and his lips thinned. The ship was heading for the same airlock that Throttle was steering the *Javelin* toward. Fortunately, the other ship hadn't shown any signs of noticing the *Javelin* yet.

"Jade-8 has thrived under my family's leadership, just like the Ross

system will. And my so-called pirates are just entrepreneurs trying to survive under Sol's smothering taxes."

"Enough lies, Ms. East," Chief said. "Surrender now, and you and your Jaders who've illegally boarded this station may live. This will be the only time I make such a generous offer."

East belted out a laugh. "Me surrender? It's you who should surrender. I have everything in your armory at my disposal. I can blow up this station any time I choose."

"Permission to fire?" Throttle asked quietly.

"Just a warning shot. I want it scared off. I don't want Free Station damaged," Chief said before he tapped the radio to speak again. "You should've taken my offer, Ms. East."

Throttle lined up a photon gun at the ship. It was a small ship, likely holding no more than six passengers. It was busy lining up to the airlock and hadn't acknowledged the *Javelin*'s proximity, though the *Javelin* was so close to the station that no sensors would detect it.

"I could say the same thing to you," East replied.

Throttle fired. The blast hit the rear corner of the pirate ship and spun it around a couple of times before the captain leveled it out.

"I thought I said a warning shot," she heard Chief say.

She shot him a grin. "Oops." She returned her focus to the other ship to fire again, but it shot away, leaving sparks in its wake that were quickly smothered by the black.

"Last chance, Ms. East. Surrender," Chief said as he watched the pirate ship disappear in the distance.

Several seconds passed, and Throttle suspected East was being informed that her escape route had just been cut off. Knowing that they were closing in made Throttle more anxious than ever to go after the crime boss from Jade-8.

Throttle maneuvered the *Javelin* in the same position the pirate ship had been in moments earlier and carefully brought the ship over the airlock to where the station's door met the *Javelin*'s, and she extended a pressurized transit tube to connect the two openings.

"Ms. East, talk to me," Chief said.

There was no response.

"She's likely onto us. We need to move quickly. Give me a ship-wide intercom," Chief said.

Throttle tapped an icon on her screen and nodded in his direction. As he spoke, she hurriedly donned her space suit.

"Peacekeepers, this is Chief Roux. We are now at the airlock on level eight and ready to go in. Best of luck to both teams. We will take back Free Station and release everyone still locked in their quarters."

As soon as he was done speaking, he stood, though Finn assisted him when he nearly fell.

"I still think you should manage from here, Chief," Detroit said.

"Just get me to the command center; then I can manage everything from there," Chief gritted out.

Throttle glanced upward. "Rusty, keep an eye out for either team. You can handle the level nine team's walk from the cargo bay. Open the doors if any of ours need to get back on. Who knows what we'll be up against in there."

"You can count on me, Throttle," Rusty replied.

"That Trappist ship computer certainly comes in handy," Chief said.

"He sure does," she said.

She and Finn took the lead to the airlock. The strongest two marshals, Jack Ames and "Munny" Munson, assisted Chief so that the group could move more swiftly while Detroit and Hank covered the group's rear.

Once they were in the airlock, Chief spoke again. "The command center will be two hundred feet in, another one hundred feet down the hallway after it turns left. There is a conference room on the right side that we'll reach first. We'll need to watch out for snipers. After that the doors should all be sealed."

The outer airlock opened, and the group moved through the small transit tube. At Free Station's outer airlock, Chief entered his code and opened the door. Everyone moved through and stood along the edges, avoiding a clear line of fire by anyone waiting on the other side. Chief stood at the panel and looked across everyone's faces. "I'm opening the inner door in three, two, one."

The door opened. Bright flashes of photon fire tore through the center, the airlock, and into the door behind them. Throttle and Finn returned fire as they hid behind the door opening. They swapped gunfire for several seconds before Finn leapt through the doorway and fired. The barrage stopped, and Throttle rushed through the opening and flattened against the wall opposite from Finn. Down the hallway lay the pirate who'd pinned them down. She wasn't moving, and from the charred holes in her body, she wouldn't be moving again.

She and Finn scanned the hallway but didn't move forward yet. When no one else jumped out, Finn motioned for the rest to join them.

Behind them, Jack and Munny assisted Chief as the trio hugged the wall behind Throttle. Detroit and Hank lined up behind Finn in a standard GP insertion maneuver. Another pirate jumped out from around a turn a long way down the hallway and threw something at them. As the round ball rolled toward them, Finn yelled, "Grenade!"

Everyone dove to the floor. The grenade went off about midway down the hallway. The sound of the boom disoriented Throttle, and the floor rumbled. Smoke filled the air and she struggled to find her feet.

"Is anyone hurt?" Chief asked as he was helped to his feet.

No one complained.

"Hurry. We need to get to cover fast. We might not get so lucky next time," Finn said, and he took the first steps forward.

Throttle kept pace until they all stopped just before the first doorway on their right—the conference room Chief had mentioned earlier. The door was wide open, which gave Throttle a bad feeling. What she wouldn't give for a grenade of her own to lob into that room right about now.

Instead, Finn pulled out what looked to be a pair of gloves from his pack and held the edge out into the doorway. Photon rifle fire burst out from the room. Finn backed up and held up a single finger for how many shooters he estimated were in the room.

They couldn't get past the room without getting shot, and they were at constant risk in an open hallway, which meant that they had to take out the shooter—or shooters—in that room sooner rather than later. Unfortunately, no one in the group had a shock grenade on them.

Chief spoke quietly. "That panel on the other side of the doorway... Run a test on the lights. Maximum brightness."

"I'll do it," Throttle said, knowing her blades gave her an edge in jumping.

"I'll lay down cover fire," Finn said.

He eyed her until she nodded. He swung his rifle around and fired nonstop into the room.

Throttle sprang forward. She didn't turn to look inside the room, focusing only on the door panel to the left of the doorway. Shots came at her, and she swore she heard a *zap* as a shot nicked one of her blades, but it didn't slow her down. In a single leap she was past the doorway and skidding to a stop at the panel. She'd lived on Free Station long enough to know the menu options forward and backward. She swiped to the administrative menu and found where she could run the power tests. In a rush, she selected to run all the tests.

She readied her rifle, standing opposite Finn on the other side of the doorway.

"You take high. I'll take low," Finn said, knowing Throttle had no knees to go down on.

As soon as she heard the sound test begin, the pair swung around and started firing.

Their shots narrowed in on a shooter using an overturned conference table as a shielded firing position.

The pirate yelled out, "Stop! Don't shoot."

"Hands in the air, and come up on your feet slowly," Throttle commanded.

A man stood. He was more of a boy, really, not looking to be twenty years old yet.

"Are you alone?" Throttle asked.

"Yeah! Is just me here alone," he answered.

"If you're lying, I'll shoot you," Finn added.

"I ain't lying! I swear it's just me." The boy held his arms up higher in the air.

Throttle covered Finn as he stood and walked into the room. He grabbed the table and knocked it over so that it sat upside down, removing the barrier. The pirate cowered yet managed to keep his arms in the air.

"Clear," Finn called out, and the rest of their group entered.

Chief nodded to Detroit. "Tie him up."

Chief stood before their prisoner as Detroit put restraints on the boy and relieved him of two knives. "Is East still in the command center?"

"Don't know. I was told to shoot anybody who tried to walk in front of me."

"How many are in the command center?" Chief asked.

The boy shrugged. "Don't know. Four maybe?"

Chief frowned and turned from the pirate. "He's just a peon. He doesn't know anything. Leave him."

Detroit wagged a finger at their prisoner. "You try to break free and run, you're a dead man. You stay here all nice and quiet like, you live. You understand?"

The boy nodded furiously.

"Can you believe that pirate used a flak grenade back there?" Detroit asked after he turned away from the pirate as if he wasn't even there. "Damned fool could've breached the hull if it'd gone off near an outer wall."

"There's a reason pirates are known for their violent streaks rather than for their intelligence," Chief said as he headed toward the doorway. "We'll hit the command center hard and fast. Chances are, the door will be locked. I just need access to the panel and can unlock it. Fortunately for us, East doesn't have someone with full administrative access to override my security. There's nowhere she can hide from me on Free Station."

Throttle and Finn continued in the lead position, and they scanned the hallway before reentering it. They knew there could still be a pirate down at the end of the hallway, ready to lob a second grenade. But they were also within ten feet of the command center.

Throttle motioned them forward as she stepped out into the hallway, keeping her rifle aimed in the direction from where the grenade had come from. At the slightest hint of movement, she would unleash a barrage of photon shots at the corner.

No grenades came tumbling at them, and she began to think a pirate had thrown one to buy himself time to escape. Not a single pirate would be escaping if the marshals had anything to say about that.

They reached the command center with no one shooting at them. Jack and Munny assisted Chief to the panel, where he used his special codes to gain access. The door opened with a swoosh, and the six marshals poured in. Shouts and gunfire erupted from the two pirates inside as they rushed to get behind three battered Peacekeepers. She noticed one specialist lying dead on the floor, who looked like he'd been beaten to death. Her stomach dropped, not at the sight of the dead person but at not seeing East anywhere in the room.

"Don't shoot!" one of the specialists cried out.

"You shoot, they die," one of the pirates said.

Chief strolled into the room, standing next to Hank in the face-off between marshals and pirates. "Put down your weapons, Jaders, and we'll let you live."

"I don't think so," the same pirate said. "I think that you'll put down your weapons and let us walk out of here and down to the docking bay, or else your Peacekeepers here will die."

"Well, then that puts us at an impasse because I will not let you take my people and use them as bargaining chips," Chief said, then changed his approach. "Tell me where Anna East is."

"She ain't here," the other pirate said.

"Where'd she go?" Chief asked.

"I said she ain't here," the second pirate repeated.

"We'll tell you where she went if you let us go," the first pirate said.

"I can't do that," Chief said. "But I'll let you live if you speak the truth."

"She went down to the docking bay, with Skully Pete's crew," the second pirate said in a rush.

Throttle's muscles tensed as she fought the urge to chase down the crime boss.

The first pirate cursed at his partner. "Idiot."

Chief eyed them. "You're lying. My people have taken or are in the process of taking control of all the stairways and elevators to the docking bay."

"We'll tell you if you let us go," the first pirate said. "And we'll take your people with us until we're safe. Then we'll let them go."

Chief sighed. "You have no chance of escape without my help."

"We do, too," the second pirate said, then shut up under his partner's glare. Then he lifted his chin and spoke again. "We tell you, and you'll let us go."

"Yes," Chief said.

Throttle frowned because she hoped Chief was lying. None of these pirates deserved to get away.

"I told you before, East left with Skully Pete's crew 'cause they got their cables cut on their ship. They's spacewalking down a couple levels to the docking bay. Then they's taking off and coming to pick us up."

"We told you the truth," the first pirate said. "Now, we're going to take these three prisoners here with us until we board the *Bendix*. Then we'll release them. You have my word."

Throttle heard movement and saw Punch, followed by Sylvian, enter the room. Relief flooded her at seeing her friend alive, though both were bloodied and looked like they'd been through a battle.

Punch looked at the row of marshals and looked at the two pirates using specialists as their shields. Then he strolled over toward the pirates, lifted his pistol, and shot the first pirate in the head. Chief shouted. The second pirate's eyes went wide the instant before Punch shot him between the eyes.

"Never trust the word of a pirate," Punch said as he turned around to face Chief. "You looked like you could use a little help."

"Peacekeepers do not execute prisoners, Marshal Durand," Chief said, his voice deeper and angrier than Throttle had ever heard.

"Those prisoners were going to kill our people. You know it, and I know it," Punch said and motioned to the three specialists who'd stepped away from the bodies and were leaning into each other.

"We'll discuss this later." Rather than walking toward Punch, Chief walked the other way and over to his chair, took a seat, and began working on the screen before him, paying attention to no one in the room. The specialists noticed and went to assist him at their own workstations like they were used to working alongside Chief.

Throttle turned her focus to Sylvian. Finn had run over to embrace his wife, and it was then Throttle noticed that Sylvian was cradling her arm, which was covered in blood. "What happened?" she asked as she walked over to the pair.

Sylvian had leaned into Finn and seemed to be using his strength to bolster hers. "We saw what was happening from the server room and came up this way to lend a hand. We ran into a bit of trouble on the way up."

Throttle nodded to her arm. "Were you shot?"

Sylvian looked down. "Oh, this? I slipped and fell in a puddle of blood. That's where all this came from. It's not even mine. I wasn't watching where I was running."

Finn glared at Punch, who seemed to be watching him with humor. Embracing Sylvian was the only reason Throttle could sense that was keeping Finn from tackling the errant marshal. "I'm going to kill him," Finn muttered under his breath.

"He protected me," Sylvian said. "He kept me behind him the entire time." She shot a hard look at Punch. "Even though I'm quite capable of taking care of myself."

"I know you are," Finn said. "It doesn't mean I wasn't still worried. When I couldn't get a hold of you on your comm-chip…"

"Oh, I forgot to unmute it." She tapped the chip and smiled. "I'm fine, and I don't want you to kill Punch. Not on my account."

Finn scowled.

Chief spun around in his chair to face the marshals. "The lockdown has been deactivated. But we're still blind with no video feeds and no Atlas."

A specialist with a broken nose spoke. "Chief, East blew the Atlas control center. We aren't going to be able to bring Atlas back up. But we should be able to get video feeds up and going. I just need a couple of minutes."

"Thank you, Meghan."

"Chief," Sylvian began, "we were watching the feeds from the Atlas server room after we brought it back online. We saw them place the explosives, but we couldn't get up here in time to stop them. Sorry."

"Nothing to apologize for, Specialist Salazar-Martin," Chief said. "We can operate without Atlas, though it'll be more difficult without being able to communicate with our teams. Our people are spread out, fighting, and I can't see who needs help."

"Get the feeds up, and we'll serve as runners," Detroit said. "We can see which areas are safe, and we'll move teams into the areas that still need help."

"You're assuming we've beaten back the pirates in any areas," Munny said.

"Of course we have. We're marshals, you putz," Detroit countered.

"Enough," Chief said. "We still have much work to do."

"The feeds are coming up now," the specialist said.

"Good. Thank you once again, Meghan."

"Do you see East on any of them?" Throttle asked as she walked over to look at the screens as well. On nearly every screen, Peace-keepers fought against pirates. There was a breach on level seven that had left an entire hallway empty. In some cases, the marshals had won or were clearly winning. In other instances, pirates were running free, with dead Peacekeepers on the floor behind them. There was no clear victor yet.

"I see my people fighting and needing support." Chief looked at the feeds while he spoke. "I need to coordinate with my people on Free Station. East isn't here, which means we have to chase her down."

Throttle spoke. "I'll go after East from outside. If she makes it onto the *Bendix*, the *Javelin* is the only thing standing between her and escape."

He nodded. "Good. I need everyone else here. I know I'm no good out there in my current condition. I'll stay here and coordinate move-ment by using you all as runners, except for you, Sylvian. You're injured and will stay here."

Throttle nodded to her two crew members and started to head out of the room. "I'll see you soon."

"We're receiving an incoming ping, Chief," a specialist said. "It's encoded with the Red Dynasty credentials."

"Broadcast an official Peacekeeper greeting," Chief said. "Hold up, Throttle."

She turned back around. On one of the external video feeds, she saw a massive ship approach the station. It was easily three times as large as the *Wu Zetian,* but it carried a full complement of weapons.

"That looks more like a warship than a reclamation ship," she said.

"I'd forgotten about them," Sylvian said.

"If you'd come face-to-face with them before, you would not find them easy to forget," Chief said.

A specialist spoke. "The Red ship received our greeting, and they responded with the following: We have arrived as part of a sanctioned operation for the Red Dynasty. We have come to reclaim the property of the Red Dynasty and to see evidence of justice against those respon-sible for its damage. Respond with proof of full compliance, and we may provide assistance with your current needs.

"How do you want to respond?" the specialist asked.

"Don't respond yet," Chief said as he scoured the screens before him. "As long as I can't prove compliance, we're in more danger from them than we are from the Jaders. Damn it, where is East?"

A response came a minute later, and the specialist translated the message. "They said: If you have failed to meet all obligations under our agreement, you are in breach of contract. Not fulfilling signed contracts is a breach of the peace treaty. Respond with proof of full compliance."

Chief sighed. "Tell them that the *Wu Zetian* is ready to be transferred to them. And that we have the ship responsible in our docking bay and that we're in progress of—wait." He pushed to his feet and focused on a screen.

Throttle saw it, too. The *Bendix* was pulling out of the docking bay. She'd never get to the *Javelin* in time.

Chief retook his seat. "Tell them the *Wu Zetian* is ready to be transferred to them, and that the ship and crew that attacked their seed ship has just pulled out of the docking bay. Tell them we left the honor of punishment to them."

"Sent, Chief," the specialist said.

"Chief, I should get to the *Javelin* in case they let East get away," Throttle said.

"They won't," he said. "I just hope they don't destroy us in the process." He glanced around the room. "You'd better all grab on to something."

CHAPTER THIRTY-THREE

ANNA EAST GRABBED ONTO YANK AS SHE STOOD ON THE BRIDGE OF the *Bendix*. The pirate ship had cleared the docking bay and was moving at full sub-speed when their viewscreen was filled by a gargantuan of a vessel.

"What is that?" she asked, fear snagging the air in her throat.

Yank didn't move, but the arm she held had become as hard as iron. "It's the Reds."

Her jaw slackened even more as she realized the force they faced. She stepped away and shoved him. "Do something, you idiot. Fly around them. Get us out of here!"

He pointed. "It's too late."

She turned back to the viewscreen. Massive photon cannons protruded from open panels in the hull of the Red ship.

She took a step forward and clutched the fabric over her chest. "No."

Bright flashes of light were the last things Anna East ever saw.

CHAPTER THIRTY-FOUR

THE CHINESE SHIP HAD FIRED NOT ONE, BUT THREE PHOTON CANNONS. A flash of light as bright as a star blinded the black sky as it shot toward the small pirate ship. All three were direct hits. The *Bendix* exploded. The batteries of all the stolen weaponry in its cargo bay blew up with it, creating a starburst of what promised to be a brilliant light show, only to be all too quickly snuffed out by the vacuum of space.

Throttle stood and stared. East was dead. Throttle had long envisioned how she'd kill the person who'd ordered the deaths of half of her crew. She'd never envisioned seeing East impersonally killed from a distance. It was…anticlimactic.

The entire room was silent until a specialist spoke. "They've responded with the following: We consider the terms of the contract fulfilled. Your obligation is complete. We will depart once we have reclaimed our property."

Chief let out a breath. "Tell them that they are our guests and welcome to stay as long as they desire while they collect their property." He stared at the screens for a moment before turning to the third specialist. "Wael, broadcast me through the emergency system."

After a couple of seconds, the specialist turned back to him. "It's ready, Chief."

Chief nodded and pressed something on his screen. "Attention, everyone on Free Station. This is Chief Roux in the command center. We have reclaimed Free Station, and Anna East is dead. All Jaders who came here under Anna East's employment are ordered to surrender immediately to the nearest Peacekeeper. Surrender now and you will live. Continue fighting and you will die. Try to escape, and your ship will be blown out of the sky. The Chinese are outside now and will see to that."

"Chief!" a specialist said. "Look. Peacekeeper ships are arriving. Most look to be coming in from Hiraeth."

"That's because they're the nearest," Chief said. "More will come now that Atlas doesn't have their ships locked down."

Punch sneered. "You're welcome."

"For what?" Hank asked.

"For bringing Atlas back online, of course," Punch answered.

Detroit glared. "You nearly got us all killed. East set off a timer to blow Free Station when you did that."

"Well, good thing it didn't blow, then," Punch answered.

"We still have work to do." Chief turned to everyone in the room. "There are still people fighting who need our help."

"That 'surrender or die' offer didn't work before either," Punch said.

"That was before our friends showed up," Chief said.

Punch's brow lifted. "I wouldn't call the Red Dynasty friends unless you believe in that 'enemy of my enemy' crap."

"I call them friends in the same way I call you a friend," Chief said.

Punch quieted; then his gaze narrowed on one of the screens. He walked closer.

Throttle's gaze narrowed on the figure who was standing in the docking bay, busily working at the dock controls of the ship she'd carried back in the *Javelin*'s cargo hold. "Is that Pete Antonov?"

Punch straightened, spun around, and eyed Chief. "I'll be back."

CHAPTER THIRTY-FIVE

Punch strode through the docking bay. There were fewer bodies than he'd expected, but there were dozens down from each side. As he walked, he noticed a heavily armed pirate with a blaster shot through his gut. Punch knew from experience that those were the most painful shots to have.

He knelt by the pirate. The Jader was older than most, looking to be near seventy, which could explain why he carried two strings of grenades—he used explosives to make up for physical weakness. Punch reached out and tugged a grenade off the body. The pirate groaned. In a flash of movement, Punch pulled out his knife and stuck it into the man's neck. Blood poured from the man's jugular, and he made a choking sound. Punch wiped his blade on the pirate's dirty jacket and sheathed the blade. The choking stopped, and the pirate's mouth and lifeless eyes remained open.

Punch stood, tossed the grenade lightly, caught it in his palm, and continued walking forward. He heard moaning as he walked through the aftermath of the battle. He ignored the sound and continued, focused on his objective.

He found what he was looking for midway through the docking bay.

Marshal Pete Antonov, also known as Skully Pete, was hunched over a dock-control panel, frantically swiping through screens. Punch crept slowly forward, careful not to make a sound. Somehow, as though he had a sixth sense, Pete looked over his shoulder. They made eye contact for the briefest instant. Punch fired as both men spun out of each other's way. Pete pulled a pistol and was firing back before he hit the floor.

Punch used a box of hardware as cover. As he knelt behind it, he saw an open section in the wall—the panel that'd been cut now stood propped against the wall. The interior of the wall revealed vertical rows of cables, several of which had been tapped into from what looked like a hacker's kit. He realized it was likely the hardline Pete had used to attach to Atlas. He chuckled, realizing how easily he could've taken down the hardline from that spot if he'd only waited. But he'd never been known for his patience, and that character flaw had seen him nearly killed on more than one occasion.

He peeked around the edge of the hardware and was nearly taken out by a blaster shot.

"That you, Durand?" Pete asked.

Punch grinned, knowing he'd made a clean hit with his first shot. "Sure am. How's the leg?"

"I thought you'd be a better shot. You're going to regret that you didn't kill me when you had the chance."

"Nah. I was aiming for your leg," Punch said.

The pirate said nothing.

"Let me guess. Still trying to get that restraining cable off your piece-of-shit ship?" Punch asked.

Pete still said nothing.

"Thought so." He heard movement and swung out to see Pete rushing him with a heavy limp. Punch rolled and fired the instant he came to his knee. The pirate raised his pistol and shot a spray of blasts. The combination of shooting while both running and injured made Pete's shots fly high and wide.

Punch's shot didn't miss. The blast hit the pirate in the calf of his other leg, and Pete went down. Punch came to his feet. Pete pulled up his pistol to fire again, but his opponent shot first and burned a hole through the pirate's hand. Pete, unable to keep a grip, dropped his weapon.

Punch strolled toward him. Pete reached for another pistol with his uninjured hand, and Punch shot a hole through that palm as well.

The pirate, grimacing, tried to crawl to cover. Punch shot him in the ass. The pirate cried out but kept trying to crawl to safety. Punch cocked his head as he considered his options and fired into Pete's shoulder. The pirate collapsed and tried to pull himself back up, but Punch had reached him and kicked him back down.

Punch cast an ominous shadow over the pirate. "You were none too kind to me. I owe you some payback."

"I've got credits," Pete gritted out. "More than you could ever use in a lifetime."

"More than you'll use in your lifetime, I'd wager," Punch corrected and shot Pete in his other shoulder.

Pete cried out in pain. "What do you want? Anything, you name it. I can make sure you get it."

Punch chuckled with no hint of humor. "You can't help me with what I want."

He was about to take another shot when Pete collapsed fully on the floor. Some of the pain left his expression as the pirate seemed to surrender to his fate.

A calm came over Punch. Pete had nearly broken him; Punch had been hell-bent on fully breaking Pete, and he'd succeeded. He looked down at the pirate. "You should've made sure I was dead. I won't make the same mistake."

Punch turned and left the pirate lying on the ground. Once he made it about ten feet away, he pulled the pin on the grenade and rolled it across the floor to where it bumped into Pete. Punch made it behind the hardware when the blast went off, followed by a horrible wind.

He grabbed onto the hardline cable still connected to the cable in the wall. "Shit," he muttered as he held on to keep from sliding toward the hull breach he'd created.

The panel that'd been propped against the wall flew, nearly decapitating him as it sliced through the air. It hit the hole with a shudder, though it blocked nearly the entire hole. But it wasn't going to hold. The panel shook as though shivering from the frozen space outside.

Near the panel, he saw an emergency repair canister. He grabbed the red tube before letting go of the hardline. He scraped across the floor as the pressure continued to try to suck him out of the station. As he was pulled across the floor, he grabbed the handle on the canister.

The distance between him and the hole was closing fast. Pete's body—whatever was left of it from the blast—was gone, and Punch was about to follow the pirate into the abyss.

He squeezed the canister's handle. A thick orange foam shot out. The foam expanded rapidly, forming a seal between the breach and the wall panel covering much of it. When no more wind pulled at him, he ran over and grabbed two more canisters and thoroughly covered the entire breach and wall panel.

Finished, he exhaled, and his breath seemed to exhale much of his remaining energy. He dropped the canisters and stood limply staring at the foam-filled breach.

He'd really thought that Free Station's docking bay walls would've been reinforced to handle a ship bumping into its walls. Once he caught his breath, he dusted himself off and strode away from the breach. He was going to make a stern recommendation to Chief about the docking bay's walls.

As he walked back through the docking bay from the direction he'd come, he still heard the moaning. He paused this time to see a young specialist propped against a wall. The man was holding a blaster wound in his hip.

Punch strode over to the Peacekeeper and bent down to pull the man up and over his shoulders. "Hang in there, buddy. I've got you."

CHAPTER THIRTY-SIX

THROTTLE STOOD IN FREE STATION'S DOCKING BAY AND LOOKED OUT the window to watch the *Javelin* undergo repairs. When the Chinese reclamation ship destroyed the *Bendix,* debris had shot out in all directions. Fortunately, the intensity of the blast had turned most of the debris into objects no bigger than a grain of sand, but there were a few larger pieces that wreaked havoc on anything they hit. The *Javelin* had only been pelted by the grain-sized debris, causing small dents across the hull. Most of the damage was cosmetic, which Throttle didn't worry about, but some caused problems with the ship's sensors and movable parts.

"It's still the prettiest ship here, even with the new dings," Sylvian said.

"Yes, it sure is," Throttle answered. She took in a breath and turned to her crew. Finn and Sylvian stood to her left. The specialist wore a brace on her broken arm. Otherwise, the pair looked in perfect health. Beyond them, Eddy wore a permanent pout. He'd spoken only to Sylvian since returning to the crew, blaming Throttle and Finn for abandoning him on the station when they took the *Javelin* up to level eight.

She glanced at a clock on the wall. "It's time. We should head up."

The group walked through the docking bay that looked every bit the aftermath of a battle scene. It was a flurry of activity, with Peacekeepers and contractors working on everything from repairing a patched hull breach to scrubbing blood off the floors.

They entered the elevator, and Throttle tapped the icon with a number eight. The elevator was smooth—she could never tell when it was moving or not, likely because the electromagnetic field was kept so much lower in all of the vertical passageways. A few seconds passed in silence before the door opened on level eight.

Throttle led the way through the hallway that was bustling with as much activity as had been in the docking bay. On this level, she saw people only in Peacekeeper uniforms. It seemed there were policies against allowing independent contractors on the highest two levels.

She led them to a wing she'd never been down before, and she had to follow the signs on the wall to locate Officer Medical Room Three. The door was open, so she walked straight in. Med bay was on level five, but there were several small private medical rooms on level eight for the officers.

Chief Roux lay semi-upright in a bed in the center of the room. A medical specialist was checking his vitals while one of the specialists from the command center—the one named Meghan—sat at his side, focused on a tablet.

Throttle and her team waited as the medical specialist finished taking Chief's vitals. Beyond them was a window, through which she could see the Chinese reclamation ship slowly pulling the *Wu Zetian* into its massive maw, preparing for a return trip to Sol.

"Everything's looking good for an on-track recovery, Chief. I'll stop back in one hour," the medical specialist said and then walked around Throttle's team on his way out of the room.

"Hello, Chief," Throttle said as she walked deeper into the room. "You wanted to see us?"

Chief motioned them closer. "Thanks for coming. I've wanted to connect with everyone who was on Free Station this week. Meghan here has been helping by scheduling everyone into ten-minute slots, which isn't nearly enough time, but it's the only way with all the work underway."

He looked across the four faces. "Each of you played a crucial role in saving the lives of everyone here on Free Station. The Galactic Peacekeepers—and I—thank you. For your bravery, I have a Galactic

Peacekeeper Distinguished Service commendation for each of you. I apologize for not standing and for not having a ceremony, but truth be told, I've never been one for ceremonies—not when we have plenty of other things to be doing."

Meghan stood and handed a ribbon to each of them as Chief continued speaking. "Marshal Reyne and Marshal Martin, thank you for leading the way to reclaiming Free Station. Your courage is exemplary. Specialist Martin, thank you for taking Atlas out of the hands of criminals and thus enabling us to launch a counterattack without our every move being watched. Specialist Edwards, thank you for your courage and fearlessness in venturing into an unknown situation alone and deactivating the explosives. You saved all of our lives."

Eddy stood proud but held up a hand. "Thank you, Chief, but I'm not a specialist. I haven't passed my exams yet."

Chief smiled. "From what I hear, you were outnumbered two to one, and you shot and killed both pirates. I'd say that more than qualifies for a passing score on your firearms exam. Welcome to the Peacekeepers, Specialist Edwards."

Meghan handed Eddy the Peacekeeper patch.

Eddy looked at it, then looked at the patch Sylvian wore, and frowned. "Why is she a specialist two, and I'm only a specialist one?"

Chief smirked. "I saw *how* you took out those two pirates. I think a specialist level one is a good fit for you at this time."

Eddy took the patch and mumbled a thank you as he placed it on his shoulder, careful to make sure it was positioned perfectly.

"Hey, Chief," Punch said as he walked into the room. When he saw the other people in the room, he held up a hand. "I'll just stop back in a bit."

Finn sneered, and Sylvian placed a hand on his forearm. Punch noticed and stared back at the other marshal.

"No. Stay. I'm just running a little behind, and it saves me from having to repeat myself," Chief said to Punch before looking across all the faces in the room. "We have learned much from the pirates attacking Free Station. We learned that Atlas can be too easily hijacked and that our security protocols on this station are lax. We Peacekeepers were overly confident. Our hubris is the reason for the losses we've suffered. We believed no one would go against us because we are the de facto protection force in this system. We've been proven wrong, tragically so. Anna East's plan was simple and flawed, yet she very nearly succeeded. It was only by chance that Free Station still stands.

"East came here to manipulate data within Atlas, but they had to adjust their plans when they found a crucial piece of technology missing—a naive Bayse router. They had to then make manual updates, which will be easy for us to locate and back out, but it will take time. I don't know where that router is or how they lost it, but we can only hope it does not turn up on the black market and end up in the wrong hands."

Eddy began, "It won't because—"

Throttle interrupted. "Pete's cargo hold was damaged when we pulled it into our cargo hold. Several crates were lost, and I'd bet that router was one of them." She noticed Punch eying her like he saw through her, and she tried to ignore him.

"We can only hope. However, I will place the router on the stolen goods list so that we can keep an eye out for it," Chief said; then his lips thinned. "During the attack, we learned that our technology and security have a great many holes, including ones that our own staff could use. We've begun to patch our systems." He looked at Punch. "The Bones files are no longer viable. While using those files helped in our fight against the pirates, they also go against everything the Peace-keepers stand for. As of now, Marshal Durand, you've been demoted from a senior-level marshal to an intermediate level. Your pay and benefits will immediately reflect the change. You're fortunate that I'm only demoting you. If I'd discovered you had those files at any other time, you would've been fired. I advise that you don't do anything foolish like that again."

"I won't, Chief," Punch said with a stoic expression.

Sylvian turned to eye the marshal, and they seemed to share a secret in that gaze. Throttle made a mental note to ask her friend about it when they were back on board the *Javelin*.

"Also, Punch, as of now, you are not allowed to take on any solo missions. You will only work with other marshals until I know I can trust you."

Punch's gaze narrowed. "You can trust me, Chief."

"No, I can't. I used to trust you, but after you pulled that Bones stunt, I can't trust you."

Punch scowled and looked away.

"And that brings me to why I had these two meetings overlap," Chief continued.

Throttle stiffened as she guessed what he was about to say.

"I have a simple yet urgent mission. A young girl, Sophia Mercier, was presumably kidnapped by Pete Antonov."

"Mercier? Any relation to Cat Mercier?" Punch asked.

Chief nodded. "Sophia is her niece and was Antonov's leverage against Cat. Cat believed her niece was still alive and being held by Jaders. Since Punch has worked with Sylvian before, I feel comfortable in having the five of you work as a Peacekeeper team."

"Hell no," Finn gritted out. "He's a loose cannon. He's reckless and almost got Sylvian—and all of us killed."

"And that's why he needs to be a part of a full team, to help him remember that the Peacekeepers are a unified force."

"Chief, put me on administrative leave. Not on a team," Punch offered.

"No. In fact, I've already placed a restraining cable on the *High Spirit*."

Throttle's heart was beating harder. "Chief, my team has worked together for years. Adding a new member—especially Punch—will hurt our dynamics."

"I'm not that hard to get along with," Punch inserted.

"Yeah, you are," Throttle said before adding, "Besides, the *Javelin* is fully crewed. We don't need another marshal on board."

"I've been on the *Javelin*, and I saw at least one empty cabin," Chief said.

"But it's not Peacekeeper property. It's my ship, and I'm the captain. I don't want him on my crew," Throttle countered.

"As long as you're using it for GP business, it is used following GP procedures," Chief said. "And those procedures state that the director can add team members to any crew if it benefits the GP's directive. You used the Bones file, and I could fire you for that. Instead, I'm putting all of you together."

Throttle gritted her teeth and forced out the words, "Yes, Chief."

"I expect you to head out immediately. If Sophia is still alive, she'll likely be sold if she hasn't been already. Since Atlas is still down, Meghan has copied all the information on Sophia and Pete Antonov's connections onto a memory card for you. By the time you get back, we should have new Atlas chips for each of you and for your ship."

"We'd prefer to go without if that's an option," Throttle said.

"That's not an option. Atlas is the GP system of record. Being connected is mandatory for all Peacekeepers and their ships," Chief said.

Throttle sighed. "Will that be all?"

Chief nodded. "You can head out as soon as the *Javelin* is ready and all crew are on board."

"If you're done beating on me, I need to move my things from the *High Spirit* to the *Javelin*," Punch said.

"You can go," Chief said.

"See you on board," Finn practically growled at Punch.

Punch sneered. "Can't wait," he said and left the room.

"We'll report in once we find Sophia, Chief," Throttle said and turned away.

"One more thing," Chief said.

She sighed and turned back to face him. With Chief, there was always one more thing. "Yes?"

"We've arrested forty-six pirates who were involved with the invasion. One of those pirates came from the Trappist system."

Throttle stood straighter.

"The ghost?" Sylvian uttered lightly.

Throttle's lips curled into a snarl. "Hinze."

Chief nodded. "He will stand trial, just like all the others, but I thought you should know."

Throttle glanced across the faces of her crew and saw they all bore the same venomous expression.

"Thanks," Throttle said.

None of the four spoke as they made their way to the brig. Throttle's mind raced with memories of Finn and Sylvian's wedding and the fire that followed. Images of human shapes burning within the fire and echoes of their screams were still as crisp and searing as the day it'd happened. The same with the face of the Trappist who'd planted the bomb.

The bomb had been intended for Throttle and her entire crew. It'd been purely by chance that she'd stepped away to talk with Aubree. Finn and Sylvian had left to consummate their vows, and Eddy had returned to the *Javelin*. Their luck had saved them that day. They'd all lost dear friends in that fire, and they all wanted vengeance. That was likely why every single one of them strode with purpose to the station's jail on level seven.

They entered the jail wing to find it overcrowded, smelly, and noisy. Each cell usually held one inmate. Right now, four pirates were crammed into each cell. Three times the usual number of marshals stood on duty. Throttle took the lead down the hallway. Finn walked alongside Sylvian, which Throttle knew he did out of his need to always protect her even though it drove her crazy. Eddy lingered behind, his anger giving way to trepidation when they came into proximity of the pirates.

Throttle slowed as they walked past each cell, searching for the face she'd never forget. Some pirates sneered and threw out obscenities. Others were quiet, having seemingly accepted their fate. The young pirate they'd caught on level eight sat on a cot, looking younger and more lost than ever. Throttle wondered how easily she could've been that kid if she'd been found by someone other than the man who'd become her adoptive father.

She continued forward, then paused. A familiar sensation had prickled her skin, a sensation she remembered feeling often back on the *Gabriela*, the colonization ship she'd captained to the Ross system. It was the feeling of being watched. Everyone on the crew had experienced the same feeling, enough so that they'd jokingly blamed it on a ghost. It was only after they'd reached the Ross system that they'd learned they'd had a stowaway watching them the entire time. A radical-turned-murderer named Al Hinze.

Throttle's crew hadn't been Hinze's first victims.

She turned back to the cell she'd just passed. Her gaze narrowed on the pirate skulking in the back corner. Even in the well-lit cell, he seemed to blend into his surroundings. His head was lowered, but she could tell he was watching her.

He hadn't changed. He was still a mess of dirty clothes and wild, greasy hair.

She stepped closer. "Hello, Hinze."

His head slowly rose. He bore that same sneer that he always seemed to wear. "Come to gloat?"

"No," she said.

Finn walked up to the cell bars. The other three pirates in the cell stepped back. "If you weren't in there, I'd take you apart one piece at a time," the marshal said.

"Still holding a grudge for that wedding gift I gave you?" Hinze asked.

"You're a bastard," Sylvian spat out. "You deserve to die for what you've done."

Hinze shrugged. "You mean for killing off a few guys who helped destroy the first ship I crewed on? They deserved to die. *You* all deserve to die."

"I hate you. You killed my best friend," Eddy said and rushed away, leaving the jail.

Hinze chuckled. "That engineer was always a little off."

"You don't get to act like you know us," Throttle said. "You slink around like a snake for fifteen years, spying on us, but that doesn't mean you know us."

Hinze took several steps closer. "I know each of you better than you know yourselves." He pointed at Sylvian. "I saw you cry every night you were awake because you hate to be alone so much." He pointed at Finn. "I saw you rummage through the passengers' bags because you thought everyone was going to figure out that you were a dromadier. I figured you out right away. I knew you were one of those cocksuckers as soon as I saw you." He turned to Throttle. "And you, I watched you most of all. I saw you fighting your insecurities. All that running and practice and reading you did just to try to make yourself good enough. Well, you're not good enough. You never were, and you never will be. You let the *Gabriela* get taken from you without even putting up a fight. You deserved losing your people, and you all should've died because you're no good to anyone."

Throttle watched Hinze for a moment. "You're so full of piss and vinegar now. You lash out at people, hoping to hurt them because you're hurting. Your insides are all rotted out from things you've done or seen or thought. I don't know which, and I don't care. You're just a shell of a human who can only feel something when you hurt others. But you can't get your fix anymore. Now you're just a rat in a cage, left with only yourself to watch in the mirror."

Hinze scowled. "I'll get out of here, and when I do, I'm going to kill you. All of you."

"I hope you do get out of there," Throttle said. "Because I very much look forward to not having these bars between us."

She didn't say anything else. She left the unvoiced threat in the air. She glanced at Finn and Sylvian, and the three of them left the ghost where he couldn't hurt anyone else.

CHAPTER THIRTY-SEVEN

"THROTTLE, MARSHAL DURAND IS TRYING TO OPEN THE AIRLOCK," Rusty said.

Throttle's eye twitched while she considered her options. She didn't trust Punch, but he was a part of her crew. She grumbled to herself before replying to Rusty, "Punch is going to be a part of the crew for a time. Give him enough access to function, but I don't want him to have access to change any of your systems. Do you know what I mean, Rusty?"

"I think I do. I've granted him crew access minus administrative privileges."

Sylvian turned to Throttle. "That's probably a good idea."

Throttle heard the airlock open and bootsteps coming toward the bridge. She ran the final preflight check and submitted the flight plan just before Punch stepped onto the bridge.

"Which bunk is mine?" he asked without any sort of greeting.

"There are two unused cabins, but Finn's converted one into a training room. You'll see which one you can take," Throttle answered and then turned her seat to face him. He carried one duffel bag, though two other large bags sat on the floor behind him. "Welcome to the crew."

"It's just temporary," he said. "Chief does this. I screw up, he slaps my hand, and then everything goes back to normal. You won't have me in your hair too long."

She eyed him. "Good, because I'm not convinced you can play well with others, and the only way a crew can function is if everyone works together as a team."

He smirked. "I'll try to play well, or at least fake it."

"I hope you can fake it well, because you're on *my* crew. I'm the captain of the *Javelin,* and as long as you're flying on my ship, you're serving on my crew. You'll do what I say, or else we're going to have problems. When we're off the ship, we're both marshals out there, but on here, you're a member of my crew. Got it?"

He watched her for a moment. "I'll defer to you, Captain."

She nodded toward the hallway. "Find your bunk and get settled in. We're launching in ten minutes."

"Aye, aye, Captain," he said and strode off the bridge.

"If he's a part of the crew, does that make him a Black Sheep, too?" Sylvian asked.

"No," she replied. "It takes more than just bunking with us to earn that title."

Sylvian smiled, clearly liking that response.

Throttle could hear two men's voices down the hallway. The volume rose in an argument.

"It sounds like Finn and Punch just ran into each other," she said.

Sylvian sighed. "I hope this is a really short mission, and Punch can return to his own ship. Otherwise, I don't think those two will survive being on the same ship together."

Throttle tapped the ship's intercom. "Listen up, everyone, we're heading out in nine minutes. Wrap up whatever you're doing and prepare for launch. Eddy, report status on the cargo hold and mechanicals."

When there was no response, Throttle rolled her eyes and looked to Sylvian.

Sylvian spoke through the intercom. "Eddy, status from the back?"

"Ready to go back here," Eddy replied a second later.

"I hope he gets over his grudge quickly because he's being a real pain in the ass," Sylvian said.

"I would've thought him earning his specialist patch would've cheered him up," Throttle said.

"I know," Sylvian said.

"I have a question," Rusty asked. "Why do people receive badges and labels, but ship computers receive no acknowledgment?"

"What do you mean?" Throttle asked.

"Sylvian is a software specialist, but I manage software processes far more complex than those any human performs."

"It's just the way things are," Throttle said. "Send through the dock launch request."

"Sending request," Rusty said.

Throttle cocked her head as she remembered the conversations that had taken place in Chief's medical room earlier. "Hey, Sylvian. I want to ask you something."

"What's that?"

"Back when Chief was scolding Punch, you gave him a look. I know that look. You know something, something that Punch didn't want Chief to know. What is it?"

"Nothing," she replied too quickly.

Throttle frowned.

"There's nothing," Punch said as he came onto the bridge.

Sylvian stiffened.

He pointed to a seat. "Mind if I take this open station?"

"No, that's Finn's," Sylvian said.

Punch grinned and headed toward it.

"This station's yours." Throttle pointed to the open seat on the opposite side of the bridge from Finn's and Sylvian's stations.

"The request for launch has been approved. We may launch at your discretion," Rusty said.

Finn stepped onto the bridge and headed to his seat, ignoring Punch as he buckled in. "I'm ready."

Throttle gave him a nod. "Let's get started on our next mission, then, shall we?" She backed the *Javelin* from its dock, turned it around and then increased the power to bring the ship forward through the docking bay. Nearly every dock was filled. Some still had pirate ships tethered in them. Others were being used by Peacekeepers or contractors, and Throttle suspected the dock she'd just vacated would be occupied within an hour.

They pulled out of the docking bay and into the black. Free Station stood behind them. Throttle increased to full sub-speed and they weaved past several ships in the vicinity. Before them loomed the Chinese reclamation ship, which was distancing itself from Free Station as it prepared to enter jump speed.

"Prepare for jump speed in one minute," Throttle announced.

"Throttle, I'm receiving a ping," Rusty said.

"From whom?" she asked.

"There are no credentials provided with the ping."

She frowned. "Can you get a visual?"

"Hold on. I'm triangulating the source. Yes, I have a visual."

A ship displayed on her screen, and her breath hitched. It was the ship she'd seen by the asteroid belt, the same one that looked eerily like the *Javelin*.

"Where's it at now?" she asked.

"It looks like it was attached to the hull of Free Station. It's pulling away now on a flight path to intercept us."

"The ping's for me," Punch said, his features deadpan.

"Is it a Peacekeeper ship?" Throttle asked.

"No. Just something I have business dealings with. Nothing that concerns the mission or any of you. This is a personal call—I'll take the call in my bunk," he answered, coming to his feet.

"They've sent another ping," Rusty said.

"Accept the call and send it to Punch's bunk," Throttle said, watching the marshal carefully.

Punch gave her a nod and started to walk off the bridge.

"That's odd," Rusty said. "The call isn't for Punch. It's for me."

Throttle tensed. "That makes no sense. What is their request?"

"They don't have one. It seems that they are sending me a data packet."

"Don't accept it," Sylvian shot out. "It could be a virus or a Trojan."

A broadcast came across the open GP channel, making Throttle jump.

"Red Dynasty Four-Oh-Two-One has detected an enemy Swarm signal. We are initiating an immediate response per Wartime Protocols of 2352. All ships in the area be prepared to take evasive actions."

"Hold off on receiving that packet," Throttle said. "Sylvian, what ship are they targeting?"

The specialist snapped her head up from her screen. "It looks like they're targeting us."

Throttle looked at the Chinese ship and saw that at least a dozen of its photon cannons were now out and aimed at the *Javelin*. She grabbed at the controls to evade at the same time the cannons were fired. No ship was fast enough to evade an energy burst that moved at the speed of light. She watched the flashes, expecting to feel a blast of heat, but the lights went over the *Javelin*.

The sounds of debris pummeled the hull as though the ship were caught in a dust storm. She scanned her screens. Yellow warning lights flashed over several system status lines. She released her breath when she saw no red lights.

"I'm showing they've hit a target not far from our location," Sylvian said. "I think it was the ship that was pinging us."

"No," Punch exclaimed as he pulled himself up from having been knocked on the floor.

"Red Dynasty Four-Oh-Two-One reports that the enemy ship has been destroyed. We are leaving this sector and will report our findings upon arrival in Sol."

Throttle leaned back into her seat and looked across the faces of her crew. She tapped the intercom. "Eddy, how are you doing back there?"

"I'm okay, but I've bruised my hip."

She sat for a moment, then turned back to Punch. "They called that ship an enemy ship."

"I don't know anything about that. I swear it," he said.

"What's a Swarm ship?" she countered.

Punch's brow furrowed as he thought for a moment. "That was the name we gave the aliens. They were our first contact. They attacked, and we fought back. But that was at least a couple of hundred years ago. And they were wiped out. There's no way that's what that ship was."

"What if they were? What was your business with them?"

"I...don't know." He grabbed his seat and slunk into the chair. He looked up, pale. "I screwed up."

He didn't say anything else. Sylvian and Finn simply watched him and watched Throttle, as though waiting for her to tell them what to do. She looked around the bridge, taking in the workstations and the technology and began to wonder…What if aliens had once operated these controls? What if the *Javelin* was a ship left over from an alien war? And what if that war was returning?

She swallowed before speaking again. "Rusty, pull up everything you can on the Swarm and the war we fought against them. If they're coming back, I want to be ready."

EPILOGUE

THE VANTAGE PROBE HAD BEEN FOCUSED ON TRYING TO CONNECT TO the Atlas network rather than on the surrounding space, so it hadn't recognized the risk of the Red Dynasty ship until the ship fired its photon cannons. With no time to jump, the probe managed to send a final QuSR data packet before being obliterated.

Numerous hostiles with dangerous armaments. Recommend imme-diate initiation of protectionism plan before hostiles detect Vantage Core.

Vantage Core considered the probe's data packet for a lengthy six point two seconds before broadcasting a message to its fleet:

All Vantage probes: Organix threat imminent. Gather all final data and return to nearest Core for reallocation to a defensive protectionism strategy.

All Comet Cores: Prioritize war mechanix replication and begin charging Leviathan fleet for the elimination of the organix threat.

President Kuznetsov stood as the Red Dynasty delegate entered his Consortium office. He smiled. "Delegate Wu, it's a pleasure to see you, as always."

She didn't return the smile. "President, I wish this meeting was for pleasure, but I bring distressing news, and I wanted you to hear it from me before you see it on the news."

He frowned and motioned for her to take a seat.

"What is it?" he asked as he sat.

Wu pressed her hands together before she spoke. "I have received word that my people have encountered a Swarm probe."

He chuckled, though inside he felt chilled. "We wiped out the Swarm three centuries ago. I assume what they encountered was a burnt-out hull of a probe."

"I wish that was the case; however it is not. It was a fully functioning probe, found in Hiraeth's orbit in the Ross system." She cocked her head. "And I believe you and I both know that the Swarm were never wiped out."

He watched her, careful to maintain a face free from any telling expressions. "Why would you say that?"

She cocked her head and raised a thin brow. "Adrian, I am quite aware of the infrequent, yet ongoing sightings of Swarm probes throughout our colonized systems."

He chortled. "Those sightings are simply UFO sightings. Nothing more."

"Oh? Then why did you order files of those sightings sealed to all except those with the highest security clearance?"

His gaze narrowed. "And how would you know of such files if you don't have access to them?"

Her features hardened. "This is not a time for games, Adrian. We each have our resources. You may not take the Swarm threat seriously, but I assure you that the Red Dynasty is quite concerned by a force that could bring harm to our people, property, and resources." She lifted her chin. "That is why the reclamation ship that identified the Swarm probe was given immediate authority to destroy it."

He swallowed. "Was it fully destroyed?"

"Of course. They were thorough."

"And you're sure it was a Swarm probe?"

"Yes. When the reclamation ship's detection systems alerted the captain of engines running at the precise frequency of the Swarm, she reported the finding to our operations center. They verified the frequency and thus provided her authority to destroy the probe upon visual confirmation."

"And how would she have known what a Swarm probe looks like?" he asked.

She gave him a droll look. "Because, unlike your Peacekeepers, we provide full historical records to our fleet. She visually confirmed that the probe was similar to the probes in the records, and destroyed it."

Kuznetsov was relieved to hear that the probe had been destroyed. It was the second probe that had been sighted within a planet's orbit in the past three months. The first sighting had happened in Gliese, but that probe had escaped. The second sighting he was learning about from Delegate Wu just now. He'd hoped the first probe's proximity to a human colony was a fluke. Two sightings back-to-back could be no fluke. The Swarm were spying on humans, and that couldn't be a good thing.

He didn't share his concerns. Instead, he remained coy. "Similar? Your captain could've destroyed a private yacht for all we know."

"Unlikely. And if that turns out to be the case, it was worth the risk of not destroying a Swarm probe when we had the chance."

He inhaled before speaking. "Not everyone has that same outlook."

"They should." She leaned forward. "I need you to be honest with me, Adrian. Should I advise the chairman to prepare our fleet for a Swarm invasion?"

He leaned back in his chair. As president of the Consortium of Sol Colonies, he often faced questions that required delicate answers. An honest answer would lead to a wave of panic across the colonized systems. But he knew that anything he said to another person, even if behind closed doors, could be—and likely would be—conveyed to others. He never would have reached the highest-ranking office across all of humanity if he wasn't careful about who he trusted. In fact, the only person Adrian Kuznetsov trusted was himself.

He gave Delegate Wu a small smile. "You may put your chairman's concerns to rest. We don't see the Swarm as a threat. You have my word."

FROM THE PUBLISHER

Thank you for reading *Free Station*, book two in The Flight of the Javelin.

WE HOPE YOU ENJOYED IT AS MUCH AS WE ENJOYED BRINGING IT TO you. We just wanted to take a moment to encourage you to review the book on Amazon and Goodreads. Every review helps further the author's reach and, ultimately, helps them continue writing fantastic books for us all to enjoy.

If you liked this book, check out the rest of our catalogue at www. aethonbooks.com. To sign up to receive a FREE collection from some of our best authors as well as updates regarding all new releases, visit www.aethonbooks.com/sign-up.

JOIN THE STREET TEAM! Get advanced copies of all our books, plus other free stuff and help us put out hit after hit.

SEARCH ON FACEBOOK:
AETHON STREET TEAM

ALSO IN SERIES

BLACK SHEEP
FREE STATION
ROGUE PLANET

Printed in Great Britain
by Amazon